Miranda Road

HEATHER REYES

'She said: What is history?
And he said: History is an angel being blown backwards
into the future.
He said: History is a pile of debris. And the angel wants to
go back and fix things ... '

Laurie Anderson,
'The Dream Before (for Walter Benjamin)'

Published by Oxygen Books Ltd. 2014

Copyright © Heather Reyes 2014

Snow-globe image in cover montage copyright © Joanna Clark 2013

A CIP catalogue record for this book is available from the British Library.

ISBN 978 099263641 8

Typeset in Sabon by Bookcraft Limited, Stroud, Gloucestershire

Printed and bound in Great Britain by Henry Ling Ltd,
Dorset Press, Dorchester

For Malcolm

Heather Reyes is the author of *An Everywhere: A Little Book About Reading* (Oxygen Books, 2014), a novel *Zade* (Saqi Books, 2004), of many short stories and articles published in the UK and US, and four illustrated books for children.

She has also edited nine anthologies of writing about world cities for Oxygen Books' *city-pick* series, and a reference work, *The Art of Rawas*, on the multi-media Lebanese artist Mohamed Rawas.

Prologue

'A DANCE TO THE MUSIC OF TIME'

❧ GEORGINA ❧

Chagall's flying lovers are parted: he drifts off over the roof-tops to some other painting, promising to be back soon, leaving me suspended in the sky, alone.

Same old question going round and round like the grubby moon: what would my life have been like if he hadn't gone? – 'If' scratching at the skin of the past like the foot of an old mongrel worrying at fleas on its neck … 'if … if … if … if … if … if … if … '

Sometimes a Chagall bride lies horizontal on my dreams. Her look hides a little balloon-man whistling in her head, his pinks and lemons and greens and violets bobbing and lifting – a fragile bunch of colour brave against a huge and thunderous sky. I try to tell the bride one doesn't marry a balloon-man: one day he'll float his colours off to another country, leaving her with just a slice of blue sky in a puddle as a reminder …

❀ ELOISA ❀

Homework   3rd Septebmer 1978

My name is Eloisa Gabrielle Hardiman.
I am 9 years old. I live in Miranda Road,
London, England,
Europ, the World, the Galicksy, the Universe.
I have brown hair that is curly and long.
I have brown eyes.
My skin is a bit brown.
School dosen't like me. I do not like other
childern much.
I don't have a Daddy but I would like one.
I live with my Mum. Her name is George (really
Georgina).
When I grow up I want to live in a very big house
and have some money not like my Mum. She only
does storys.
The picture I drew is my Mum with her
tipewritter and me beside her. I am asking her
what she is writting about.

                                    by Eloisa Hardiman

Quite good. Copy spellings 3 times.

Europe   Europe Europe Europe
Galaxy   Galixy Galaxy Galaxy
doesn't   does't does'nt doesn't
children   children children chidlren
stories   storeis stories
typewriter   typewritter typewriter typewriter
writing   writing writing writing

❧ GEORGINA ❧

A little while after I get back from taking Eloisa to the school Christmas party it starts to snow – slow, floppy flakes drifting past the half dark between the open curtains. The first snow of the winter. Hands still circling the empty coffee mug, taking the dregs of its warmth, I go to the window to watch. As the drift of flakes thickens and swarms, a little film from my childhood flickers on the other side of the cold glass.

… Six years old, holding my father's hand. His big leather glove – brown with seams all around the fingers – pulls my blue mitten so there's a cold gap around my wrist. We're walking home from school. It's snowing hard so the Infants have been allowed home early. My father starts to sing.

'*I'm … dreaming of a white … Christmas …* '

'Don't be silly, Daddy. We've had Christmas.'

'But I'm already dreaming of the next one, honey.'

'Did it snow at Christmas when you were a little boy in America?'

'Yep. You bet.'

'And you used to make snowmen, didn't you.'

'Bigger than any other kid in Chicago. And snow ladies: don't forget the ladies. And snow children and snow dogs and snow cats … '

' … and snow mice and snow birds and … and … and snow *elephants*. I bet you made snow elephants.'

'Well, I could've done if I'd thought to. There was enough snow for a whole herd of elephants. But the truth is, Georgie, I just never thought of it. I guess I didn't have your imagination. You get that from your mother.'

'Where did *she* get it from? Poland?'

'I don't know, sweetheart – though she never went to Poland. It was only her parents came from there.'

'Then where did she get it from?'

'Maybe from all those books she's read.'

'Can we make a snow elephant when we get home? Please can we?'

'We'll see how your mother is first.'

'Is she still in bed poorly?'

'Yes, honey.'

Making a snow elephant. A baby one because it's just small English snow, he says. It starts as an African one, but the ears keep breaking up, so in the end it has to be an Indian one with small ears. When it's finished he sits me on the top, holding me in case it collapses. My mother looks down from the bedroom window, drawing aside the net curtain. Pink fluffy dressing-gown. Waving slowly. Smiling. I wave back from on top of the snow elephant. Then the net curtain drops and I can only see the vague shape of my mother for a moment before she moves away from the window, going back to bed.

By the time we go in she's asleep. My father – so large in the small kitchen – makes me ham and eggs for tea, bathes me, and begins to read me a Winnie-the-Pooh story that has snow in it. But I am so tired from playing outside in the cold that I fall asleep before he reaches the end.

(My mother died in the night. I didn't hear a thing.)

I ought to close the curtains to keep the heat in. But the snow-light's so beautiful. And I ought to do some work on *Never Too Late*. That page has been sitting in the typewriter for three days, the same words whispering from the desk every time I pass it.

He felt the inside pocket of his linen jacket for his passport. He checked his watch, the one she'd given him. "Time to go." He took her in his strong arms one last time, tipped up her face towards his own. Her cheeks were quite dry now: she was past crying. The softness of his kiss still astonished her. But even as her body began to melt with the sweetness of it ...

But I can't concentrate, even on that stuff.

Okay, if I'm not going to sit down at that desk and write, I should at least do something useful while she's at the party. Like wash jumpers or something. Will her red one still fit her? If I can find it in the mess of her cupboard.

Snowlight. I leave the curtains open in her room so I can enjoy it and just switch on her reading lamp. I look down into the quiet of Miranda Road, its decade of familiarity made strange by the snow. The longing to move on has gradually evaporated into an accommodation with its short-comings. As with many things in my life. But at least I have Eloisa – the unignorable reality of the past.

So touching, a child's room when they're not in it. Even the mess is forgivable.

I re-unite the pink slippers and place them at the foot of her bed, close the sock drawer and pick up the drawing book and coloured pencils abandoned in the middle of the floor. Then I rescue the splayed, face-down library book from the rumpled bed, insert the homemade felt bookmark and place it on the bedside cabinet. But in doing so, I knock over the little photo of herself she keeps there – the most recent regulation school photo and the best one so far, which is why she likes it. Those big brown eyes looking out of the oval window in the grey card mount. Butter wouldn't melt in her mouth. Though the hair suggests otherwise – that wild, dark aureole of loose springs. I find myself giving the photo a little shake and muttering, 'Monster!' then kissing her on the nose. The white school blouse shows up her colour.

I prop the photo up again as best I can (the little cardboard triangle at the back has already gone floppy and ineffectual), and go to her wardrobe to look for the jumpers to wash.

There are shouts from outside. Kids are playing snowballs in the road.

❦ ELOISA ❦

Our new headmistress, Mrs Oliver – aka 'The Bouncer' (on account of her bosom) – had got it into her head to start teaching us ballroom dancing so we could 'have a really lovely time dancing with our mummies and daddies' at the school Christmas party. She said round about nine or ten is a good age to start. Her eyes were shining and she clasped her hands rapturously together as we no doubt whirled through her imagination in our lovely dresses and dainty shoes.

It turned out that most of the class had 'two left feet and no sense of the beat'. We were supposed to learn about five or six different dances but all we could manage by mid December was the waltz and a rather chaotic Gay Gordons (we all loved the twirly bit).

Mrs Oliver had already introduced 'Prize-giving' and had been disappointed when nobody came in a hat. My mother had turned up in trainers and The Bouncer wouldn't speak to her, even though I'd won a prize for 'Composition', as she called it.

We were supposed to practise our dancing at home, the boys with their mums, the girls with their dads. I pleaded with my mother to find me a father for the party.

'You haven't got a daddy and there's nothing I can do about it.'

'Can't you get someone to pretend, just for the party?'

'You really want a pretending kind of life? Sorry, my prawn, but it's foot-down time. And I don't care if I do tread on Mrs Oliver's exposed toes: she should wear more sensible shoes. We're not playing those games.'

When it came to it, my mother claimed she already had something on for the evening of the Christmas party. I didn't believe her, but it was actually fine by me. I was one of the lucky ones: most parents would *be* there, dancing in public and embarrassing their children.

Trousers weren't allowed and I was absolutely freezing in the one summer dress that still almost fitted me. Rosemary's mother had made her a special dress and a pink satin cape. The Bouncer told her she looked like a princess. All she said to me was, 'Take that cardigan off. You can't dance in a cardigan.'

The school hall was looped with green paper chains and red balloons like giant holly-berries. There was a tall, spindly Christmas tree stifled with tinsel, and a terribly sequined Mrs O got up on the stage to welcome everyone and to announce that there would be prizes for the children. She'd be judging us while operating the tape-recorder for the music. The first waltz was just for us children – a kind of 'demonstration' waltz – then we could dance with our mums and dads. I'd been given Matthew Turnbull to steer round the room – not so much 'steer' as drag after me as I moved backwards mouthing '*one*-two-three, *one*-two-three', trying to keep Matthew on the beat of the music. At least I was warmer, moving about, and Matthew's hands were hot and damp with nerves.

The parents clapped us. The next waltz: mainly the boys dancing with their mums and the girls with their dads. It was a lifeless and corny version of 'Somewhere, my love' from the film *Dr Zhivago*. (We had the proper version on a record at home.) I leaned against the wall and kept my eyes on the patch of floor in front of me as if deep in thought and not really bored (was it?) to tears.

Then I seemed to see two feet in the patch I was staring at. I raised my eyes slowly up long legs ... to the waist ... the chest ... A voice seemed to say, 'Shall we dance?'

I couldn't see his face, but he whisked me up and held me to him, my arms around his neck, my face against his slightly rough cheek. He held me to him and we spun round and round ... round and round ... *one*-two-three, *one*-two-three, *one*-two three …

I was dancing with the most wonderful father in the world … a father better than all the others in the room … a father that was making all the other children wish they were me … *one*-two-three, *one*-two-three … As we spun past The Bouncer, she glowered, but still we kept dancing – *one*-two-three, *one*-two-three, *one*-two three …

Before the prizes were announced it was 'refreshments'. A pushing of children. A spilling of orange squash. The parents chattering over their wine, some around The Bouncer, all smiling and laughing, putting on an act. My mother would've hated it.

Nobody spoke to me at all. You feel a bit stupid, stuck on your own at a party, so I took a mince pie for something to do. I got some of the brown stuff on my dress. The more I tried to rub it off, the worse it got. In the end I gave up. It was an old dress, anyway. It didn't really fit me any more so I'd probably never wear it again.

While Mrs Oliver was making her speech and announcing who had won the prizes, I made my eyes search the floor for Dora's necklace (less boring than listening to Mrs O): I'd heard Dora tell Clarissa it'd come off during the twirly bit of the Gay Gordons and she couldn't find it: I hoped that if I managed to find it for her she might be nicer to me.

Then I heard my name being called.

' … a special prize. Not on my original list, but I think she deserves it, don't you, ladies and gentlemen? A prize for the SOLO WALTZ!'

I had to walk out in front of everyone. The clapping was a bit over-enthusiastic, as if the parents were embarrassed or trying to make up for something. And The Bouncer's face looked different and quite kind when she held out the prize to me. (It was just a bar of chocolate.) Then one of the fathers with a big voice got up on the stage and said thank you to Mrs Oliver and wished everyone a happy Christmas, and the party was over.

I went to find my cardigan and duffle-coat. I put them on and waited for my mother. Mrs Oliver was standing on her own by the Christmas tree. No-one was talking to her now and she looked tired. I couldn't help feeling sorry for her. I don't suppose the ballroom party had been as lovely as she thought it would be: just the usual old school Christmas thingy with a bit of dancing of the kind no-one really liked any more. I managed to catch her eye, over the heads of the departing parents, and waved to her, trying to cheer her up. She waved back and gave me a nice smile. 'Well done, Eloisa,' she called. 'You're a good little dancer.'

It was the nicest thing a teacher had ever said to me.

❧ GEORGINA ❧

Smell of wet wool. I'll have to hang the jumpers up to dry when we get back. It's time to go and collect Eloisa from the party. I rake out her wellingtons from the back of the cupboard and put them in a polythene bag (it wasn't snowing on the way there). I find a hat that doesn't look too silly with my big coat, grab the brolley and the door-key and go out into the snow.

A new place – all the tawdry grime of Archway turned white and amazing. But against the light from the street-lamp the flakes look dark as swarming insects …

The weird whiteness of everything. Only the main road is unwhite where the hot traffic hisses and the flakes don't get a chance to build up. Everything moving so slowly you can hear the flop and squeak of wipers in the strange, muffled quietness. Then the unsettling blue light of a police car.

People are already pouring out of the school, all the good mummies and daddies who went to the party. There's still a bit of a rebel left in me: I just couldn't face it, not with that woman Mrs Oliver telling everybody what to do all the time, like she did at prize giving. Prize giving! Who does she think she is: headmistress of Roedean? Couldn't she just have let them enjoy an ordinary Christmas party – employ a Father Christmas or a magician? Have games and crackers?

A few resentful looks as I push against the flow of departing parents and children. I can see Eloisa just inside the hall door wearing her coat already.

I make her put on her wellies at the door. 'Nice party, Tootsie?'

'I had a mince pie. And I won a prize for dancing on my own.'

'Well done! So tell me … '

'It was embarrassing. I don't want to talk about it.' She stares ahead.

Oh dear. We walk in silence. Then I try, 'Are you excited about Christmas, Toots?' She shrugs. Back to silence.

Finally I say, 'It's snowing really hard,' trying to make it sound exciting.

'I can see that,' she says.

Oh dear oh dear. I try again. 'Shall I put the brolly up?' She just shakes her head and we walk on, not talking. She's gone into one of her strange, distant moods. To try to haul her back to me I stop, tip back my head and stick out my tongue, like my father had shown me, to catch the little sting of a snowflake landing on it, then melting away on pink warmth. She just looks the other way. I try again.

'D'you know, Tootsie, they say every single snowflake is different … like every person who's ever lived is different from anyone else. Can you believe it? Every snowflake different.'

'You just said that.'

Oh, dear oh dear oh dear.

Then she suddenly says, 'Is it true you can't dance in a cardigan?'

'*What?!*'

'Mrs Oliver said you can't dance in a cardigan. She made me take it off and I was freezing.'

'Of course you can dance in a cardigan. You can even dance in a coat … and gloves and boots and carrying bags. I bet Mrs Oliver just never tried it. But I *have*, so I know what I'm talking about.' I turn and grab both her hands. 'Come on. You know how to waltz now. Side to side steps – one-two-three – one-two-three … Not too fast … '

'It feels funny in wellies.' But she keeps going.

'Only till you get used to it.' I start to hum that jazz waltz *he* was always humming, then I start singing it out loud, beginning to turn to it … '*Laa – – , laa – la, laa – – , – la la, laa la la, laa, la* … ' Waltzing and smiling and saying, 'See, Toots, you can dance in anything, as long as you can hear the rhythm in your head.' Our heads going with the music, waltzing and turning and the snow coming down thicker and thicker and singing at the top of my voice and her finally starting to smile ... '*Laa – – , laa – la, laa – – , – la la, laa la la, laa, la ...* ' Round and round in our boots and our gloves, dancing with the whole sky coming down on our heads, like Chicken-Licken. And when she slips over I scoop snow off a car and throw a snowball at her, and once she's got up she does the same to me, though I keep ducking between the parked cars, still singing the waltz at the top of my voice, holding on to it – even when there are people on the other side of the road, staring at us, laughing. Then I grab her and we start waltzing all over again ... '*Laa – – , laa – la, laa – – , – la la, laa la la, laa, la ...* ' – waltzing and singing and laughing and the snow coming down on our heads ... down and down and down and down ...

The Tuileries. Sudden snow. Hardly anyone about, just him and me and a couple of old Parisians bundled up against the cold, one with a short-legged dog that left a dribble of yellow urine on the beautiful white. The two of us shouting and dancing to an audience of blank-eyed statues being steadily clothed with snow ... Tomatoes falling out of the bag. He makes a snowball with a tomato in the middle, but I duck and it hits one of the statues. Tomato-pips dripping from its groin ... Laughing ... laughing ... Then him singing out that Shostakovich 'Jazz Suite' waltz, grabbing me and dancing me round and round in the snow – round and round and round and round ...

1

'MY BRILLIANT CAREER'

❦ ELOISA ❦

Homework   My Earliest Memorys

I rember crying when my hair was brushed
because of the tangels.
I remeber Sunday school and the time my uncles
came to see us and I asked why they were fat and
my mum was a bit cross with me. And other
children being nasty to me. Sometimes I think it
was because they had a mother and a father and
I just had a mother and an old grey typewriter
she called Qwerty. She called it her friend. She
used to say it brought home the bacon – which
was silly because we are vegetarian. I used to hear
my mum working on her tipewrighter when I
was in bed.

Quite good but try to write more next time. Do your spellings.
Remember to date your work.

Memories   Memories memories Memories
remember   rememember remember remember
tangles   tangles tangles tangles
typewriter   tyepwriter typewritter typewriter

❧ GEORGINA ❧

One of my earliest memories.

My stepbrother Archie invites me into the cupboard under the stairs to 'see some magic'. I don't know how I'm expected to see it in the dark and I'm afraid of the cupboard, anyway: I'd seen a large spider run down the hall and disappear under the door into the cupboard.

'You'll like the magic,' he coaxes. 'It's really interesting.'

'Can *I* come in, too?' His younger brother, Sam, has a high, wheedling voice.

'There's not room for you,' says Archie. 'Georgie's little. She can squeeze in.'

They're both 'big boys', fleshy and ungainly and often called names because of it. It's true: there *isn't* room for both of them in the cupboard.

Before going in I tuck my trousers into my socks so no spiders can run up my legs.

Archie has a torch with a red light. He closes the door. I say I'm scared. Archie puts his arm around me. 'You won't be scared when the magic starts. And you must promise not to open the door once we begin. Do you promise?'

Feeling just a little bit scared is quite nice in an odd sort of way. So I promise.

'Close your eyes.'

There are noises as if he's moving things about. It seems *ages*. I cheat and open one eye just a little bit. He's messing about with something, his back to me, the bulky shape of him seeming even bigger in the dim red light and the smallness of the cupboard.

'Can I look yet?'

'Not for a minute.'

'What are you doing?'

'I have to get it ready,' he says. 'Nearly there.'

There's a strange smell.

'Right, now you can look. Watch carefully … '

On the floor, next to what looks like a machine of some sort, is a square white dish with smelly water in it. Using grey plastic tongs he slips a rectangle of thickish white paper into the liquid.

'This is when the magic happens.' He puts his arm around me again. His hand squeezes my shoulder and I can feel the fatness of him against me.

The white paper begins to get patches of pale grey. Some of the pale grey darkens.

'It's like the magic painting book I used to have,' I say. 'You put water on it and the colours come. Except it's not colours.'

'It's not water, it's chemicals.'

'What's chemicals?'

'Never mind. Just watch … Look! Who's that?'

The patches of pale grey and dark grey and bits of black and bits of white are slowly making themselves into a person.

ME!

I'm holding my big doll by the hand, making her 'walk'. We're in the garden.

The moment it's just dark enough to be clear, Archie pulls the photo out and slips it into another square white dish of liquid.

'That's the fixer,' he says. 'That will stop you turning too dark.'

The doll's name is Margaret: a 'walkie-talkie' doll, as they were called, though she doesn't really talk – just makes a moaning kind of sound when you tip her backwards and forwards. But she can do a stiff-legged walk if you hold her and propel her in the right way, her head moving from side to side in tandem with a slow, clunking goose-step.

It makes me cross when people call her my 'baby'. Babies

don't walk. And I'm not in the least maternal, anyway. Margaret is my friend, listening to my stories – my very first stories – when nobody else has time.

They're mostly stories about America, embroidered around facts and anecdotes I've heard from my father, Lieutenant Miles Hardiman Jnr, very smart and serious in the one picture there is of him in his USAF uniform.

War is very, very bad, he says: lots of people get hurt. 'Though if it hadn't been for that nasty old Mr Hitler, honey, you wouldn't be here. I'd never have come to England and met your sweet, sweet mother. So I guess a tiny little bit of something good can be got out of even the worst situations, if we try, eh, Georgie?'

❧ ELOISA ❧

My mother spent a lot of time with 'Qwerty' (as she called her typewriter) – probably more time than most women spent with their husbands. And a *lot* more time than she spent on housework. The wild-beast roaring of the vacuum cleaner was a rare and terrifying event accompanied by a cross look on my mother's face. The usual sound of 'home' was a friendly little horse tap-dancing, sometimes very fast, sometimes hesitating, irregular, as if it'd forgotten the steps.

A childhood full of words – too many words, always rising up out of Qwerty's long straight mouth with a dark roller for one lip and a metal bar for the other, words rising and rising on the square breath of paper … pages and pages of them screwed into loose balls that filled the waste-paper basket, even spilling onto the floor. Wasted words. Words thrown away. I felt sorry for those, all screwed up and not wanted.

'Why are you always playing with Qwerty?'

'I'm not playing, Tootsie. I'm working. I make up stories and type them out and people pay me money for them. I've told you lots of times, I'm a writer.'

'Will you read me the stories?'

'No. They're stories for grown-ups, sweetheart.'

'Do the people pay you a lot of money for them?'

'It would be nice if they paid me more. But it helps. It's money.'

Money. That was something we always needed more of. My 'new' coat was from a stinky old second-hand shop. We had *some* money, she explained, because an old lady had left us a 'leg-at-sea' which brought in a 'trickle of money'. (And it was so clear to me, that old lady's leg sticking out of the waves, kicking water towards the shore, foamy waves running up the beach and then trickling back to leave gold coins sparkling on the sand, and my mother crouching there, bare-footed, picking them up.)

My proper remembering started with Sunday school. I must have been nearly five because it was just before I started 'proper' school. Not that my mother was religious – not in the normal sense (though she did believe in being nice to people, she said): it was just a way of grabbing an extra hour for herself. I heard her say as much to her friend Alma. She told *me* it was to help me get used to going to school.

Whenever I asked a question at Sunday school I was just told to 'be quiet and listen'. (Not like home.) So I tried to listen. But they were such terrifying stories. Blood. Threats. Cross old men ... Did my mother know what was going on in that awful Sunday-morning room that smelled of wet dust? – what nasty stories they were telling us?

I didn't mind it so much if I got the wobbling chair you could jiggle against the floorboards when you didn't want to hear what they were saying. And I liked it on rainy Sundays when the enormous shiny bucket appeared in the middle of the room and there were plink-plink-plink sounds to go with the stories. Some of them were all right, of course, like the one where all the hungry people got fed – though I felt sorry for the fish (we didn't eat fish, of course, being *proper* vegetarians). I told the Sunday-school lady it would have been a better story if they'd just had bread. I don't think she liked me much.

I thought, 'Now, if I had a daddy, he could take me to the park while mummy has an hour to herself.'

At Christmas, the Sunday school would be putting on 'an activity play' about the Furchin Mary and Baby Cheese-us, and because all of us would be acting in it, all our mummies and daddies 'must come and watch us'. I put up my hand and told the lady I didn't have a daddy so would it be all right if just my mummy came along to watch me be an angel?

28

The Sunday-school lady said not to worry about not having a daddy because G – O – D (she screeched out the name in yellow chalk on the blackboard) was Father Of Us All and was watching us all the time (which I found a bit scary) so He'd be there, watching me be an angel, just like all the other daddies. We were all part of His family. She was trying to be nice to me, I supposed.

But the pictures of God and His family and His angels showed I was nothing like them. Golden hair, they'd got. And there was God's big nose and his skin haggard white. The long pale face and yellowy beard of Jesus. They had nothing to do with the fountain of loose brown springs erupting from my head or my skin like the paler sort of toffees.

'Why aren't there angels *my* colour?'

'I've told you before, Eloisa, unless you can be quiet and listen, you'll go back down to the babies' class.'

The goody-goody children with no questions in them stared at me. I stared back, wishing I was at home even if I did have to be quiet while my mother got on with her Qwerty work.

29

❧ GEORGINA ❧

A dark face at my white breast.

She arrives on a bleak Monday afternoon. February 1969. Eloisa Gabrielle Hardiman. A normal birth. All fingers and toes present and correct, a lusty cry and, right from the start, sucking efficiently from my inexperienced breasts.

I use feeds to read my way through the first volumes of *A Dance to the Music of Time*, laying the book face down on the bed so as not to lose my place while I manoeuvre her to the other breast. I finish the first volume while still in hospital. The ward sister seeing the title – *A Question of Upbringing* – says it makes a change to see a young single mother (I'm nearly twenty-four) taking her responsibilities seriously.

The woman in the bed opposite is reading Angela Carter's *The Magic Toyshop*. The other women are just reading their babies, so I go over and stand at the side of her bed. She's stopped reading and is looking into a small hand-mirror. I say, 'Hi. I'm Georgina and my hair needs washing too.'

She slips the mirror back into her wash-bag and laughs. 'I'm Alma and I'm not usually so vain. Was that a ghost of an American accent?'

'Father from Chicago. As a kid I used to deliberately imitate him so as not to sound like my stepmother's family. They were from Kent. North Kent.'

'What's your baby called?'

'Eloisa. Yours?'

'Apple.'

'What a lovely name!'

'I hope she'll like it.'

'It's different. Different's good.'

'I think so, too.'

When it's time to take our babies home, Apple's long-haired and bearded father is there to carry her over the hospital threshold and out into the world in his hirsute arms.

Me? I splash out on a taxi back to Miranda Road. The driver is kind, carries my bags up the stairs, waits till I've opened the door and puts them inside for me.

'And the very best of luck, mate,' he says. 'I've got three of the little perishers at home. Sucked all the sparkle out of my wife, I can tell you.'

I manage to wait until he's gone downstairs and slammed the front door before bursting into tears from the sudden, over-whelming feeling that this is someone else's life I've strayed into. Georgina Hardiman was supposed to travel the world and be free and become a great writer! How ... *How* could I have let this happen? I've never even held a baby before. Then the tiny, odd creature in my arms begins to shift about inside her shawl, a livid surge coming alarmingly to her face, then subsiding. She begins to turn her head, nuzzling. I stop crying, sit on the edge of the bed and feed her with my coat and boots still on: the flat's freezing.

Such long evenings alone. But isn't this the perfect opportunity to get going properly on my writing career? Having a baby isn't going to stop my career plans. Look at George Sand! *She*'d had children. *And* lovers. Alfred de Musset ... Chopin ... (Though she'd also had plenty of money, of course.)

I try to write a novel based on my life so far – but it just won't come out right as a 'story'. And I get so tired, always up in the night to feed and change Eloisa while the people above and below sleep, praying she won't cry and disturb them.

I soon get used to the strange yellow stools from milk and become quite an expert at dealing with it ... not getting it everywhere, like at first. And the nappy-bucket routine. Letting her kick without her nappy on for a while after changing.

Leaning over her, talking, making silly noises. No-one else around to hear. Looking into dark eyes that are gradually learning to focus. What does she see? Does she sense my love? My anxiety? Does she hear my weary little sigh when she wees the second I lower her buttocks onto a clean nappy and I have to start all over again? ... And the nappy-bucket is full already and there's no garden to dry them in because it belongs to the downstairs flat.

Then there's my fury and humiliation at the way that Health Visitor scans the flat, looking for things to criticise and, presumably because she finds none, says, 'The trouble with children like that, how are they supposed to know which race or culture they belong to?' And my clipped, admirably controlled reply, 'They have the undoubted advantage of belonging to more than one. She will be able to choose.' Refusing to be beaten, the woman goes on: 'If you don't mind my asking, where exactly is the father now? Do you still have contact with him?'

'*I do mind you asking. And frankly it's none of your business. You've done your job – checked that, despite being unmarried, I am not living in a state of sordid filth, and ... *'

Oh how I wish I could've said that! But unsure of the power of such people, I restrict myself to a highly responsible-sounding, 'Actually, it's a little past the baby's feed time already. Would you mind leaving?'

But it's hard. And more than once I get so tired and frustrated I even begin to wonder if I should've put her up for adoption like that dog-faced woman at the hospital suggested.

Then comes the night when, for the first time, she reaches out and touches my face. I pick her up and hold her to me, crying and crying at the thought that I might have given her away.

Then there are the beautiful rewards of those little sounds, like tiny balloons, rising from the cot in the mornings, the sounds that will one day turn into talking. The funny hiccoughing intake of breath – the start of laughter. That terrifyingly visible flicker of pulse in the fontanelle slowly being hidden by hair. Then is that 'Mama' I hear? And it isn't long before the finger learns to point at pigeons and dogs and cats and the mouth bunches for the effort of meaningful speech and makes the word 'dod' ... and soon 'oof' ... and then 'dog' and almost 'woof'. Already she has favourite foods, loves sweet things more than savoury ... can hold her bottle by herself.

A few days before her first birthday (my diary records it as the day the Equal Pay Act goes through Parliament – though it doesn't materialize for another five years) comes Eloisa's delighted defiance of gravity: her first tottery steps. No-one to tell – except my stepbrothers and they don't know what to say, really, having no idea about anything to do with babies or children. I can't even phone Alma: it might sound like boasting as Apple is a long way from walking. They have a joint first birthday party, but we have to leave early because Eloisa starts screaming every time she catches sight of Apple's long-black-bearded father.

I hate having to buy second-hand things for her, but with the cost of living going up so fast I have to. Three weeks after her second birthday I take her on a huge women's liberation march. Alma takes Apple, too. Apple in a brand new buggy, Eloisa in an old one with a dodgy brake. But I'm determined to stay in London, no matter what: a suburban childhood has convinced me it will be worth it even though times are getting harder, especially with the miners' strike and the resulting power-cuts. I read by candle-light or torch-light (when I can get batteries – they're like gold-dust!), or by the light of a dangerous little oil-lamp of the kind that suddenly appear in the shops, imported from goodness-knows-what country with low safety standards ...

At three-and-a-half, Eloisa is already quite a handful, but so wonderfully curious, full of energy and words – talking, talking,

talking from morning to night, full of strange questions.

'Is there a country where the rain's made of milk?'

'Do cats grow up to be dogs?'

'But *why* aren't frogs born frogs?'

'Has that tree got different leaves because it's a girl tree?'

And one day suddenly terrified of daisies, standing there, petrified, screaming to be lifted off the grass in the park. 'I don't like them! I don't like them!' 'But they're daisies, sweetheart. You like daisies. Pick some for Mummy.' 'NO! *NO!* They're eyes!' She's seen them as white irises with yellow pupils everywhere, staring up from the grass, watching her.

Then comes the day when I see the advertisement. I try my hand at it, after reading a few to get the general idea. I have the imagination and soon pick up the knack of giving them what they want. I guess you'd call it 'selling out' ... or intellectual schizophrenia – reading *The Female Eunuch* (lent by Alma) while writing ... what was that first one called? ... *With a Will and a Whip* ... ? A compromise Alma never quite forgives me for. But at least I can work from home and bring up my daughter myself.

It isn't quite the kind of writing career I'd wanted. I'd seen myself more as a cross between Dorothy Parker and the Virginia Woolf of the late twentieth century. But maybe I'll move on eventually. As long as I use a pseudonym for this ... 'commercial' writing.

I try to carry on writing poetry, but most of it is about motherhood in one way or another. And, of course, I write things for Eloisa, too.

❧ ELOISA ❧

By the time I was five, my mother had taught me to read by rhymes and stories she'd made up herself, stitching them into my own little books. I remember a particularly weird one about a yellow woman and a blue man and their green baby. And poems, of course. Lots of those. How I wish I still had them! The only one I can remember by heart is the one about a Manx cat, probably because I could never work out whether it was funny or sad. (It *sounded* funny, but having such an important thing missing from its life meant it had to be a sad poem, surely. Never thinking it could be both at the same time.)

When you look at a Manx cat
you certainly know that
there's something not right —
something's missing!

It's got two eyes for seeing
and the right bit for wee-ing,
but something's not right —
something's missing!

It has four legs for walking
and a mouth for cat-talking
but something's not right —
something's missing!

There's its head, looking thinky.
There's its nose sort of pinky.
But something's not right —
something's missing!

It's got fur soft and stroky
and whiskers all poky ...
But WHERE'S ITS TAIL?
Oh no!!!
It's missing!

Then I started school and met a very different world to the one I was used to. It wasn't a world where people answered all my questions and wrote poems and stories just for me. And it was a world that included the 'Janet and John' reading scheme where a suited daddy came home each evening and the mummy never wrote poems or wore black and the children's skin and hair just didn't look like mine at all. At first I pretended I couldn't read, trying to be like the other children as they stumbled over 'Run, John, run' ... 'Look, Janet, look' ... But that soon got boring, pretending not to know things. When I took the books home, my mother wrinkled her nose at them. 'That school! It's so old-fashioned!'

For me, though, 'Janet and John' was the least of my worries at school. I soon turned into a wild little doll stuck with the pins of words that hurt and hurt ...

'Curly-wurly girly-wurly. Curly-wurly ... ' 'My daddy says you're a mongrel.'

I tried to get my own back one break-time. Put in the classroom alone (for hopping down the corridor when we were supposed to 'walk nicely like young ladies and gentlemen'), I took the red pencil off the teacher's desk and scribbled out the faces of all the drawings on the wall we'd done of each other, except the one of myself. My desk was put in the corner for the rest of the day, my back to the class, paper pellets and bits of rubber bouncing off me whenever the teacher wasn't looking.

After that I refused – absolutely and utterly refused – to speak to anyone once I was inside the school gates.

❧ GEORGINA ❧

Things begin to go wrong soon after she starts school. Eventually they send for me.

'There's something wrong with her,' they say.

'I don't think so,' I reply.

They say, 'She's what's called an elective mute.'

'Better than being an elective bully,' I suggest (which doesn't go down too well).

'Does she speak at home?' they ask.

'Never stops,' I say, with considerable feeling.

Stories. She's always telling stories. (Maybe she'll have the brilliant career I'd hoped might be mine.) From my desk, as I work on that seedy soft porn – and, a new departure, Mills and Boon-type romances – I can hear her telling her innocent but meaningful stories to Lucy (just as I used to tell mine to walkie-talkie Margaret), her one-eyed doll with brown felt-pen scribbles on her cheeks.

'*I'm going to tell you a story, Lucy, so you have to keep very still like at school. Once upon a time there was a girl called Lucy only she wasn't a doll like you she was a proper girl like me only her name was Lucy and she wanted to go to the moon like the spacemen because she didn't like going to school but the people in charge of the rockets said, "Oh, no, you can't go to the moon, only boys go to the moon.' So Lucy went away very sad but then she had an idea and she dressed herself up as a boy called John and they let her go to the moon and it was lovely walking on the shiny silver stuff and she looked down at the world all small and she was happy because there was no school on the moon and it was all quiet and the teacher said, "Where's Lucy today?" and one of the children said, "Lucy's gone to the moon" and when I got back from the moon they said what was it like on the moon and I wouldn't tell them and the teacher got cross and she said, "When Richard went to Spain when he came back he stood up in front of the class and told everyone what it was like in Spain so now it's your turn because you've been to the moon" and she made me stand in front of the class only I wouldn't say anything because there's no words on the moon and it's very quiet.'*

I wish scribble-faced Lucy had had a tape-recorder inside her so I could play them all back, those stories: they'd make a thesis on fiction – on how we metamorphose truth to make it truer. And I could have played them to her teachers to prove just how un-silent she was at home.

Are stories a way of covering silence? Absence?

When she's old enough to start asking about her father I tell her a kind of truth: a very nice man who had to go away – though I hope he might come back one day.

What I can't explain to her is how the 'not knowing' keeps me chained to our past. It's ages before I can even contemplate getting involved with anyone else, let alone a long-term commitment. Supposing he came back? – like those war films where a woman's been told her husband is dead and she re-marries and then he turns up …

The first temptation is David.

David. His big toe ludicrously longer than the rest. His tousled fair hair. His old blue jumper against my skin when I go to make tea after love – like a dress on me … pushing up the bulk of its sleeves. That story he tells about the day next door's parrot escaped: laughing for a week each time I think about it. A dour girl in Boots looking at me from her white coat as I laugh, all by myself, in front of the Tampax. The little wooden Buddha he goes back to the shop and buys me when all the time it's the paper-weight I was really pointing to when I said,

'That's lovely'. And not having the heart to tell him.

It feels like a gross infidelity at first because it isn't just 'physical': I begin to really fall in love.

Even Alma likes David – which is really something because she's rapidly shrinking from good-natured feminist to radical man-hater: her husband went off with one of his Sociology students. David and I bump into Alma on Highgate Hill one day, and the next time we meet for a coffee she's full of dire warnings: he's 'too nice to be for real'. 'I think you're jealous,' I laugh. 'You bet I am,' she says, 'especially if he's good in bed.' I don't reply and try not to smile.

But of course there's Eloisa, so it isn't always easy.

❀ ELOISA ❀

One day the teacher got so cross about me refusing to speak that she said out loud I was 'the pupil from Hell' – giving the class another pin to stab me with. (That chanting in the playground. '*Hell*-o-is-a Hardiman … *Hell*-o-is-a Hardiman … ') Miss Jones who played the piano was the only teacher who smiled at me, asking me gently why I was so silent. Wouldn't I talk to her? … just a little bit? … Or sing? … OK. Maybe another day. But I was happy standing next to her, watching her hands on the piano while the others sang, her long fingers flowing over the white notes and the black notes, making a lovely sound by mixing them all together.

Then I went one better than silence: I played truant.

It was my birthday – my seventh, maybe. Or was it my eighth? I'm not sure. But I do remember that the present I wanted more than anything was to stay at home. An icy mist breathed on our windows as I was bundled into extra layers plus big red scarf and mittens. A suffocating kind of panic: I was really *not* going to get my own way.

I tried everything – absolutely *everything* – finally resorting to a downright lie.

'I can't go to school today: I've got a headache.'

'No you haven't, sparrow.'

'I have.'

'Little girls don't get headaches on their birthday: it's a well-known fact.'

'Perhaps whoever gives out the headaches doesn't know it's my birthday.'

'Well, if a little headache got in there by mistake, supposing I get it out and have it for you.' She put her lips to my forehead, pretending to suck the pain out. 'Ouch! Yes, that *is* a nasty one. I can already feel it just above my left eye.'

Cross, defeated, I pulled away. 'Don't be so silly.'

All the way to school she chatted, trying to make me cheerful. I met it with a wall of sullen silence. I had the feeling she was really desperate for me to be in school, out of the way, that day. From my bedroom, a couple of nights before, I'd over-heard part of a phone-call ... She was talking to someone called David. They were making 'arrangements' ...

At the school gates I refused to kiss her and walked even more slowly than usual towards the edge of the playground, well away from the noisy, rough children running about. When the headmaster came out to ring the lining-up bell I slipped away, under cover of the mist, to a gap in the railings at the far corner of the playground. I knew the way to my favourite place: Waterlow Park.

The mist hung there like wet washing and smelled of metal. It was thicker in the park than in the streets. A man was magicked to nothing a few yards ahead of me, and a lady with a dog appeared in the same place as if the man had turned into her. The dog ran up to me, black and high as my waist, sniffing the air around me as if I were a plate of food up on a table. Big wet nose ('all the better to smell you with ... '). I ran. And the dog ran after me. A bossy voice called, 'Here, Belzy. Good boy!' But he took no notice. I ran faster. So did the dog. On my left the rail-ings were partly overgrown with bushes and trees. I lunged into them and, with the agility of panic, used them to hoist myself up so I was standing on top of the railings, clinging on to a thin bendy branch and looking down at awful spikes and at the dog leaping and barking and at a small red flag – one of my mittens caught on the bush below. As he leapt and barked, the dog's teeth were very white against his black fur and pink mouth ('All the better to ... '). Half jumping, half falling, I landed in a heap, scrambled to my feet, then ran until the sounds of the dog and the voice of the woman were smudged away in the mist.

41

I found myself on an overgrown path in a dreamscape. I moved forward slowly, like a sleep-walker, wide-eyed in the fantastical ghostliness. Between and beneath the trees stone monuments froze in the white air. Rags of snow lay scattered on the ground. Then I realised it was the place where they buried dead people. There were big stone crosses, and smaller ones. Plain ones and fancier ones, some with ivy climbing around them and hanging from their outstretched arms, or padding the tombs like old green eiderdowns for the dead people to sleep under. I walked on and on, watched by stone angels that hovered in the mist, looking down at me with sweet and gentle smiles – not giggling, behind-the-hand smiles that would open to call me 'bush-head' or 'toasty'.

Footsteps!

I found a hanging blanket of ivy big enough to hide behind. I kept stone still, only my heart throbbing away in my chest and ears. Wheezy, ghostish breathing came very close. I could make out a tall shape on the path. A man? Or a ghost? Maybe my father was really dead and this was his ghost coming to see me – or coming after me.

The footsteps and wheezing breath grew fainter. Overcome by curiosity, I edged out onto the path again. I couldn't see anyone. But I suddenly felt scared all alone there in the mist and thought maybe I'd go home … if I could find my way out of that place of dead people. I could say I'd been sent home from school because … I felt sick. No, they always phoned your home if you were ill and your mum had to come and fetch you from the secretary's room. I could say … I could say …

I began to see how many hops I could do to take my mind off the immediate problem of how to explain why I wasn't at school and to make me feel less scared of being in this place with the mist getting thicker and thicker …

I was hopping and watching the little ghosts come out of my mouth and blend with the cold, misty air when I turned a corner and saw a big stone head staring down at me – the wide face, big eyebrows and bushy beard of a stern father. (Was mine like that?) I sounded out the letters of the name carved into the stone beneath the enormous head.

'K – A – R – L   M – A – R – X'

Then I heard footsteps coming towards me again. The man – or the ghost of my father – must have heard me saying the name out loud. He'd turned around and was just a few yards off now. I could see him peering at me through the mist! He was coming closer … But he didn't say anything. If he'd *said* something I might not have been so scared. It was the way he was just walking towards me, staring …

I ran and ran like Goldilocks … ran till I found the gate, ran back through the park, crying, ran and ran till I got back to Miranda Road and to our front door and hammered on it with my mittenless fist. Hammered and hammered because nobody came, and I called, sobbing, through the letter-box.

But who was this unusually pink mother who finally opened the door?

And why was she in her chrysanthemum-patterned dressing-gown? She'd been all dressed when she'd taken me to school!

On the way up the stairs she put her arm around me and I buried my wet face in her oddly hot body.

When a tall man came out of her bedroom, I was so surprised that I started crying all over again because I thought, for a moment, the ghost had followed me home. I screamed and screamed and told the man to go away.

In the end he did.

❧ GEORGINA ❧

'I want you. I want you now … now … ' Her breath was coming fast, her body moving against him. His cock was growing, hardening again, ready to take her.

'And this time, no interruptions.' He locked the door and put the key on top of the high cupboard where she couldn't reach it. He pulled out the phone plug. He pushed her towards the bed, then pulled something from the pocket of his jacket hanging on the door. Four pieces of rope.

'What are you doing?' Her eyes widened. He pushed her so hard she fell back onto the bed.

'I said there'd be no interruptions this time.' Then his whole weight was on her, pinning her down while he tied first one …

Coitus well and truly *interruptus*. But nothing's ever wasted when you write fiction (especially the kind I end up writing most of the time). You just take life and turn it a little, pat it into the required shape for consumption.

Not ready for a 'fully committed' relationship, perhaps. Sorry, David. I'm too 'haunted by the past'. How can I *not* be with Eloisa's face before me every day? And I still spin myself B-movie-type stories about him being kidnapped then escaping after years and years and making his way back and … Or an accident leading to amnesia and then a miracle day when something will happen to jog his memory into the past and he'll hurry back to me as soon as he can … Or he meets someone else out there and married but then realises he's made a mistake and comes back to me … or his wife will die and he'll come back to me and … Even though I despise myself – despise myself utterly – for giving in to such fantasies (the stuff I have to write is clearly turning my brain), what are you left with when someone … ?

David and his wife had already parted before we met, but when she becomes terminally ill he goes back to nurse her. I am not sufficiently convinced as to our long-term prospects to support him selflessly in this. And she takes longer to die than expected and it all becomes too difficult anyway. So I'm on my own again. But after the first 'big' abandonment, you know you can cope. The sun comes up the next morning. The plants carry on growing. Children have to be fed. Not the stuff of novels, really.

2

'A ROOM OF
ONE'S OWN'

❀ ELOISA ❀

Homework
What I did in the Christmas Holidays
7th of Jan. 1979

It was just my mum and me for Christmas like usual. I did not have many Christmas presents because of what we were going to do straight after Christmas which we have never done before. We went to France. I was sick on the boat. We stayed in Paris. The room was very small. We met people my mum knows from a long time ago. We went to a restoront. I got a souvenir of a dancer that goes round and round.

3/10

Try to write more, Eloisa. This is not your best work, though your spelling is getting better. (Just 'restaurant' is wrong, but that's quite a difficult word, anyway.) It must have been very exciting to visit Paris. Please write a proper description of what you did and what you saw there, then I can give you a better mark! (Give it in on Wednesday.)

❧ GEORGINA ❧

Giordano Bruno supported himself for a while by giving private tuition in the system he'd invented for improving the memory. It included placing each memory on a 'big wheel'. You turned the wheel when you wanted to retrieve a memory. But inside it you created five concentric wheels on which memories were also placed. By turning the wheels, new combinations of memories were created and this could generate new knowledge.

(The Inquisition burned him in 1600.)

A system for forgetting would sometimes be more … useful.

'*STOP! Someone's drowning …* ' The gendarmes looking on.

Gilles Tautin. The name floats to the surface. A student. They'd been chased into the Seine. We went to his funeral. June 15, 1968. My fist raised and clenched like the others, but my eyes on that internal calendar: five days late.

Insomnia. A night longer than the last ten years.
Paris. Tomorrow. TOMORROW!

To think, I was going to 'travel the world' and here I am getting all excited about going back to Paris! Taking Eloisa for the first time. It's a bit sad, really, to be so … agitated.

Supposing I'd gone first to … Madrid, say, instead. Or Rome. What would I be doing now? Would I still be free? Had the career I wanted? Or would the same thing have happened … only with someone else?

Contingency? Or inevitability?

A healthy young woman with a viable womb. 'YOUR SPECIES NEEDS YOU!'

And what if I'd ...

But I can't imagine a life without our daughter. Who else is there? Not even my stepmother (cervical cancer during my second year at university), or my father (he crumbled utterly, went back to the States to be with his younger sister even before I left for Paris) ... After a certain length of time has passed it gets harder and harder to keep in touch. Especially when one's life has gone in such a different direction. And I thought he would be ashamed to know I had a child without being married. But now I regret just letting go of him like that.

So it goes.

Would we be such strangers to each other? He'd probably be a really good grandfather. No, I mustn't start thinking like that. Regrets, sentimentality and all that paraphernalia. The things our generation tried to get away from. Let's face it, I've abandoned him and it was a dastardly thing to do. Sentimentality and love are not the same thing. I hope to God Eloisa never abandons me, though. She's the one thing that goes on giving meaning to ... all that we were, her father and I.

Or that I thought we were. Part of the 'post-war generation'. So full of hope. Or was that just because we were young. Is every generation the same?

But, no. It was *different being young then. For the first time the young had 'status' – that's what they say, the social historians (though we're scarcely 'history' yet, are we?). We weren't afraid to let our voices be heard.*

And how we raised them! Against war, inequality, injustice of any sort. Our voices adding to the shouting of the banners we carried. Believing we could do something. Believing in ourselves. *Believing in the banners we carried and the slogans we shouted and painted on walls.*

Those months when the walls of Paris had mouths. (Not that I ever did that. Too scared of being caught, paint-brush in hand, and sent packing, back to England ... without him.)

'Nous ne nous tairons pas!' *No, we won't shut up.*
'Osons!' *Let's dare.*
'Seuls nous ne pouvons rien faire.' *Alone we can do nothing.*
'Ecrivez partout.' *Write everywhere.*
'En tout cas, pas de remords!' *In any case, no regrets.*

Pas de remords?

Is that possible?

Looking for reassurance, rifling quietly (so as not to disturb Eloisa) through my desk drawers to find the small red diary with one grubby corner (dropped in a muddy puddle on the rue Soufflot more than a decade ago). Bits of poems covered in crossings-out and illegible insertions. Titles of 'must read' books. Quotations. Names and addresses. All jumbled together and punctuated with copied-down graffiti ... 'Je déclare l'état de bonheur permanent' ... 'L'imagination prend le pouvoir' ... 'Ayez des idées' ... 'Vivre au présent' ... *There it is:* 'En tout cas, pas de remords!' *Just another version of* 'Non, je ne regrette rien', *really. Easier said than done ...*

A movement from Eloisa's room. I push the door open a little, just enough to check her but without letting the light through to wake her. She's kicked the duvet almost off. I tip-toe in and place it gently across her again. She's so beautiful I want to cry. She's growing more like him. What will she make of Paris?

Oh, God! Won't morning ever come?
   What will it be like, going back?

3 a.m. ... Pulling back the curtain. Someone's Christmas-tree lights left on ...
   Same old stains on the moon ... Windy. Doesn't bode well for the boat. Hope she won't be sea-sick ...

❧ ELOISA ❧

The ferry rose and fell as it lurched drunkenly across a winter sea. We tried to stay on deck: my mother said you got less sick that way. But it was so cold I thought I was going to die. Then, when we went below, my stomach felt as if it were in my head and my insides kept trying to escape from anywhere they could. My breakfast ended up in a brown paper bag (as did my mother's).

I was still very queasy as we climbed into the big French train at Calais. My mother's eyes were glittering oddly in her pale, sea-sickened face. I curled up in the corner of a window seat and slept with her big jumper over me till just before the train drew into Paris.

It was so weird. Everything different … but the same. We arrived at a big station rather like King's Cross, but the sounds and smells were different. There were a lot of small, darkish-skinned men standing about, not doing anything in particular. They looked quite poor. I didn't understand the words on any of the signs or the advertisements. My mother held my hand very tightly and we went down some stairs with a lot of other people.

The underground train made a swishing sound as it came into the station, not clattering like the ones in London. The smell was definitely different: more like a public toilet in some parts. We sat on tip-up seats by doors that had little metals handles you flipped up when you wanted them to open at a station. Beside me was a picture of a small animal getting its paw caught in the door.

Then something odd happened. Two stops before we had to get off, a French girl – about the same age as me – came onto the train with her father. His skin was quite dark, but not black. She was paler than he was. And she looked more like me than anyone I'd ever seen before. Even my mother looked twice. I couldn't take my eyes off her. It was as if I'd been living a parallel life as a French girl all along. Then my mother stood up and heaved the big rucksack onto her back. (I hadn't bothered to take off my little one.)

'Next stop, Tootsie. Ready to get off.'

She pushed me out as people started crowding into the carriage. I had a final glimpse of my double's familiar hair as the train swished her away into the tunnel.

Walking up the stairs, surrounded by French people, I tried to pretend I was that other me and that this was all quite normal. In my head I said the few French phrases my mother had taught me: '*Bonjour, madame ... Bonjour, monsieur ... Comment-allez-vous? ... Je vais très bien, merci ... Il fait beau ... S'il vous plaît ...* ' But it began to feel a bit silly, so I stopped. And I went back to being English me again, holding my English mother's hand.

And there we were, out on a Paris street. It was dark. A thin, icy rain was making the road and pavements a confusion of lights. A lot of traffic. A screech of brakes. Angry horns. Someone knocked into me and said something though I didn't know what it meant. Was it 'Sorry' or 'Get out of the way'? I stood there, shivering and hungry, waiting for my strange-faced mother to finish thinking whatever she was thinking. She looked as if she were seeing all sorts of things inside her head – things I couldn't see. It felt like a wide, dark river between us and I was tired and miserable and wished we hadn't come.

❧ GEORGINA ☙

In Paris, Verlaine, I saw your soul
at aperitif hour on a terraced café,
your fingers fiddling with a miniature roundabout
enchantedly twirling the painted horses
and humming under a lilac-lipped smile:
'Tournez, tournez, bons chevaux de bois,
Tournez cent tours, tournez mille tours,
Tournez souvent et tournez toujours,
Tournez, tournez au son des hautbois.'
Then the bead-eyed waiter came
and the painted horses slowed and slowed —
Tournez —
Tournez —
And there was left the broken roundabout
And the forced joy of the blind street-player.
(Georgina Hardiman, 1968)

Head suddenly bursting with the sounds and pictures of 'then' … Momentary panic.

I shouldn't have come back.

Standing there on the wet pavement in the dark, close to the hiss and blare of traffic, in a kaleidoscope of reflected lights. A once-so-taken-for-granted street. I try to face down the memories with a wry smile. Humour is what I need. Distance.

Nothing doing. The memories swarm, settle on me, agitated, clambering over each other with a deafening drone. I keep still, just trying not to get too badly stung.

Places … Words … Touching … Music … People … Eating … All the small things by which we got to know one another. The films we watched, agreeing and disagreeing about the actors, the direction, the intention, the originality or otherwise, talking our way to a café or bar afterwards … sometimes running into his friends there … Had they seen it? … What did they think? Being part of what was going on – good to be young, then – against war, against the tyranny of the old and the past (so soon to sneak behind our lines and get its own insidiously back).

The books. Him reading out to me a little post-coital Camus, the way some people might have lit up a Gitane. Or some Boris Vian. And poetry, sometimes – Prévert, Rimbaud, Verlaine, of course … though I didn't understand most of it.

And music. Above all, music, of course. All kinds of it. Having my ears opened to what I'd been missing, all that had been kept from me … apart from Sunday-school hymns and my father's childhood songs and a few by Schubert we sang at school. We made love to Bach cello suites or jazz, ate dinner to string quartets or the songs of Boris Vian, Serge Gainsbourg, Leo Ferré, Georges Brassens. Once I even tried to get a sound out of his saxophone ('a cow having a baby' he called the strangled honking that was all I could manage: I didn't try again). He tried to get me to sing, but I was too self-conscious. He sometimes got annoyed with me for my lack of confidence. 'If I'd had your wealth and education,' I'd say, 'then maybe … ' And he'd feel dreadful … and guilty about his own privileged childhood and youth. I said, 'I am what I am: take me or leave me.'

And of course, in the end, he did both.

❧ ELOISA ❧

The people my mother used to 'au pair' for – Pierre and Claudine – were preparing supper for us. We were greeted with lots of emotional hugging and kissing. (Quite over-the-top, I thought. Why did the French insist on kissing everyone twice?!) Their *apartement* was beautiful: I was almost afraid to sit on the yellow and white sofa in case I made it mucky. Enormous, Chinese-style table lamps gave out a relaxing, drowsy light. It was all such a contrast to the tearing wind on the boat and the sea-sickness and the crowding on the *Métro* that I felt exhausted with all the sudden differences. And then my mother was trying to talk in French – talking much more slowly than she usually did, as if she were having to think very hard to find the right words – words I didn't know. She was turning into a stranger from a world of words I was excluded from. I felt terribly small and alone. I hadn't realised that my mother might know people who led a life so very different from our own. I tried to imagine them visiting us – sitting in our living-room ... They would look so odd! Everything about them was smooth and perfect – Claudine's blond hair held in a perfect shape; her bright lipstick exactly the same shade as her nail varnish; wrinkle-less tights on her elegant legs; beautiful shoes ... Several silver rings. And Pierre, his lightly tanned skin smooth as china, with his slightly greying hair sleeked back, coolly attentive to my mother and directing to me the occasional reserved smile. Once or twice they all looked towards me and I heard my name and knew they were talking about me, but didn't know what they were saying. I can't say I really liked them. They didn't make much effort to make me feel 'comfortable'. At one point Claudine brought over a framed photo of two boys in their teens. My mother put her hand to her face as she looked at them, as if she couldn't believe what she was seeing. Then she leaned over and showed me the picture. 'These are the boys I used to look after when they were very young.' They shared the smooth, rich look of their parents. I didn't say anything.

Strange food. But I was too hungry to care. (My mother made signs with her eyes that I should *not* take a third helping until others had had seconds.)

Eventually the meal was over and they stopped talking. They took us to a building nearby, the place where my mother lived when she worked for them. Claudine owned some rooms that were let out to students and people like that. My mother's old room wasn't occupied just then, so we would be staying there.

The tiny lift juddered past a number of floors, as far as it could go and when we got out we still had to walk up some corkscrew stairs to a room in the roof. Part of the ceiling was sloping. There was more kissing and then we were left on our own.

Silence. The look on my mother's face was even more peculiar than when we came up from the *Métro* and she'd just stood there in the rain, gazing about.

In the end she remembered I was in the room, too, and put her arm around my shoulders. Her mouth smelled of wine. 'It's so strange … so strange, being back here … Not quite real, somehow. Strange, but … kind of wonderful, too.'

Wonderful??!! I, personally, was blind to its charms. The room seemed terribly … *basic*. I'd thought it was going to be nice, like Pierre and Claudine's place only a bit smaller. I'd thought it might have those soft, bride-veil curtains at long windows. But it was scarcely as big as my bedroom at home and it smelled as if too many people had lived in it. Not very clean people. It had grubby green walls with pale rectangles and lots of pin-holes where posters had been fixed. And just one small, square window high up. No curtains at all. And a grimy rug in the middle of the room. There was one proper bed and a small camp bed for me. The white bed-linen was the only clean-looking thing in the room. A single bulb on a wire gave out a mean, urine-coloured light. There was a reading-lamp on a shelf by the main bed: the room looked a bit better once that was turned on. A tiny basin with all its pipes showing huddled in the corner. Two shelves for books. A plain wooden table and chair under the window.

'It hasn't changed at all,' she said, gazing about and remembering the 'old days', I supposed, before I was born. I felt abandoned again. I thought she might tell me off if I climbed onto the table and looked out of the window – better than being ignored while she relived a life I was no part of. But she didn't say a word.

The building was on a slope and I realised, from the spread of lights, there'd be a lot to see from there in the day time. I ran a finger down the glass. Filthy.

She was still ignoring me, so I struggled with the foreign window-fastening until I managed to open it. A bucket of cold air hit my face. But at least it smelled crisp and clean. And the view was suddenly sharper, not veiled by grubby glass, and city noises were vivid on my ears. I thought of the girl on the train being out there somewhere, perhaps in one of the buildings silhouetted against the reddish night sky of the city.

Then it burst like a firework in my head. The girl on the train and me: we were *twins*! All that stuff my mother had told me about my father 'having to go away' was lies. We were twins born in France but our parents fell out, and as there were two of us the same, they took one each. How did they decide which one? 'Heads or tails'? 'Eeny meeny miny mo'? Was I nearly that *other* girl? – living in Paris and speaking French? I might've had a father and no mother. Or just a stepmother. I might've been rich and had lots of nice clothes. New ones.

I gave my twin a name. 'Minette'. Like the girl in the library book, *Minette's Day*, which was supposed to tell you what it was like to be a French girl but only showed things like the

Eiffel Tower and eating *croissants*. I imagined us meeting, talking … in the stilted little bit of French I could just about manage.

'*Bonjour, Minette.*'

'*Bonjour, Eloisa. Oû habitez-vous?*'

'*J'habite Londres.*'

'Close the window, *chérie. Il fait froid,*' interrupted my mother.

'What?'

'It's cold. I know it needed some fresh air in here, but that's enough. This old radiator's no warmer than it used to be.'

It was all so much worse than home: I couldn't for the life of me imagine why she wanted to come back.

❧ GEORGINA ❧

The feel of French in my mouth again. Like stumbling about in borrowed shoes that are too big. (I was never very good at languages, anyway. And he didn't really help – impatient with my incompetence or liking to show off his own knowledge of English.) And I spend the evening high on the adrenalin of anxiety, hoping Eloisa will behave herself.

I'd forgotten how beautiful Pierre and Claudine's place was ... and is. Strange to think I used to clean it. (I feel as if I should be doing the washing up after the meal!) A shame the boys aren't here – away ski-ing with their cousins – but Claudine shows me a recent picture, Michel a handsome teenager now and naughty little Jean (he'd been an *abominable* two-year-old: I'd nearly given my notice more than once on account of him) already doing very well at the *lycée*. Pierre is greying at the temples now, though he's as slim and tanned as ever, and Claudine doesn't seem to have changed at all – still petite with perfect nails. They tell me I haven't changed either. (The usual civilized niceties by which we try to keep each other cheerful?)

They say kind things about Eloisa ... now yawning uncontrollably. We decide it really is time to walk around the corner to where we'll be staying, before Eloisa falls dead asleep.

And so the moment I've been longing for and dreading in equal measure: the room that was mine during the brief time that would shape the rest of my life ...

1967. Arriving in Paris with virtually nothing – not even my virginity (a stringy lecturer in Middle English, big on the *carpe diem* theme). Just half a dozen of my favourite books, the school magazine containing my first published piece of writing, a couple of outfits, and enough knickers to get me through a week. A piece of paper with the address of the people I'd be working for – arranged through an 'au pair' agency in London. Yes, basically, I was in Paris to do housework ...

But the excitement! Heady with freedom and avid for every sight and sensation. Stupidly exhilarated by the smell of market strawberries, the faces of old men in half-light at *le zinc* ... 'My life.'

Living on bread and cheese and apples for the first fortnight – until Claudine found out and fed me constant omelettes – which caused other problems. (Not easy, being a vegetarian in France.)

The shelf gradually filling with cheap books from the stalls along the river and from those sad *prix réduit* boxes outside the shops on the Boul' Mich and the rue des Écoles. Finding a cheap Moroccan bowl for fruit (only slightly chipped), and filching an empty jar from Claudine's bin for bits of foliage and damaged flowers I'd rescue from the ground at markets. I used to put them just there, on that table beneath the window.

After the claustrophobic luxury of Pierre and Claudine's, it was always a relief to come home to simplicity. I'd sit cross-legged on the bed, munching an apple and reading or trying to write poetry. Even though the window was so high you had to stand on tip-toe to see out of it, I loved the view from there so much I tried to draw it, once, though I hadn't drawn for years. Not very good, but I pinned it to the wall, beside the joyful poster of Truffaut's *Jules et Jim* I'd splashed out on (the bit where the three of them are having a race across the bridge and Jeanne Moreau is dressed up as a man).

Sometimes Pierre and Claudine needed me to baby-sit and I'd have to stay there for the night: a little bed in the children's room. Too warm and airless. (In trouble, once, for opening the window. *'la sécurité* ... ' Not a problem where *I* was living.)

And then *he* stumbled into my life and the room was full of him, too – even when he wasn't in it. The old record player he bought me used to stand in that corner ...

Him on the bed – *that* bed – stark naked, toes to the ceiling, hands behind his head, his satisfied '*sexe*' floppy, snoozing. Talking about music. Couldn't believe I'd never heard of John Coltrane. I teased him it was because he was older than me that he knew more: a five-year start. And as a musician, he ought to know all that, anyway. Instead of criticising my ignorance, I said, he should think of me as one of his students: he should try to *enlighten* me ... which gave him the excuse to hold forth while I peeled oranges or made the bitter coffee he liked.

How will I be able to lie down on that bed again?

❧ ELOISA ❧

When we came back from the smelly toilet halfway down the curly stairs, I shivered into my pyjamas then got between the stiff linen sheets of the wobbly camp bed. No duvet: just two bald, hard blankets and a funny sausage pillow that hurt my neck. I wriggled and shuffled and scrabbled about in the bed, trying to get comfortable, hoping it'd warm up. My mother buttoned her blue winceyette pyjamas right up to the neck (humming happily in her own world), turned off the overhead light so just the reading-lamp was on, then slid into bed.

I got out of bed, pulled my socks and big jumper back on with audible humphing noises, got back into bed and lay on my back, gazing at nothing.

She got out of bed, put *her* jumper and socks back on.

'I bet it's not as cold as this in your friends' flat.' I gave an exaggerated shiver.

'No, I imagine it isn't.'

'They could've made it a bit nicer for us.'

'They probably thought I'd like it to be the same as when I lived here. I did say to them it'd be like old times.'

'More like "cold times".'

'Oo. Very funny. Being chilly obviously sharpens your wit.'

I grumbled into a foetal position, my back to her, my face to the grubby wall. I heard her snap open the case of her reading glasses.

'Mummy … '

'Mmmm … ?'

'On the Underground … I mean the *Métro* … there was this girl … '

' … who looked a bit like you? But only a bit, Tootsie.'

'Enough to make you look: I saw you.'

'Yes, because the chances of another girl about your age

being as gorgeous as you, my jewel, are … '

'Unless she's my twin.'

She just laughed at me. 'If you had a twin, I think I might've known about it – might've noticed I was having to push out two babies instead of the regulation "one".'

I was silent for a while. There was just the whisper of her turning pages. Then my deepest question forced itself out.

'Why are we here?'

She repeated my question slowly, playing for time, I suppose.

'Why … are … we … here … ? *C'est une grand question, ma petite philosophe.*'

'Don't say words I can't understand. It was horrible when you were talking to *them* and I didn't know what you were saying. You were like someone I didn't know.'

'Are you as cold as I am, sweetheart?'

'Colder.'

'If you pop in here with me, Toots, we'd both get warm.'

She made me go next to the wall in case I fell out in the night, she said. There was extra warmth from the reading lamp clamped to the shelf above us.

'What's your book called?'

'*Memoirs of a Dutiful Daughter.*'

'Don't you mean *beautiful* daughter?'

She turned it so I could see the title. 'No. Dutiful. Only she wasn't really.'

I'd never heard the word 'dutiful' before.

'What's it about?'

'A French woman who wanted an interesting life and not to fritter it away on doing things just to be "respectable". She wanted to think and have the kind of life that was best for *her*. She didn't want things to be boring and stupid.'

'How do you know all that? You're still at the beginning.'

'I've read it before.'

'Are you reading it again because we're in France?'

She narrowed her eyes and put on a comic French accent. 'You know, Inspecteur Clue-zo, I zink you may be on to somezing.'

'Read it to me.'

'Okay, *ma fille*. Here we go. "*In the Luxembourg Gardens we were forbidden to play with strange little girls: this was obviously because we were made of fine stuff …* "'

'No. From the beginning. I want to know what it says right from the start.' I was sure this book was somehow connected to why we were there, though I didn't know how.

She turned back to the beginning and began to read in her soft, story-telling voice that used to get me to sleep when I was little. '*I was born at four o'clock in the morning on the 9th of January 1908 in a room fitted with white-enamelled furniture overlooking the boulevard Raspail. In the family photographs …* '

❦ GEORGINA ❧

Ouch! ... Those sharp knees. The bed's too small for both of us. (However did he and I used to manage?!) It'll have to be the camp bed or I won't get a wink of sleep, especially if she starts doing that thing with her arms I've seen her do in the night.

God, it's cold. They might at least have put a kettle in the room. And a curtain at the window. Or am I just getting old?! It didn't bother me then. It was all part of the excitement, the difference. The glamour of poverty! ...

He likes coming to my room, even when it isn't to make love – says it's less claustrophobic than his mother's spacious and comfortable apartment.

'Too many carpets, too many curtains, too much padded furniture. Like having cotton-wool in your ears.'

'Why don't you get your own place? You must be able to afford it, with your teaching salary.'

'I couldn't afford it emotionally. My mother is rather lonely, you know. If I left I think it would "break her heart", as you say.'

'Do you mean you'll never move out, even if ... '

'Even if I got married? No, that would be different for her. It would be natural to leave her then. Before that, she would have it badly, I think. She has enough of unhappiness, still, with my father leaving her.'

I wish he'd said, 'Even if WE got married.'

I go quiet, feeling suddenly unsure of what I am to him. Just a bit of fun until he finds the right woman to 'settle down' with? Or is it just a casual male use of the customary 'I', rather than 'we'? ...

'Why are you not speaking, Georgie? What is in your head that you're not saying?'

'It doesn't matter.'

'Yes it does.'

'It doesn't.'

'But it DOES matter. You must learn to speak what is in your head. You must learn to defend your ideas.'

'That's easy for you: you're a man. And you had a good French education.'

'But surely in English schools the *professeurs* encourage their students to … '

'Some did … '

(Miss Rose: 'Think for yourselves, girls. Think, question, scrutinize.' One of her favourite words. Scrutinize. Making fun of her pronunciation, the sound of the 'u' closer to how it would be in 'rut' than in 'screw'.)

'Oh, the English!'

'But I'm not properly English. I'm half Polish and half American.'

'American. Yes. Even worse! But educated in England.'

'So you don't like me. You don't love me because you despise … '

'Of course I love you, you stupid English girl! I love you in spite of the fact that you are a strange kind of Polish and American English girl.'

'Then why do you love me?'

'I love you for your shoulders.'

'For my SHOULDERS?!'

'Yes. You have very nice shoulders.'

'You're making fun of me again. You're not taking me seriously.'

'What does it mean, this "seriously"?'

'Oh … YOU!!'

He laughs at me. And soon I'm laughing too.

Would we really ever 'settle down' to an ordinary domestic life together? When he says 'love', maybe he doesn't mean what I mean: deeply, for ever, whatever.

Would I have to put up with him having 'contingent loves'? ... like that jazz singer with the amazing hair he's on such 'good terms' with? Does he ... ? Do they ... ? Or maybe just an 'old flame'. You can usually tell, seeing people together, whether they've known each other nakedly. Something to do with the eyes ... the thoughtlessly casual way of touching ... or the over-careful avoidance of touching ... or the moment of hesitation before touching ... Why does it seem to matter so much? It shouldn't, if one were rational. But I think even de Beauvoir minded, though she pretended not to. Probably afraid Sartre would accuse her of 'bourgeois values' or something. Yes, I think she was hurt. I think ...

❧ ELOISA ❧

I stirred to a dull grey light at the uncurtained window and plenty of room in the bed. My mother was in the camp bed. Under the green blankets her curled-up body made a landscape of hills and valleys, her brown hair a tangled winter forest, the bed-linen patches of snow. Drifting into a dream ... watching a very tiny me running across the landscape, making for the forest of her hair because I am looking for something or someone (My father? The girl on the metro?) and words in my head say lost things might be found in a forest ... I am running and running ...

But someone was calling me back ... calling my name ... 'Eloisa ... Eloisa ... ' telling me not to go looking.

'Eloisa ... Eloisa ... '

The landscape turned to a blue ocean close to my face. Sound of the sea.

'Come on, dormouse. Wake up or we'll lose the best of the day.'

My mother was sitting on the bed, near my head, in her chunky blue jumper. The waves were rows of knitting and the sound of the sea just city traffic. The backs of her fingers stroked my cheek, coaxing me into my first Parisian morning.

❧ GEORGINA ❧

We make a game of it: I invent an 'air camera' – the photographic equivalent of 'air guitar'– since we didn't have a real one, persuading her to pose for it. She's embarrassed at first. 'Don't! People are looking. They'll think we're mad.' 'So what! Relax, Tootsie. Let's have fun!' I'm hoping it will help to fix certain places in her mind. But of course, as I line up the imaginary shots, a scrum of ghosts appears around her, almost crowding her out – though I am the only one who can see them.

The pages of our 'air album' begin with Eloisa on Pont Neuf, a grey Seine narrowing off into the distance. She's wearing her duffle-coat and big red scarf; the wind's pushing her hair forwards from behind; her shoulders are raised against the cold; her mouth is trying to smile but her eyes are anxious … (*The piece he wrote called* Pont Neuf *, his voice explaining how the harpsichord-like beginning was the time of the bridge's origin, the 'anguished' saxophone section the cartfuls of the condemned rumbling over the bridge during the Terror … the theme metamorphosing into something lighter, the bridge as a place of fun, entertainment, romance … and finally the cacophony of modern traffic fading into lovers by moonlight, and a scarcely audible kiss.*)

Eloisa rather stiff and serious beside the statue of Montaigne, *rue des Écoles*. He sits, one leg crossed over the other, leaning forward with a slight smile as if listening intently, wisely amused by what he's hearing. The inscription on the plinth just visible: 'PARIS A MON COEUR DES MON ENFANCE … ' (*'You have never read Montaigne? Incroyable! What is wrong with you English? … Ouch! That hurt me! Put on your coat. We go to a bookshop … NOW!' … I wasn't up to the French version, though, so bought a second-hand Penguin translation* at *Shakespeare & Co, without letting on to him so he'd think I'd read the* Essaies *in French. And that old Penguin was the one a certain little girl later 'illustrated' for me with a red crayon when she was three and I'd taken my eyes off her for a few moments and I got uncharacteristically cross, out of all proportion, when she started to rip out the offending pages …*)

Several photos on the *boul Mich* – one outside Gibert Jeune. (*Those cheap little* Livres de Poche *I used to flick through there, wishing my French were good enough to read them and cure my ignorance of French literature, afraid he'd find me boring if I didn't 'know things', afraid to admit how uncultured – how unprivileged – my background was compared with his. He could take so many things for granted that he didn't even realize what they were.*)

Another photo looking along the *boulevard* … (*A jostle of ghosts carry banners and chant, the road haunted by sirens and the surreal figures of riot police like something out of* Dr Who *in the filthy fog of tear gas.*)

Looking up the *rue Soufflot* towards the *Panthéon* (*… where we sheltered from the tremendous storm that afternoon and talked about Voltaire and what he really meant by* 'Il faut cultiver votre jardin' – *though I can't remember what we decided in the end, only wanting the storm to be over so we could go back and make love.*)

Eloisa looking a bit more cheerful in the Luxembourg Gardens, with leafless trees and the big round pond in the background. (*Summer days there, reading on those uncomfortable metal chairs, moving them from sun to shade and back to sun again. Meeting Aline for the first time there, by accident, as she walked with a friend. My embarrassment: it was before he'd 'taken me home'.*)

Eloisa small and dark against the domed white bulk of *Sacré Coeur*. (*He called the domes of Paris the city's 'breasts' and the Eiffel Tower its 'phallus'.*)

A close-up profile of her leaning on a stone ledge just below the church, that tear-jerking panorama of Paris spreading into the distance, brilliant in the gift of brief winter sunshine breaking through that afternoon.

And we end up back at the Tuileries. (*All I could see was the snow and the two of us dancing even though weighed down with coats and boots and bags, and just feeling so happy and alive and full of music and wanting to dance for ever ... But then, by summer, the Tuileries statues had had their lips painted red by the students ... which was funny if you could see it as lipstick, but terrible if you could only see blood. And everything had changed because someone had led six million skeletons out of the family cupboard and the dancing and the music stopped dead.*)

❧ ELOISA ❧

On our third evening in Paris, some 'old friends' (as my mother called them) were taking us out to dinner at a proper restaurant. We'd have to 'spruce ourselves up a bit', she said. She even abandoned her jeans for a pair of black trousers, so I knew it was serious. She persuaded me into my grey woolly tights and blue school skirt (the only skirt I possessed and which I didn't know she'd packed), but I was allowed to wear my favourite red polo-neck. She worked my impossible hair into something like a pony-tail and checked my nails were clean. Not used to this kind of mother, I was fidgety and anxious. What on earth was it all about?

In the end I came out with it. 'Why are we trying to impress your friends?'

She dampened a handkerchief and rubbed at the sandy mud on my shoes before she replied. 'It's too complicated to explain, Tootsie.' She rubbed at my shoes a bit more before saying, 'Just go with it this time, can you? I'm a bit nervous as it is, seeing these particular friends after so long. And my trousers are so creased and there's no iron.'

'What am I supposed to do when we meet them?'

'Just be your usual charming, intelligent self, my jewel, and eat as much as you can – without appearing piggish.' (Veiled reference to my ravenousness on the evening of our arrival, I assumed.) 'They're paying and it's a good restaurant. If we camel-it, we can last the rest of the holiday on minimal eating and have enough money left for you to choose a souvenir.'

(Was that a little bribe hanging in the air between us?)

A table for nine. Three people were already there when we arrived: Monsieur and Madame Bonnat and their daughter, Monique, with whom I shook hands, English-style, while my mother did the multiple kissing thing, calling them Thérèse and Patrice and looking rather emotional as Thérèse gave her a long hug that seemed to be saying something they both understood but I didn't. Monsieur Bonnat smiled at me and winked, as if to say, 'These women!'

Monique eyed me coolly. Only a couple of years older than me, she had an assured, rather chilly manner. Plumper than me, with straight, dark brown hair cut just below her ears and a precise fringe, she was wearing a very smart blue-and-green tartan skirt with crisp pleats, a grey jumper with a white blouse-collar showing at the neck. Between her blue leather lace-ups and the hem of her skirt were grey woolly tights, just like mine. Did she find them itchy, too? Thinking I'd found a good conversational opening, I smiled, pointed at my grey-clad legs, then at hers, and made scratching movements. She put on a questioning kind of face. Her mother, noticing my gesture and guessing its meaning, translated it for her since Monique had, it seemed, failed to understand my sign language. Monique – sophisticated, assured, twelve-year-old Monique – gave a condescending little smile. And that was the end of our relationship for the evening.

The words of my mother's book came back to me – how the French lady writing the book hadn't been allowed to play with 'strange little girls' because they were made of different 'stuff'. Was I a strange little girl, then? – not made of good enough 'stuff'?

Four older people arrived: Monsieur and Madame Pinot, and Monsieur and Madame Laumain. I offered my hand, but the women insisted on kisses. I had to stop myself coughing from their perfume. They said something gabbly to my mother who was smiling oddly, her face an unnatural pink.

She said to me, 'They think calling them Monsieur and Madame is a bit formal. They'd like you to call them aunts and uncles.' I wasn't sure from the way she said it that she was entirely happy with this. 'So … ' (She took a deep breath.) ' … this is *tante* Aline … ' (A smart, grey-haired lady in black: lots of silver jewellery.) 'And her husband, *oncle* Alphonse … ' (Tall, distinguished, sparkly blue eyes and a big, bony nose.) 'And this is *tante* Maude … ' (A browner, rounder, shorter version of Aline – sisters – in a green suit straining a little at the buttons and seams: lots of gold rings.) 'And *oncle* Maurice … ' (Plump, balding little man with a permanently 'apologizing' expression.)

'That's funny,' I said, 'the letters go together: Aline and Alphonse, Maude and Maurice. It makes it easier to remember who goes with who.'

Maman stumblingly tried to translate what I'd said. They smiled and said some things, looking at me in a really nice way.

'What did they say?'

'Something like you have a very quick mind, as well as being beautiful and polite. I think you have a fan club, Tootsie.'

I felt like saying I didn't think Monique was a member, but I didn't want to spoil things.

I did my best to eat as much as I could, but it was unnerving, them keep looking at me in a really kind but curious way. I felt there were reasons for it, but couldn't tell what they were. *Tante* Maude, in particular, looked as though she were searching for something in my face. I gave her one of my best smiles because she looked so kind. But tears suddenly came into her eyes when I did that, even though she was giving me a big smile back. What a strange bunch of people!

But they let me order strawberries. In January. (They were that rich.)

❦ GEORGINA ❧

I keep my promise of buying her a souvenir as a reward for behaving well (and eating plenty) the evening of the restaurant. But she's *ages* going through the shelves of plastic bits and bobs. I'm desperate to make the most of our last few hours in Paris, not knowing when we'll be back, and there she is absorbed in tourist junk. Plastic Eiffel Tower thermometers. Little wind-up musical boxes that play the cancan (almost) as a little plastic dancer with a red net skirt and her leg up high in front judders round and round on top. A small plastic box you put to your eyes and click the lever at the side to see different views of Paris. And dozens of little plastic snow scenes, *boules de neige* to shake into a blizzard: the Eiffel Tower in a snow storm ... *Notre Dame* in a snow storm ... *Sacré Coeur* in a snow storm ... She insists on testing them all as I feel the seconds dripping away into precious last minutes.

In the end it's a toss-up between the cancan dancer and the Eiffel Tower snow-globe. A protracted 'eeny-meeny-miny-mo' finally gives her the little dancer. I pay quickly then grab her hand and virtually pull her into the street: there's one more place I really want to go to.

Then, a few yards from the shop, she says she's changed her mind: she wants the Eiffel Tower snow scene instead.

'It's too late,' I snap. 'You have to learn that once you've made a decision in this life, you're stuck with it and have to make the best of it.' More gently, I add, 'Anyway, I think your little dancer's really sweet. Are you going to give her a name?'

'Yes,' she says.

'Well, what is it?'

'Eiffel Tower,' she says, looking straight ahead. 'Eiffel's her Christian name, Tower's her surname. I'm making the best of it, like you said.'

77

At which point I mutter something I would rather not record.

Time to go home.

(In my diary for '68 I'd noted that, on several walls near *Les Invalides*, some 'wag' had painted 'FROGS GO HOME'. And I'd written, 'Where's home? A landscape of the mind. Portable. Packs into a soft grey walnut the size of a head. You can take it with you wherever you go.' Well ... maybe.)

Leaving the first time was worse. Convinced a bulge was visible already, I bought a cheap ring at the flea market – for 'going back' – then stuck to my guns and didn't wear it.

But, all the same, I was a defeated army shambling home.

Stolen from myself. That wasn't supposed to happen to Georgina Hardiman.

Georgina Hardiman was going to be ... something. I had things to say, didn't I? – though I wasn't sure, then, exactly what they were. But I wanted to shake the world by the shoulders, show it things it didn't seem to see. I'd go *everywhere*, look at *everything* – Russia, Katmandu, South America ... deserts, forests, snow, oceans, mountains, villages, cities ... and I'd meet so many people and talk to them and give them the benefit of my experiences and knowledge. I'd open eyes, make people think. All those books I would write ... poetry, stories, novels, travel books, maybe even philosophy ... I was Georgina Hardiman and I could do it all!

Probably just hormones, of course, all that energy and enthusiasm of the young. Really just the body getting ready to reproduce: it's all the energy you're going to need for raising children.

As the boat-train cleared *Gare du Nord* on that October day in 1968 (Maude, crying, waved me off), I'd strained for the last glimpse of *Sacré Coeur* – wedding-cake-cum-sepulchre – my mind a dog chasing its tail around a clot of darkness.

Now our beautiful daughter is sitting there opposite me, watching *les banlieus* run past the window. 'Be back soon,' I say, to reassure her – or myself.

'Do we have to?'

'I thought you liked Paris.'

'But I don't like the beds. Or the pillows. They're uncomfortable.'

'Sounds like you're older than I thought, Toots. Children your age aren't supposed to care about things like that. You're supposed to want to go everywhere, see everything, do everything. Or … ' (I lower my voice, leaning towards her) ' … are you really my grandmother in disguise?'

'What do you mean?'

'Oh, never mind.' (Leaning back. Weary. Houses thinning already.) 'It's … '

'I know: "too complicated to explain," isn't it.'

'Hole in one, Tootsie.'

Bleak winter fields of northern France. Mud. The occasional little scab of a war cemetery. Lest we forget.

❧ ELOISA ❧

Not long after we got back from Paris, my mother received a long letter from *tante* Maude. She told me the letter said some very nice things about me and included a special message: what would I like for my birthday? My little plastic dancer having already snapped off below the knee so only her stump turned gruesomely to the musical-box cancan, I asked for an Eiffel Tower snow-globe like the one I'd nearly chosen instead.

My mother left the letter on her desk while she went to have a bath. Vanity urged me to sneak a look. Even though it was in French and I wouldn't understand all the 'nice things' *tante* Maude has said about me, I'd at least be able to see just how many times my name was mentioned ... how much of the letter was about *me* ...

Not at all in the first paragraph, as far as I could make out from *tante* Maude's unusual handwriting. But there it was in the second one. And on the second page it was there again in a sentence that had two other names in it, but not names of people we met in France or that I'd ever heard before. One is Colette. The other is a strange name I hadn't heard of. It looks like 'Amadon'. Perhaps it wasn't a person at all. It was a bit like 'Amazon', so maybe it was a river ... or a place. But why was my name in the same sentence? How was I connected with those names?

Idea! Copy out the sentence then, once I knew French, I'd find out. Or I could find someone who spoke French to tell me. I couldn't ask my mother because I shouldn't have been looking at the letter at all. We had strict 'privacy' rules when it came to anything written that was in the area of her desk, because some of the things she wrote for money weren't the sort of things I should read, she said, and she couldn't forever be remembering to put them away.

But I only got as far as copying out the two names when I heard my mother coming back from her bath. I stuffed the piece of paper and pencil into my pocket and tried to look innocent. On her way past the desk, she picked up the letter and I never saw it again. But the names went on dancing together through my head – a spiky, worrying sort of dance that didn't make any sense.

Two days before my birthday, a small parcel arrived from France. The Eiffel Tower snow globe.

'It's called a *boule de neige*, Tootsie. *Neige* is French for snow. *Il neige* means it's snowing.'

It was bigger and better than the ones I'd seen in the souvenir shop. I made it snow and snow.

I kept it on my bedside table, as close to my pillowed face as possible. The muted glow of my 'going-to-sleep' lamp shone softly down on it. Somebody liked me enough to send me a birthday present all the way from France! It was a good feeling.

While my mother went through the bedtime ritual of closing the curtains, tucking me in, pushing my slippers under the bed, I reached out from under the warmth of the duvet and shook up a blizzard in Paris, then watched it calm and settle. Shook it again. Watched … Calming and settling … calming and settling …

3

'THE HEART OF THE MATTER'

❧ ELOISA ❧

Things I like	Things I don't like
Strawberrys	School and other childern
Peoms	Piggens
Cats	Smell of other poepels poo
Chockolate	Orange (colour not froot)
My not school cloths	Itchy tites
	Plasters when there
	taken off
	Banarnas
	Apple (the girl not froot)
	Those coff sweets with
	shugar on
	Pitcher of lady with no
	cloths and not real face
	over my Mum's desk
	Other childern

❧ GEORGINA ❧

Alma suggests an animal. (The school is putting pressure on me about the 'not talking' business and they want to have her 'referred', so anything is worth a try.)

'She doesn't have any problem talking to cats and dogs.' True, she's always crouching down or reaching up to stroke and exchange intimacies with cats, or asking strangers the names of their dogs. 'If she talks to an animal on a daily basis, maybe she'll eventually transfer it to children.'

A goldfish is the only possibility in our small flat.

Wriggles, we call him. He becomes a kind of father confessor to us both. Eloisa spends hours, nose squashed against the curve of his bowl, confiding her thoughts and little misdemeanours. And when she isn't there I sometimes find myself saying things I normally keep inside, especially after it all goes wrong with David. 'Let's be lonely together, Wriggles.' 'Each in the glass globe of their own head, eh, Wriggles? Staring about and mouthing off … nothing.' 'Life's an open and shut case for you, isn't it, Wriggles?' 'We're alike, you and me, aren't we, Wriggles? Both were meant to live in open water, and look how we've ended up? – you in your small goldfish bowl and I in mine … '

But the 'transference' to other children doesn't happen: she still refuses to talk at school. An intense relationship with Wriggles is enough for her.

After a few months I guess it all gets too much for him. He floats to the top of the water and refuses to swim any more, no matter how much Eloisa encourages him with a spoon. We bury him in a plant pot as we don't have a garden. She insists on a cross (two worn-down pencils wired together with deconstructed paper-clips) and for ages I can't look at the spider-plant without thinking of its green being fed by poor Wriggles' progressive disintegration among its roots.

❀ ELOISA ❀

In Memmory of My Gold Fish

A poem by Eloisa Gabrielle Hardiman

I had a little goldfish
And Wriggles was his name.
But I have'nt got him anymore
And that is such a shame.

When things were bad at school
I told him all my trubbles.
He never told me off.
He just blew me lots of bubbles.

In his little goldfish bowel
He swam happily around.
Then one day he flowted.
He was quite dead. He drownd.

The world my mother made for the two of us seemed so different from other people's way of going on that I was confused. I longed for a life that was more normal than mine. A Janet-and-John life. A house with a garden and resident puppy. Brothers and sisters (well, one, at least). A daddy with a car and a mummy who baked cakes and cleaned the house properly instead of pulling stories out of her head like bright silk scarves from a magician's sleeve (those sheets and sheets of paper she pulled up out of the mouth of Qwerty).

The gap between the life I thought I should have and the life I actually had was a big one and the only way I sometimes found of responding was with hysterics or granite-like silence.

As part of her campaign to get me talking to other children

again – after the death of 'Wriggles' – she decided I should start going to birthday parties. (I suppose she thought that if I had fun and played games at parties, then the rest would follow.) She'd never forced the issue before, and my will had always been stronger than hers on the matter. (I could throw a really mean tantrum!) But, with the school breathing down her neck to 'do something' about my refusing to talk, she became unshakeable in the face of my fury.

The first party invitation to come my way after her decision was from Dora. And Dora's mum made it clear it was to be a proper party-dress kind of party: she didn't hold with letting girls 'scruff about' in dungarees or trousers.

The Oxfam shop didn't have many party dresses: the only thing small enough was an ex-bridesmaid's. 'A nice delicate yellow,' the woman called it. 'It's wee-wee coloured,' I hissed. The shop-woman gathered her mouth in an ugly way at me. I was made to try it on, my mother wrestling it down over my deliberately awkward head and suddenly non-bending arms, not bothering to remove the over-large jeans I was wearing. I was dragged to the mirror by the rack of smelly old suits for men.

The ghastly garment was all puff and gather, shiny in a cheap kind of way, and a pale grey dumpling of once-white artificial flowers hung heavily near the left shoulder. In defiance of all the dress stood for, my hair corkscrewed out madly above it and my jeans concertina-ed round my ankles. (Hell is other people's clothes.)

When we got to Dora's house and I realised I actually was going to have to go through with it, I looked my mother straight in the eye and said, 'I hate you'. She didn't bat an eyelid as she replied with, 'Enjoy the party, sweetheart.'

You had to wipe your shoes on a 'Welcome' mat (they were still checked before you were allowed to proceed to the pink carpet), then go and put your presents with the others. Dora wasn't allowed to open them until after tea. There were lots of felt-tips, going by the shapes of the parcels. But there was one huge box – more than half as high as Dora herself – wrapped in shiny silver paper and tied with a huge pink ribbon.

There were games (in which I did not join) and then tea (which I did not eat) and then the undoing of the presents. The enormous one was for the end. Dora ripped at our gifts, hungry for surprises. Books, coloured pencils, felt-tips … And then the Big Box. She approached it with trembling anticipation. Some children began calling out what they thought it was. 'It's a pony!' 'A big stuffed dog!' 'A tree house!' The bow undone, the silver paper ripped off, the top open. Some of us stood up to get a look … and were made to sit down again before Dora was allowed to continue.

'It's wrapped in newspaper,' she announced, tearing at it and flinging the bits everywhere. Then, 'Something red! I can see something red!' and she drew a red-wrapped parcel out from the depths of the enormous box, her face rather flushed as she turned her attention to this more modest-sized gift. 'More paper!' She smiled, but her eyes were over-bright and she didn't look at her dad who was snapping away with his camera. Tissue paper. It suggested something delicate. The guessing started again.

' … princess crown … ' ' … cuckoo clock … ' ' … jewellery box … '

'I can see something green.' She pulled out another even smaller box.

' … bracelet … ' ' … hamster … '

Now a little tiny earth-brown box. Dora's eyes glittering. I looked at her parents to see if they were worried because Dora might be going to cry, from the look of her. But they had smiles on their faces, but not nice smiles: the kind of smiles people had when they were teasing you.

'It has to be a ring,' someone called out.

'You're all wrong,' announced Dora, with a Gargantuan effort to see the joke. Between her thumb and forefinger she held up, by the stalk, a very small, mouldy brown apple core.

And she didn't cry after all, I'll give her that. I did it for her. Cried and cried while everyone else laughed. Cried so much (and they didn't know why) that my mother had to be telephoned to take me home early.

'I think she's sickening for something: she wouldn't eat any tea,' said Dora's mum. 'I thought she looked a bit peaky when she arrived.' (Without doubt the yellow dress effect: it really did make me look horribly sallow.)

As we walked home and my sobs gradually subsided, I told my mother about the cruel trick Dora's parents had played on her. I made my mother promise she'd never force me to go to a party again. She promised. (Victory!)

At the corner of Miranda Road we saw an arch-backed dog doing its business on the pavement. The stuff coming out of it was orange. For some reason, we both laughed. Then I was crying again ... then laughing and crying at the same time.

When we got indoors she gave me a big pair of scissors and let me cut up the yellow dress for cleaning rags (lovely crunch of the blades through the cheap, shiny material). She said she'd use the greyish dumpling of flowers for cleaning the sink. She said she was sorry she'd made me go to that party and agreed that some grown-ups could be horrible – absolutely horrible. Even to their own children. I asked her why. She said she couldn't even begin to imagine and she hugged me very tightly as if there was something in her mind that she was not actually saying but I didn't know what it could be.

And I still wouldn't talk at school.

❧ GEORGINA ❧

'Pottery,' says Alma. 'She can go with Apple. It's Saturday mornings. I bet that'll get her talking to other kids again.'

Thus begins her relentless production of piggy-looking creatures that are supposed to be dogs – and a strange kind of love affair.

It's at pottery that Eloisa meets Katy (gentle and ginger with milky skin and rusty freckles) whose life is as different from her own as chips from broccoli.

Katy has all the things she *doesn't* have: a television, a brother and a sister, a whole house to live in – with a garden – a mother who wears a pink cardigan and dainty pearl earrings and 'does a proper job'. And a daddy.

She nearly drives me mad, talking about Katy and what Katy has and what Katy has told her. But at least she's talking to another child, so I grit my teeth … and finally invite the girl to lunch.

'What will you give her to eat?' demands Eloisa, arms crossed and a thunderous scowl on her face.

'Oh, just the usual beetles on toast with a glass of bats' blood. What do you *think* I'm going to give her to eat, Eloisa? We always have salad for lunch on Saturdays. Salad is not peculiar. Even people with televisions eat salad.'

Exit Eloisa. Slammed bedroom door.

❀ ELOISA ❀

The pottery class was held in a big dusty room that called itself an Arts Centre and was run by a woman who dressed a bit like my mother's friend Alma (big, dangly earrings, long skirts smelling of something my mother said was called patchouli and a CND badge on her baggy jumper).

To begin with I sat on the same table as Apple, but, when she said my first attempt at a dog looked more like a pig, I threw a piece of clay at her and got moved to another table. I was made to sit next to a girl called Katy who was told to be nice to me.

Katy was a quiet and gentle girl. She had a sweet, sad sort of smile and told me she liked the dog I was making. I told her I liked her cat ... only it was a lion (but she didn't get cross with me). I sat on her table again the following week. And it wasn't long before my mum got talking to her mum and Katy was invited to have lunch with us as it was such a rush for her mum to pick up her brother from football and her little sister from dancing and get to the pottery place in time for Katy.

We talked a lot while our fingers prodded, rolled, pinched and smoothed the clay, so by the time Katy came to lunch she already knew I didn't have a father or a television. But I was afraid that if she saw there were too many weird things about me she might not want to be friends any more. I was desperate to make our flat look more what I thought was 'normal', but in the end all I could really do was remove the dead joss sticks from the plant pots, hide the little wooden Buddha (Katy had said her father thought people should be Christians), tidy my room and do a bit of cleaning when my mother wasn't looking. But the thing that worried me most was the big picture above my mother's desk (it was a Modigliani nude). Would Katy be all right about pubic hair?

As we walked in through the door, I saw Katy's eyes flick around the room. They caught on the nude lady … then moved on and she didn't say anything. And she ate up all her salad.

After lunch we went into my bedroom (a bit bare and startled from being tidied up) and sat cross-legged on the bed.

Katy said, 'Your mum's got nice smiley eyes. I bet she's happy all the time.'

'I bet she's not as happy as *your* mum, though … with a proper house and a husband. And a television.'

'I don't think she *is* happy, not most of the time.' Katy looked hard at a patch of bed-cover. 'Can you keep a secret? A really terrible secret?'

It was the first time anyone had ever thought me worthy of a *secret*. 'Of course I can. Anyway, who would I tell? You're my only friend.'

'Do you *promise*?'

'Cross my heart and hope to die.'

'Well, once I saw my dad … hit my mum.' She looked up to see the effect of this revelation. (Frankly, I was disappointed: I thought it was going to be about her mum having a secret boyfriend or something. Or maybe she knew something terrible like who'd done a murder.)

'Just the once?'

'Once was enough!' Katy looked hurt that her 'terrible' secret hadn't made more of an impact. But any kind of physical violence was so far removed from my experience that it didn't really mean anything to me.

I tried to put things right between us by saying, 'What I meant was maybe it was the only time. Maybe he just lost his temper the one time and you just happened to see it. It was probably just that once.'

Katy's eyes had gone rather wide and damp. 'Or it could be happening all the time, when we're not around, and the time I saw it he didn't know I was there.'

On the patch of bed-cover between us, I tried really hard to imagine the scene into 'terribleness' – an angry man waiting for the children to go to school then lurching towards Katy's mum like a glowering gorilla, raising his arm and …

'Has anyone ever hit *your* mum, El?' I think she was hoping for proof that it was somehow *normal*. But it wasn't the kind of thing you could lie about.

'I don't think they'd dare!' A snorty little laugh came out as I conjured a scene in which someone tried to get violent with my mother. (There he was, laid out cold on the floor, my mother considerately calling an ambulance …)

'Do you know *why* he hit her?' I said, still hoping for some juicier revelations.

'He's just a bit like that, my dad. Mum says he's just a normal man who always has to have everything his own way. *I'm* not going to get married in case my husband turns out like my dad. Mum says he was all right to start with but … '

The perfect solution leapt out of my mouth. 'You could be a lesbian!'

'What's that?'

'When two women live together instead of a man and a woman.'

'Like you and your mum?'

'No, silly. It's like man and wife only it's wife and wife. That way you wouldn't be lonely but you wouldn't have to put up with a man. My mum knows someone called Janice who works at the greengrocer's and *she's* a lesbian and she's always very happy!'

Later we took Katy home. Her house wasn't as big as I imagined it. They had more rooms than we did but all of them were small. There were three bedrooms: Katy shared with her little sister, Alice. I decided all the books and records must be kept in the big bedroom where her parents slept (the door was closed) as there weren't any in the rest of the house.

Katy and Alice's bedroom was amazingly tidy, almost bare. The bunk beds had matching pink candlewick covers tucked in tightly all around. The walls were painted an awful turquoise colour. There was a white wardrobe and chest of drawers with a little square orange plastic clock on top. There was a mirror with a shelf underneath where two identical brushes and combs (one red, one blue) were set precisely parallel, diagonally. The woven rush linen basket in the corner had two matching teddy bears on top, one honey brown, one dark coffee-ish.

'I tidied my room, too,' I said, 'when I knew you were coming.'

'Ours is always like this. There's trouble if it's not.' She rolled her eyes.

'Is your mum that strict?'

'No. It's him.' She pointed down from the window to where a thin, smallish man, ginger-haired like Katy, was disappearing into the shed. (The garden was mainly a concrete yard: the shed was in the far left-hand corner.) 'He's going in there because your mum's in the kitchen. He doesn't like that sort of thing, women having coffee together and talking. He'll probably be in a mood the rest of the day.'

When we got home from school on the Monday, my mother said we needed to have a little talk. She'd had a phone call from Katy's mum, Louise.

'Eloisa, why were you talking to Katy about lesbians?'

I felt my face begin to go hot; from my mother's voice (not angry, but definitely serious) and the fact that she called me by my proper name – not 'Toots' or 'Tootsie' or some made-up thing like she often did – I realised something bad must have happened and that it was probably my fault. I didn't answer straight away, so she said it again.

'Eloisa, why were you telling Katy about lesbians?'

'Because she didn't know. Why?'

'After we left, Katy's dad was in a bad mood and smacked Katy for some silly little thing and she told him men were horrible and she was going to be a lesbian. He got really quite ... cross and ... well, he hit Katy a lot and wanted to know where she'd heard about lesbians from and ... well, he doesn't really want Katy to come here anymore. And I don't think it would be a good idea for you to go to her house, either.'

'Don't worry, I wouldn't want to. He's *horrible*, Katy's dad. She told me about him. Did he hit Katy *very* much?'

'I don't know, sweetheart. Louise didn't say.'

My mother put a protective arm around me and gave me a little loving squeeze as if to say it wasn't really my fault.

It crossed my mind, fleetingly, that maybe *my* father had been horrid, like Katy's dad, and that it was really my mum who'd 'gone away' from him, rather than the other way round. I had to ask.

'My father wouldn't have done that to me, would he?'

Her face went a bit strange when she replied: 'Oh, no, sweetheart, no ... not in a million years.' And this made me cry, because I missed him – this nice 'stranger' I'd never met – though my mother probably thought I was crying for Katy and the awfulness I'd inadvertently caused.

❧ GEORGINA ☙

Louise phones me a couple of times when her husband isn't around. I could do without the interruptions when I'm trying to work during the day, but I get the feeling she really needs someone to confide in, so I suggest we meet up for a coffee. It's then that the whole picture gradually emerges. Not a very nice picture. A life so far removed from Eloisa's perception of their perfect family life that it would be laughable were it not so dreadful.

I tell her she shouldn't put up with violence – not towards her nor towards the children. She claims he's got worse as he's grown older. When they first knew each other he was just a little bit 'spiteful' from time to time, but she believed in the power of love to change that ... instead of which the daily rough and tumble and pressures of family life have just made him worse. The only way he feels in control is with everything obsessively neat and tidy and regular and everybody obeying his orders to the letter.

I say it sounds like a condition that might need some help.

She says she values her life too much to suggest it.

She cries a little.

'It's not fair,' she says. 'My sister Myra was always the more wayward and selfish one. She used to be a harassed single mother but now she's ended up with Jack, a really lovely man, and a spacious house. And she doesn't even have to go to work any more.'

Jack is the only one she's been able to talk to about the shitty life her husband imposes on her and the children. He encourages her to take the children round to his and Myra's house on Sunday afternoons – one of the worst flash-points of the week: they are expected to be utterly quiet at home because 'father' likes to sleep then.

'He lives on his nerves, you see,' she says, 'so he's always tired.'

'You're making excuses for him, Louise,' I say.

'It's just how it is,' she says. 'But being able to take the kids to Jack's certainly helps. I don't spend the whole week dreading Sunday afternoons now.'

Louise knows about my writing from that fateful Saturday afternoon chat we had over coffee in her kitchen. One week, waiting for the children to clear up after the pottery class, she asks how *Dangerous Dawn* is coming along and I mention I'm having trouble meeting the publisher's deadline. To give me a few extra uninterrupted hours she offers to take Eloisa with them to Jack's house the following Sunday.

❧ ELOISA ❧

A big front door wonderful with coloured-glass birds and leaves and flowers. Door to a different world. Katy was allowed to push the white ceramic door-bell. A mellow 'ding-dong' (not a rasping single note like the one to our flat).

The door opened and a tall, thin man with dark hair and eyes and a longish head and bristly little moustache was smiling down at us. Jack.

'Come in, come in … ' He stood aside and made ushering-in movements with the arm not holding the door. Once Katy, John, Alice and myself were through, he gave Katy's mum a big hug. 'Myra's in the kitchen, Lou, doing something with a cake, I think.' He didn't seem to notice Louise had one too many children with her.

Katy tugged me across the hall and through a doorway … (I glimpsed a rambly, dishevelled kitchen where two very differently dressed ladies with almost matching faces had their arms around each other: Katy's mum and a woman in blue dunga-rees) … and through to the big room at the back. Now I realised why Katy's uncle hadn't batted an eyelid when Louise walked in with four children instead of three.

'Is it a party?' I whispered to Katy.

'No, they're just my cousins – except those two. I don't know who they are.'

The little boy sitting on the floor playing a board game with the two non-cousins looked up and said, 'They're my friends, that's who they are.'

'They're Edward's friends,' repeated Katy, 'and that's Josephine.' Katy pointed to the corner of the room where a very tiny girl with pig-tails was arranging shells on the floor, singing quietly to herself.

A plumpish girl with glasses was lying in the middle of the

floor, a small ginger cat balanced on her stomach. 'I'm Natasha,' she said, not taking her eyes off the cat's face, 'but you can call me Tash like everyone else.'

'And that's Jamie … ' A skinny, teenage version of Jack.

'Hello whoever-you-are,' said Jamie.

'She's Eloisa,' said Katy.

'Where did you get that name? And that hair?'

Cheeks suddenly hot. Wanting to run away, to be back home on my own.

'Don't take any notice of him,' said Natasha, from the floor. 'He doesn't know how to talk to people nicely, especially girls.'

At this, Jamie suddenly growled like a big dog and the little ginger cat leapt off Natasha's stomach and shot into the garden through the tall glass doors that were open … and at which a long, thin girl now appeared in skinny-fit jeans and flip-flops.

'That's Dee,' said Katy – by which time Natasha had hurled herself at Jamie, toppled him onto the sofa, and was pummelling him for having scared the cat. As he battled to grip her wrists and stop her, she shrieked, 'Mind my glasses! Mind my glasses!'

I was bemused, overwhelmed, fascinated by this sprawling, boisterous family life.

Then Jack appeared at the door, carrying Katy's little sister Alice. Noting the tussle on the sofa he said, without much conviction, as if it happened all the time, 'Cut it out, you two. Mind Tasha's glasses, Jamie.' Then he called across to the diminutive girl in the corner. 'Hey, Josie, Alice would like to play with you. Would you like to show her your shell collection?' The pig-tails shook a silent 'no'. Jack stood Alice down, went over and squatted beside Josephine, whispering something. A pause. He whispered again. The pig-tails nodded agreement. Jack said, 'Josephine's ready to play with you now, Alice.' Alice ran to Josephine's corner and sat cross-legged, in imitation of her cousin who didn't look at her but said, 'You can only touch the ones I say.'

Then Jack turned and spoke his first ever words to me. 'Hello, Eloisa. It's really nice to meet you. Don't let this rabble scare you … ' (as if he'd read my mind). 'They're quite harmless really.'

❧ GEORGINA ❧

She comes home bubbling over with it all – Jack, Myra, the five children, the pets, the big house … She's fallen in love with the whole package. My heart sinks. It's so utterly different from the life I can offer her – that I *want* to offer her – that I feel … What? Guilty? Defeated? Hurt? Disappointed?

❦ ELOISA ❦

It was after my second Sunday afternoon visit that I announced to my mother I wanted to write a novel and wanted her to tell me how to do it.

'A novel! Don't you think that's a little bit hard for you?'

'But you do it all the time, so it can't be *that* hard!'

She laughed and made a funny face ... but then explained about character notes and research and plot lines and found an old red exercise book (the kind with tables and weight and measures on the back) for me to write in.

Katy proved a useful source of information on the family – which she traded for the honour of being included in my novel ... as long as she could be pretty and have nice clothes and no freckles and be called Dolores.

MELANIE FINDS A FATHER
by
Eloisa Hardiman

THE CHARACTERS ARE THESE

JACK   40 yrs old. Very tall and thin, a bit stoopy because he has to bend lots of times like for talking to ordinary size poepel and spechally children with a little mastarsh that's a bit sticky out. His skins nice and brownish his head sort of long with dark eyes that look at you in a nice way. Very kind and makes poepel feel all right about everything. His mother is from India but his father was from Scotland only he died he was a doctor but for poepel with things wrong in their heads (like mad poepel). Jack's hands are long and thin he used to be a teacher but now he teaches other poepel how to be teachers. He likes it when Josephine sings and plays her violin even when other poepel don't like it. He never makes fun of poepel he is a very nice man he is the hero because everybody loves him speshally Melanie.

MYRA 34 yrs old Jack's wife. He was married before but his wife died. Myra was a art teacher that's how she met him. After his wife died. Not very tall not like Jack. Her hair is a brown plat. A loud voice and a bit bossy. He should of got someone nicer to be his wife.

DEE Nearly 15 yrs old long and skinny like her dad with long hair that's blacker than it should be because she puts stuff on it. She wears tight black trousers and big shoes with laces that come over her ankels. Myra is not her mother Jack's 1st wife is. Dee is short for Deerdree. She wants to be a artist.

JAMIE 13 yrs old long and skinny like his dad. His mother is the same one. He has got a nice cream powlow neck jumper. He likes reading and winding poepel up by saying what's supposed to be clever things. Speshally girls.

NATASHA 11 yrs old. She is a bit fat next to the others and wears glasses and short hair. Myra is her mum but Jack is not her dad. Myra had her before she was married to Jack. Jack is very nice to her and she loves him like evrybody does even though she is not his real dorter.

EDWARD 8. Small and thin. He has a action man but he makes him not be a solider. Dee has made him some cloths that are not soliders cloths because she says war is wrong. Jamie painted the action man jeep so it looks like a normal car not for war. Jack and Myra are his proper parents. Josephine is his proper sister.

JOSEPHINE is 6yrs old she is very tiny for her age. Dee calls her a fairy. She has pigtails mostly. She is always singing quietly to herself and it sometimes drives the others mad because she never stops. She can play the violin already she has speshal lessons with a Japanees man.

DOLLAWREZ She is their cousin. She looks nice and has nice cloths. And no freckels.

MELLANY doesn't have a dad she loves Jack and wishes he was her dad.

MELLANY'S MUM is very nice. She doesn't have a husband. She is the heroin.

THE STORY IS THIS

One day Mellany is bord because she is on her own and her mum is busy type writing as usual so Mellany goes for a walk to where the houses are really nice. Just as she is crossing the road a car comes speeding along and nocks her over. The car drives off but some one in one of the nice houses hears Mellany scream he comes running out and finds Mellany at the side of the road. She is not badly hurt so he dosen't bother calling an ambalans but he picks her up in his arms and carries her into his big house and puts her on a big sofar and gives her a drink of lemonaid and she meets all the children. They like her. They stay friends. She goes to play very often. Jack likes her very much he is always nice to her. He feels sorry she hasn't got a daddy Mellany wishes he was her daddy. Then tradegy strikes the family. Jack's wife gets ill and dies. Mellany goes to the fewnerel but her mum comes too because she dosen't want Mellany being sad on her own. At the fewnerel she meets Jack. He tells her to still let Mellany come round to play even though his wife is dead. One time it's raining very hard when Mellany and her mum arrive so instead of Mellany's mum going strait home to get on with her type writing Jack tells her to come inside and wait till the storm stops and they get to know each other and they fall in love and the children like Mellany's mum and say they should get married and they do and Mellany and her mum end up in the big house with all the children and she dosen't have to do her stories anymore and best of all Jack is Melanny's dad.

❦ GEORGINA ❧

'Mother duck, father duck, and all the little baby ducks ... '
That's what she wants. But I long to tell her about an old grey
Citroën and what it meant to me in my growing up ....

A childhood bulging with relatives. Eight years old when my
father remarried – a sweet, hard-working, dumpy little woman
with lots of affection but little in her head, rather 'put upon'
by her large family but too nice to complain. A marriage of
love? Or of convenience? Both left with children to look after.
A reasonable arrangement. A marriage of affection and mutual
support rather than passion – I assume.

After my mother died my father quickly became an overweight, rather stooped and sad man, only a flicker of his old
spirit lighting up his Chicago drawl. My stepmother's husband
had spent all their savings on a 'dolly bird' (as the family
referred to her) then died of a massive stroke in the midst
of enjoying her pampered body at eight o'clock one Tuesday
evening when he'd told his wife he was having dinner with the
boss as a promotion was in view ... which would solve their
monetary problems. No life insurance. His wife got a job in a
local bank – which is where she met my father. Together trying
to rescue some kind of life out of the devastation inflicted upon
them by other people's faulty biology and, in my father's case,
by the toll taken on his mind from losing so many friends and
seeing so many 'bad things' in the war.

My stepmother? – nice enough in a conventional kind of
way, but with a sprawling family who spend a lot of time
together – maybe having nothing better to do. The first poem
I have published is about the family. Only in the school magazine, but I'm so excited – especially as the magazine's editor is
Miss Rose. *She* chose it. And it's on the first page!

'The Loss of a Beach Ball'

Georgina Hardiman L. VI A

Haunched into sand
the family sat circled,
molared on sand-gritted sandwiches,
grinned with breaded teeth.

Only a granite-eyed gull saw it go –
the bright, the coloured ball,
the light ball.
It trickled
with the silence of a breath
held,
down the easy slope of washed sand
to the lapping edge of endless
grey, was licked gently afloat.

Alone as a person barely sane,
bright butterfly on the heave of ocean's steel,
drawn out far and farther by
the muscular pull under moon-shackled waves.

Though the tide would turn some time and
nudge it back towards the beach,
I could have told them it would stay
Just beyond the family's antic reach.

But I can't show it to anyone at home, not even my father. It's really rather unpleasant about the family and draws attention to how 'alienated' I'm feeling ('alienation' being a concept I've recently come across for the first time). People might be upset by it (if they understood it). So one starts leading the schizophrenic existence of a woman – being good and helpful and law-abiding on the outside while throwing bricks through windows in one's head.

When 'the relatives' come to our little house – which is often – I'm always having to take round plates of sandwiches (there are usually too many people for our small dining table), and smile and pick up things they drop and ask them whether they want coffee or tea and then find they've changed their minds and when is the sugar coming and is there a weaker one or one with less milk and 'Oh, dear! I've spilt it in the saucer. Georgie, could you go and get ... ' And always having to dry the dishes. Because I am a girl.

And not just at our own house. If we go to one of *their* houses it's the same. The boy cousins and the men will be playing football or something in the garden and I'll be stuck in the kitchen with the women.

By fourteen I start catching my step-uncles looking at me in a certain way. And I'm always being asked, 'Have you got a boyfriend?' I'm seventeen before I get up the courage to reply, 'No, but I've got a girlfriend,' – giving them something to think about. No, I don't actually have a girlfriend, but if married life has to be like the examples before me, then any alternative is worth considering. I'd rather be like Miss Rose and Miss McHale.

Sometimes I wish I'd told Eloisa about Miss Gwendoline Rose and Miss Annie McHale.

Miss Gwendoline Rose (humorous blue eyes ... an old grey cardigan ...), English teacher *extraordinaire* who has her sixth formers to tea and shares a house with Miss Annie McHale (dark, hooded eyes ... a red polo-neck frayed at one wrist) whose school trips to France were known to be life-changing for many a girl of slender experience (most of us ... in that part of Kent). Off school premises they are Gwen and Annie to us, insisting, despite our awkwardness at calling teachers by their Christian names. Advance guard of a coming revolution? Or after-shocks of an earlier one? Anyway, they put ideas into our heads.

Despite two professional salaries, their house is a small one because they have another in France. A framed photo of the French home hangs in their hallway. We see them making their escape to it within half an hour of the 'breaking up' bell. The sight of their old grey Citroën in the school car park, packed to the roof and ready to go, always adds an extra *frisson* to the last day of term. (How we longed for our own freedom!)

The sitting-room – where Miss Rose and Miss McHale serve us tea that tastes different from that our mothers brew and slices of what we learn to call *tarte aux pommes* and *tarte citron* – is lined with books. Dust furs the tops of the older volumes, but most spaces between the vertical books and the shelves above are filled with others, more recent-looking, crammed in horizontally. While waiting for 'Gwen and Annie' to bring in the tea, some of us read the spines. I memorise whole litanies of them – mantras to repeat in my head when my stepmother's family visits and the talk is of how much better things were during the war and how the whole country is going 'down the pan' with young people no longer respecting their elders and more and more immigrants and in the old days clothes were made to last and women …

(' … *The Kiss and Other Stories* … *The Idiot* … *Notes from the Underground* … *Crime and Punishment* … *Dead Souls* … ' – ' … *Nausea* … *Words* … *The Age of Reason* … *Iron in the Soul* … *The Reprieve* … ' – ' … *The Voyage Out* … *To the Lighthouse* … *The Waves* … *A Room of One's own* … ')

Then there's the 'subversion' method Miss Rose sometimes uses for teaching Shakespeare's sonnets, getting us to replace words to make our own new meanings.

'*The expense of Sunday in a waste of time*
Is stupidity in action … '
'*Shall I compare thee to an abattoir?*
Thou art more bloody and more ravenous … '

That last one I dedicate to Uncle Pete who always asks for the bloodiest bit of the roast. '*Uncle Pete likes bloody meat*' – a distant cousin chanting, for the sake of the swear-word he can get away with in the context. My silent vow to be a vegetarian as soon as I have my freedom. I can't wait to get away.

My mind an old grey Citroën packed and ready to go …

But I suppose each generation must find its own adventures. Eloisa is trying to find her own path, I suppose. To her, a big house and a big happy family *would* be an adventure, new territory. But her obsession with Jack is a little hard to swallow. Maybe it's just a phase that will pass. I hope so …

4

'WOMEN IN LOVE'

❀ ELOISA ❀

Dear Mummy,

I am having a lovely time I hope you are too. This post card shows a picture of the beach near where the holiday house is. You can hear the sea. All the time. Even at night. I am being good.

Love from

ELOISA XX

Dear Mummy,

I am still having a nice time. This is a picture of the life boat that went to rescew some people. The sea was ruff. There was a big scary storm. The sea is too ruff and cold for swimming. Jack says I am being very helpful. (His wife not here.)

Love from ELOISA XX

PS Jack is very nice to me

❧ GEORGINA ❧

Am I glad I went back to Paris? I guess so – in a self-lacerating kind of way! … though Alma was wrong when she predicted it would be a 'laying of ghosts and griefs'. 'There's no such thing,' I tell her. 'What we call "laying ghosts" is just learning to live with them – like new houses built right at the bottom of your garden: you simply have to get used to them being there and they become the new normality.'

If anything, it's been a painful resurrection of ghosts. 'Love is so short, forgetting so long.' Who said that? Somebody.

And I come home still picking daisy petals: 'he loved me … he loved me not … '.

I *think* Eloisa liked the trip: I can't really tell. And Maude, not surprisingly, was in thrall to her smile. The *boule de neige* birthday present clinched the bond between them. (Mercenary little beast!)

Despite coming back with a terrible cold (everyone in Paris seemed to be coughing or sneezing or sniffing) the trip has given me new energy and a sense of purpose – the way that Paris can. And, even more importantly, it results in Eloisa being less obsessed with Jack and his family … till the end of April, anyway.

In May, Jack resurfaces with a vengeance. For a week and a half – from the arrival of the invitation until the event itself – she nearly drives me mad, flapping and fluttering round me, telling me what to wear, what not to wear, which earrings will go with which outfit and so on and so on.

I'm patient at first, understanding that it means a lot to her, in her own perverse little way, this first time of my meeting Jack. Once or twice I just say something like, 'Stop poppling, my robin. Please.' But my fuse gets shorter and shorter the more she fusses until the morning of the visit when she screams at me, 'Aren't you even going to wash your hair?!!' and I scream back, 'For Christ's sake, Eloisa, we're only going to lunch with a couple of ex-school-teachers: I'm not auditioning for a Hollywood movie!' And she hisses back, 'He might only be an "ex-school-teacher" but at least he doesn't swear at his children.'

(She storms into her bedroom and slams the door.)

Yes, well, they are very *nice*, of course. Eloisa had described them all pretty accurately. And that lovely house. Jack proves to be charming and civilized. Nice way with the children – of which there are ... rather a lot. I like Dee: arty and rebellious. You wouldn't catch *her* smiling above plates of sandwiches. OK, she might help out, but not in the desperate-to-please kind of way that *I* used to. Perhaps things *have* moved on.

The little kids are sweet – especially Josephine.

And Myra? Well, I can't say I warmed to her. A little bossy and insecure. Of the two sisters, I prefer Louise, conventional though she is.

Do I understand why Eloisa has fallen hook, line and sinker for the whole package? Not really. Though I guess it's because she has nothing to compare them with, except the 'friends' in France, but they're too far away in more senses than one.

Jack's a decent, solid guy: I can see that. But when you place Eloisa's wished-for father next to her *actual* father, it's just ... FUNNY.

They want to take her on holiday with them, as a friend for Natasha, so she won't be the odd one out. They realise I won't let them take Eloisa away without meeting them first, hence the invitation to lunch. Normally they take Katy, but her father isn't allowing her to go this year. Even Jack hasn't managed to persuade him.

Three weeks. Suffolk … so not too far away. If she becomes unhappy or ill, it'll be easy for them to bring her back or for me to collect her. It seems a good idea for her to learn a bit of independence before starting secondary school, so I say yes.

❧ ELOISA ❧

I was *so* excited. Jack was going to be my father for three rapturous weeks. That's twenty-one days. Or five hundred and four hours. Or thirty thousand two hundred and forty minutes. Or one million eight hundred and fourteen thousand four hundred seconds.

I just *knew* what it'd be like. Wide sandy beaches. Sunshine. Playing in the waves. Jack teaching me to swim, maybe. Picnics. White sea-birds riding the breeze high over head. Being a child in a big, happy family …

They had to take both cars and I was put with Myra and the three youngest. Tasha sat in the front with her mum, and I shared the back with Edward, Josephine, assorted bats, balls, bags of toys and games, as well as Rags, a young black mongrel recently rescued (by Tasha) from certain death. He wouldn't settle on the floor and ended up on my lap (giving me pins and needles in my left leg) with his head resting on the wound-down window, ears flattened, eyes narrowed, panting into the wind as we drove along. Josephine hummed and murmured little songs under her breath right next to me *all* the way and, not used to travelling by car, nor to the smell of warm dog, I was sick half way there. (Myra managed to pull over just in time, so I wasn't sick actually *in* the car.)

Jack, Dee and Jamie were already there when we arrived and were unloading all the stuff into the house. They rented the same one every year during the last three weeks of August. It was a spacious, weather-bleached, carpetless place where you could put wet stones and seaweed on the windowsills and it didn't matter, and wet towels on the furniture didn't matter either because it was old and tatty. And all that separated the house from the beach was a path and a low wall.

But there was hardly any sand: the beach was made of stones – fawns, greys, whites, blue-greys, soft lavenders. The sea's slow heart beat against them, all day, all night. Or it sighed and cleared its throat like an old man sleeping. The North Sea, grey and cold.

It's true there were sea-birds, as in my imagination, and they did ride the breeze overhead … but only after they'd squawked me awake too early each morning.

And there was a life-boat always at the ready, suggesting there might be catastrophes.

❧ GEORGINA ❧

At first I can't settle, imagining drownings, car crashes, fires … The length of a school day is the most time we've ever been apart. I keep thinking I can hear her voice or the sound of her moving about in her bedroom.

But after a few days I grow used to it and, if I'm honest, it's a nice change not to have to consider anyone but myself. I eat at funny times, stay up half the night reading, then sleep in late. In the evenings, when I've finished working, I play old records she'd have made a face at – Charlie Parker, Juliet Greco, Nina Simone … I even spend some time trying to write something other than the usual semi-rubbish that keeps our bank balance just out of the red. Nothing much will come, though: all I can fish out of my head is an old drowned doll of myself, eyes blanked to the future and a head full of salt-water stories. And I don't want to write sadness: that's too easy.

It's while she's away that it suddenly hits me: only seven or eight more years and she'll probably be off to university and I'll be left a middle-aged woman with only the ghost of a lover for company and a career in writing books I hope my daughter will never read. But if my generation has been about anything, it's about looking forward. We've tried to free ourselves from the diving boots of the past, to make the old world new, not keep circling it like the moon in a clockwork nightmare.

Ironic that, like Orpheus, like Lot's wife, the impetus to look back is what ruined everything. If only he hadn't … And we ended up as refugees from our own possibilities, tramping the dusty roads of the past after all.

Maybe it's time to move on. Finally. Not that I haven't tried. The months with David had been … quite good, even though it didn't work out in the end. But that wasn't my fault. And now I'm ready to try again.

So, while Eloisa is away, I look for places to go where I might … meet someone suitable. (OK, yes, I do basically mean to pick up a man.) And that's how I come to be at a rather tedious poetry reading in a bookshop and, emboldened by a couple of glasses of cheap red wine (included in the price of the ticket), start chatting to 'STEPHEN UNSWORTH: MANAGER', as his little plastic badge announces him to be.

I begin by congratulating him on the splendid display of books by Camus (some chat-up line!). He's using the twentieth anniversary of Camus' death to promote his work. A gesture, nothing more. He feels like Sisyphus, he says, trying to promote 'literature' when most people came in for books on gardening or sport or cookery or military history.

So. Camus. We take it from there …

It's about half way through Eloisa's time away – the Tuesday morning – that Louise phones to say she can't make our monthly coffee date. Something terrible has happened.

On the Sunday, her husband had gone berserk after Katy, bored out of her mind, had said she wished she'd been allowed to go to Suffolk with her cousins, as usual, because 'home' was so horrible. Her brother John had joined in, saying how stupid everything was in their life, and he was going into the garden with his football whether it was Sunday afternoon or not because nobody else he knew had the stupid rules their family was supposed to live by. When Louise tried to stop her husband lunging for the children (little Alice screaming in the corner), he went for Louise herself. She managed to get away, with the children, and ran to a neighbour's house, leaving a madman smashing up the home since there were no longer any people within reach. The neighbour called the police, who eventually managed to restrain him and carted him off.

The children were physically all right, though very shaken, but Louise had had to go to casualty. Myra was going to be arriving any moment, she said, to help clear up the house and get her and the children back to their parents' home in Bristol. It had made her finally realize the situation was unsaveable: she just wanted to be free of him and to heal her children, give them some fun and make up for the last five years when their father, for whatever unfathomable reason, had become increasingly like a monstrous rodent chewing at the centre of their lives.

Naturally, I am deeply upset for her. But, to be honest, my main thought is that, if Myra has come back to London, my daughter is up there in Suffolk without a woman in the house. And even though I tell myself not to be silly, I feel … mildly uneasy.

❦ ELOISA ❦

It was the evening of the second Monday. Jack and Myra had just started the washing up while Dee was putting 'the babes' to bed and Tasha, Jamie and I were setting out Scrabble on the kitchen table, when the phone rang. Jamie went out into the hall to answer it. It was Louise, and she wanted to talk to Myra. So I offered to dry the dishes, even though it wasn't my turn.

'Isn't it nice to have a goody-goody in the house,' sneered Jamie.

'Eloisa's mother has clearly succeeded in bringing up a polite and helpful human being,' murmured Jack, 'which is what I seem to have singularly failed to do.'

Exit Jamie to throw stones at the sea. Exit Tasha behind him, in a rare act of solidarity with her step-brother. Exit Myra with, 'It's his age, Jack,' as she closed the door into the hallway to take the phone call.

So it was just me in the kitchen with Jack, next to his long brown legs and his old blue shorts. Happiness. Even the old red-and-white tea-towel in my hand seemed special.

'This is jolly decent of you, Eli.'

'Oh, I'm used to doing things at home as my mum hasn't got a husband to help her.'

'She seems to get along pretty well without one.'

'I think she'd like one, but it's just a case of finding the right sort. He'd have to be intelligent … and very kind. I don't think he'd have to understand her poetry or anything, so long as he didn't mind her writing it.'

'I didn't realize your mother was a poet. Is she published, or does she just do it for her own satisfaction?'

'She used to get them in magazines, but she says she's too busy for that now.'

'You get on really well with your mum, don't you.'

'Mmm ... All right. But I've always wished I had a dad. I'm trying to find one for my mum to marry, but no luck ... so far.'

He laughed, then said, 'We humans are funny, aren't we, always wanting most what we haven't got.'

'You don't, though, do you? Is there another tea-towel? – this one's sopping.'

'Top drawer of the dresser ... on the left. It is true of me, actually. Coming here every summer, for example. When I was a child, we always had holidays in Scotland or the Lake District – my father was Scottish – never the seaside. And a different place every time because he wanted to show my Indian mother different parts of the country: you never knew what to expect. So now I drag my family here to stare at the same bit of chilly sea every year.'

'I like it here. Thank you for inviting me. When I'm grown up, I'm going to get married and have a big family and bring them on holiday to a place like this.'

'But have a career, too. You're a clever girl and you'll end up being frustrated if ... '

Myra erupted into the kitchen, tearful and distressed. 'Jack, something terrible's happened. Eli, can you go outside with the others. I need to talk to Jack in private.'

Before bedtime, we were summoned to the kitchen and told that Myra was going back to London next morning to 'help her sister' for a couple of days or so. She wanted us to promise to be good and helpful while she was gone.

Trying to prove just how helpful I could be, I said, 'We can look after Edward and Josephine, can't we, Tasha.'

Black look from Tasha. 'I've got Rags to see to. *You* look after them if you want.'

'Oh, for goodness sake, Tash ... ' snapped Myra.

But Jack came in with, 'Good thinking, Tasha. The last thing we need is a neglected and miserable dog on our hands. You look after him properly, and Eli and I will manage the babes between us.'

I was probably the only one to go to bed happy that night: I was going to be Edward and Josephine's big sister and help 'our' father to take care of them. Paradise. I couldn't wait for Myra to go next morning. And the sound of her car pulling off was the overture to three of the happiest days of my life up to that point – three days when imagination and reality coincided … more or less. I even got to call him 'Daddy' when talking to the babes: 'Daddy says you'll need a sweater if you're going to the beach, Edward … Come on, Josephine, let's get your pigtails done to save Daddy a job, shall we?' I even took Josephine down to the water's edge early each morning so she could play her violin without driving the others mad. (She'd screamed the place down when they'd tried to get her to leave the instrument at home because *they* needed a break from her violin-playing, even if she didn't.)

Jamie and Dee grudgingly helped with the shopping and cooking, but skived off every chance they had to be with the friends they met up with there every year. One of them was Ben, dark, handsome, and intelligent, adored by the girls. They all met up on the beach in the evenings when Tasha and I hung around the edge of the group, too young to be properly included, too old to be in bed.

On the Thursday evening, after I'd read the babes their bedtime story, Jack sent me out to be with the others on the beach. I'd have preferred to stay in with him, but he said, 'Time to be young again, Eloisa. Go on. Out you go. It's a lovely evening.'

There were eight or nine of them sitting in a ragged circle on the stones. The tide was up. Natasha was there, on the outside, hanging onto Rags's lead as he bit and pulled it from side to side out of boredom. I went and sat near Tasha, but not too near: things were rather strained between us just then. Jamie and Ben were the centre of attention. They were talking about things they'd learnt in History. 'Boys showing off,' I thought to myself. Ben was getting very passionate regarding what people were taught about the past, and what they weren't taught – what was kept from them. He said his parents had told him the *real* stuff that had gone on in the Second World War, not just what was in the school text books, because it had been done to people they knew, people in their family.

'We all know *that* stuff,' Jamie said.

'What stuff? What stuff?' taunted Ben.

'The gas chambers.'

'Huh! That's just the *basics*, man.'

What Ben went on to tell us changed forever the feel of certain words in my head … 'lampshade' … 'soap' … 'shower' … 'experiment' … 'camp' … and, for a long time, I couldn't hear the word 'bayonet' without seeing a baby speared on the end of it.

I thought Ben would never stop. It was almost as if we were trying to get rid of it all from his own head by putting it into ours. None of us could walk away, transfixed by this past which was such recent history – our grandparents' past.

The sea turned from grey to black as the last light faded to dark, and still we sat there.

Suddenly I felt afraid of the sea, just a few feet to my right – a vastly black and powerful liquid, full of slimy and alien life. The ageless stones were hard beneath me. The sky was black as the sea. On my left, just beyond the beach, the feeble gold rectangles of lighted windows that showed people reading and chatting didn't seem much against all that blackness.

After what seemed a thousand years, I saw the silhouette of Jack standing on the sea wall, calling us to come in: it was late.

An angel of mercy. Protector. Father.

❧ GEORGINA ❧

I can tell from her voice there's something wrong the second time she phones to say she's having a great time. A mother's fear leaps automatically to something sexual. But no. Not a too early initiation into sex: into history. And there's no cure for that – except, maybe, love.

Love … whatever that is. At this stage, I am prepared to put the definition on hold and go along with Isadora Duncan's view that love might be a pastime as well as a tragedy. (Isn't making love 'frivolously' what sets us apart from the animals?)

My relationship with Stephen is fundamentally Platonic … with a bit of sex thrown in for exercise and practice. And for the comfort of flesh. Discussing Thomas Mann is his idea of foreplay. (He's wasted in that bookshop.) Yes, he sometimes lacks humour but is never unkind in word or deed which, when the chips are down, is not an inconsiderable thing.

Eloisa has grown in the three weeks she's been away, I swear it, and her colour has deepened in the sun and she is so beautiful it makes me afraid. But she's come home with a shadow of knowledge stitched to the heel of her smile: she's too young for that uncensored film of history, people falling from the screen to die in three-dimensional agony in front of her all-too-ready imagination. I'd planned to open the doors to the past for her gradually, one by one at the right time, like some kind of unsentimental Advent calendar. But once your child begins to run free in the world they bump into all sorts of things and you're powerless to kiss it better any more.

Not that she lets on in any direct way. (She could be secretive as an oyster.) I only find out from her English exercise book, soon after the start of that first term in her new school. They have to write a story called 'The Dream' … only she makes it a nightmare. It starts with a girl on a stony beach in the dark, hearing a conversation, then tells how it all comes through in her dreams that night. But mothers aren't fooled by narrative devices. No eleven-year-old could've made that up: the details are too gruesomely historical. Lampshades made from human skin.

I ask her where such information has come from, and the truth tumbles tearfully out. Is it true, she sobbed. She knows I never lie. I put my arm around her and hold her tight, wondering how the teacher would 'mark' such a piece of work. '*Powerful images. Watch your spelling. B+*'? I just hope they don't think she's got it all from me.

The start of a particularly difficult time for both of us. Not only is Eloisa having to cope with the move to secondary school, she's also not reacting too well to the rather delicate matter of Stephen Unsworth.

Selecting what she considers appropriate letters from his name, she dubs him 'Stunt' – 'As in "stunted",' she kindly explains. True, he is no Adonis, but I point out the wisdom of Shakespeare's '*Love looks not with the eyes but with the mind,/ Thus is winged Cupid painted blind.*' But Stephen isn't Jack, and that's that. It would be only a minor exaggeration to say that she is making my life *hell*.

Some samples …

'How could any sensible person fall for a *specimen* like Stephen Unsworth when there are people like Jack in the world!'

'Stupid name … Stupid man … He even *looks* stupid. And his hair's floppy and boring because *the brain underneath it* is floppy and boring … even if he *does* work in a bookshop. And what's more his glasses are always crooked.'

'*And he's younger than you!* That's disgusting … '

That's a very old-fashioned line to take, I point out. 'Besides, he's a kind and sensitive man.'

'Yeah! So sensitive that when we went on that picnic in Holland Park and he spilled red wine down his white trousers, it didn't bother him to go around the rest of the day looking as if he'd been stabbed in the thigh or was having a period or something. That's how *sensitive* he is!'

I always check her homework and her marks – a situation Eloisa makes use of in her own inimitable fashion. Her English teacher encourages their imagination by setting 'story homework' every week, and it seems to come naturally to my daughter that fiction isn't just entertainment but can be used to make a point. And she makes her point. Over and over.

A story about a mother lured to the book-lined castle of Count Septicus, only the book shelves are trick doors to thirteen torture chambers where the remains of his previous victims hang from rusty chains. (Teacher's comment: *Well written, but try to be more original.*) In another, an angel has a spell put on her eyes by Satan and falls in love with a smelly camel so she loses her wings and is condemned to ride the camel back and forth across the desert for all eternity, blood dripping from the shoulder-blade wounds where her wings had been torn off. (Teacher: *I like this take on the Oberon/Titania story we talked about in class, though a happier ending might be nice!*) The story of a mother so obsessed with a man that she doesn't clean the house and her daughter gets ill from the germs and dies and the mother doesn't care. (Teacher: *Is everything OK at home, Eloisa? Talk to me if you want to.*)

I manage to confine my reactions, in front of Eloisa, to a raised eyebrow and a nod.

Then she starts nagging about France. Are we going back? Wouldn't Stunt and I like a romantic weekend in Paris? 'Not a bad idea,' I say. 'You could go and stay with Alma.' Which is unpleasant of me: I know she doesn't mean us going without her. But I am almost at the end of my tether and we're both building up quite a head of steam.

It's one Thursday evening (when I'm trying to get her to bed because Stephen's coming round to supper) that the safety valve blows in the form of a question that must've been pacing back and forth in her mind like that polar bear in London Zoo across its patch of warm concrete.

'Who's Colette and Amadon?'

I gaze at the cross and desperate little stranger in front of me, my mind scuttling madly about, searching for clues as to where she's got the names from. Then the truth dawns: that letter.

In a controlled and icy voice I say, 'Colette is dead. And it's not Ama*don*, it's Ama*dou*. Clearly you misread Maude's writing when you took it into your head to read my personal mail ... which I politely request you not to do in the future.'

'*But who's Colette and Amadou?*' It comes out almost as a sob.

I took a deep breath. 'Well ... Colette was the older sister of Aline and Maude. Amadou was ... Colette's child. They lived on their own, rather like you and me.'

I've always told her that her father's name was Marc – actually his middle name, so it's not really lying – but when she wrote it down for the first time and spelt it the English way, with a 'k', I didn't correct her. Maybe this was the moment for the truth ...

I find myself pulling her to me, hugging her ... hugging her too tightly so she squirms against my arms then pulls away. 'Eloisa, ... ' But I hesitate a moment too long. She starts on about Stephen and the opportunity slips away. I do nothing to call it back.

'Do you promise me you're not going to marry Stunt?'

(A momentary, perverse vision of myself in a white dress, emerging from a church door on Stephen's arm to a peal of bells ... At least it makes me smile.)

'I cannot imagine such an unlikely situation ever arising.'

And it's that evening, after supper, that Stephen breaks it to me that, after Christmas, he'll be moving to Birmingham to manage a branch of the bookshop up there.

Predictably, our friendship does not survive that departure to … another country.

❧ ELOISA ❧

The phone rang. My mother answered it.

'It's for you, Toots. It's Natasha.'

Things had been frosty between us ever since Suffolk and I couldn't imagine why she should be phoning me. She'd never ever phoned me before.

'Hello.'

'Guess what, Eli … '

'What?'

'We're going to America!'

There was that wonderful moment when I thought she'd put aside our little Suffolk 'difficulties' and was going to say she – and the rest of the family – wanted me to go with them on holiday, like before.

'America instead of Suffolk?'

'Not on holiday, silly. We're going to live there!'

… at which point something weird happened to my body: I felt all shaky and red.

'What, all of you? … even Jack?'

'Of course Jack.'

'But what about his job? He works here.'

'Well, he's got a new job … over there. It's so exciting!'

'Will it be … for ever?' (I knew I was going to cry.)

'It's just for a couple of years to start with, then we'll see, he says.'

Did I realise, at the time, that Natasha's decision to phone and tell me the news was probably a trump card of spite? – a gloating punishment for my getting on so well with her stepfather, and maybe even for having the body and looks she might have preferred? Probably I didn't. I was probably too upset to think of anything but losing my 'father' to another country.

❧ GEORGINA ☙

'After three months, not longer, I will come back, I promise you.' On the way through Paris to the airport thinking, 'Shall I tell him? ... Will he be angry I didn't say anything before? ... If he still went and we parted with bad feeling between us after so much happiness, I think I'd ... I couldn't bear it ... ' Looking down at his dark hand over mine on the fawn leather seat of the car. Should I? Still time ...

Then the airport, everything noisy and hurried and unreal. As he turned for the final wave, I could still have called out, 'I'm pregnant!' But it would've been too like a corny film. He turned. I waved. He waved.

When the news comes about Jack going to America, she cries and cries. I am sympathetic for the first two days, but by the third (a Monday, and she's made herself too ill to go to school), I am beginning to get a little fed up with her histrionics and say firmly, 'Look, this has got to stop, Eloisa. It's not as if he's dying of some dreadful disease. It's just for a couple of years ... ' – which only prompts a new symphony of sobs and moans. I suppose one forgets how long each day is for the young: two years is the difference between a four-year-old and a six-year-old, between a primary-school child and a girl coping with the start of periods and the stresses and strains of secondary school.

'But I ... won't be ... able to ... *see* him ... and ... and ... he might ... never come *back* ... and we'll never ... never *ever* be able to ... afford to go to ... America!'

I try to comfort her with wise words, saying how we don't always have to be literally *with* people we love: if we're really close to them we carry them around inside us. They go on being part of us, even if they're on the other side of the world ... Even if we don't see them or hear from them for a long time.

'That's silly,' she sniffs.

'No it isn't. I can tell you from experience that it's true,' I persist.

But she doesn't really want comfort: she wants her own way and she can't have it.

It's such a shame. She's really started to settle down in her new school (after the departure of 'Stunt' from our lives) and is beginning to shine in some subjects as I always thought she would. But the departure of Jack – dropped into the stew of hormones bubbling up in her – will, I fear, send my daughter hay-wire again. And the first sign comes when she plays truant for the second time in her life. (Only this time she doesn't come home in the middle of the morning and catch me in bed with a man!)

Fortunately I am an observant woman: I can *smell* she hasn't been to school.

❀ ELOISA ❀

I pushed a pair of jeans and a T-shirt into my school-bag in place of books, kissed my mother goodbye and left the house at the usual time … but caught a bus into Central London and walked into the National Gallery. (The fact that it was free meant I'd known it from an early age.) I changed in the toilets then checked my bag into the cloakroom behind a Spanishy-looking couple whose daughter had hair a bit like mine so I could feasibly pass for their 'other' daughter. I smiled coyly at the attendant as I took the little tag with the number on it and followed the Spanishy family up the stairs. They turned left into the religious section my mother had always steered me clear of, saying, 'You don't want to go in there: it's all blood and misery.' I decided it would fit my mood of Jackless despair.

There were many, many Marys hanging around crosses and open tombs. Mournful angels helping to hold dead Jesuses with varying degrees of droop. Dreadful crowns of thorns every-where: they made me wince … as did the arrows stuck in Saint Sebastian – a helpless voodoo doll, eyes rolled up to the sky. But it was the holes in the Jesus hands that finally got to me – especially the one with the bruised blue flesh around the ragged wounds. I began to feel faint. 'Whatever I do, I mustn't faint or they'll find out I'm not a Spanish tourist at all and that I should be in school and … I mustn't faint … I mustn't faint … '

I got to a bench just in time and tried to close my eyes against all that awful history of blood and sadness … and real-ised I was terribly hungry, having surreptitiously binned my breakfast because I was too nervous to eat it (on account of my truancy plans).

Looking at the floor so as not to see any more of the suffering on the walls, I made my way down to the café. I had just enough money for the cheapest sandwich and my bus fare home.

It was quite crowded, but I managed to find an empty table. My mouth was stuffed with the second ravenous bite of my sandwich (shedding bits of grated cheese) when an old lady with a powder-pinked face asked, 'Do you mind if I join you?' (Scottish.) 'There's nowhere else.' I nodded, mouth too full to speak. She stirred her cup of tea and waited for the crucial moment between my swallowing and taking the next bite before asking, 'You're not here by yourself, are you?'

'Oh, no. My family's upstairs ... you know, looking at pictures. I was hungry.'

'No school today, then?'

Was she a retired truancy officer doing a bit of under-cover work? Just my luck!

I bit, then chewed visibly for a few moments, giving myself time to think.

'I'm over here from America. I'm not American, of course: I talk normally. My dad's got a job in San Diego for a couple of years. We're here visiting ... my gran. For her birthday.'

'Do you like it over there? ... in America?'

Biting. Chewing. Thinking. Be careful ... 'It's all right.'

'Have you got any brothers or sisters, deary?'

'Oh, yes. *Loads* ... '

Her hand shook as she lifted the heavy cup to her lips. 'You're never lonely then.' A brown tear dripped from the bottom of her cup onto her cream blouse.

I shook my head and chewed and chewed.

She put the cup down into its puddled saucer. I didn't want to see her pick up the cup again. Didn't want to see the brown tears fall silently down her front. It made me feel nervous, waiting for the moment of the drip, so I said, 'Have you got any? ... brothers and sisters, I mean.'

'No, dear. I'm told I had a brother once, but he died as a wee baby. It was just my mother and myself at home. I don't remember my father. She told me he died when I was very small, but I have my doubts.' (she pronounced it 'doots'.) Then she leaned forward, conspiratorial. '*I* think he was in prison.'

Prison. It was like the drone of an aircraft coming relentlessly closer and louder until it roared in my ears: MAYBE MY FATHER HAD REALLY BEEN IN PRISON ALL ALONG! Maybe it was all lies, that stuff about him being 'a very nice man' ... Maybe he'd committed some unspeakable crime ... Maybe the violence I sometimes felt inside myself was inherited from *him* ...

The old lady picked up her cup again. The brown tears dripped. I swallowed the last bit of sandwich, almost choking.

'Must get back to my family now. They'll be worried if I'm gone too long. Nice talking to you ... '

'Goodbye, dearie. Enjoy the rest of your visit.'

I drank from the tap in the 'ladies' to get rid of the sandwich-lump (was it?) in my throat. It was still ages before I could start for home and confront my mother with my suspicions – because that was what I intended to do. I wanted the TRUTH, once and for all.

I wandered aimlessly through the galleries while, through my head, staggered a murky parade of crimes for which my father was undergoing years and years of imprisonment ... (I just hoped Jack would never find out.)

I timed my arrival home perfectly. We sat down to tea as usual, my mother saying, 'So, tell me about your day, butterfly.'

I invented the result of a French vocab test: nine out of ten.

'Now tell me about your *real* day.'

I felt the blood rush to my face. 'I don't know what you mean.'

'Yes you do, Eloisa. That school blouse didn't acquire the look of a crumpled handkerchief from being on your body all day. Besides you don't *smell* of school ... and that vocab test's tomorrow: you don't have French on Tuesdays. Now tell me: WHERE HAVE YOU BEEN?'

I looked down. 'The National Gallery.'

There was a moment's pause. 'Well, I guess that's ... different. There can't be many truanting kids who head straight for the National Gallery.' Another pause. I detected a slight pride in the way she said it, but I kept looking down at my hands, the knuckles tensing with my pent-up question.

'I take it you had a good time, Eloisa?'

I shrugged, uneasy, not sure where the conversation was going. What kind of corner was she steering me into?

'In any case, I imagine you had a better time than I did, stuck here all day over Qwerty when I'd've loved to take myself off to an art gallery. Don't you think *I*'d sometimes like to play truant from my everyday life, too? Don't you think *I* sometimes get fed up and lonely and miss people I've loved and that "life" has taken away from me? – just like you miss Jack?'

I finally looked up. 'You can't mean that Stunt bloke.'

'No, I don't mean "that Stunt bloke".'

'D'you mean my father?'

She didn't reply, but I knew the answer was 'yes'.

'He's in prison, isn't he. He didn't disappear, like you said.' (The words just fell out of my mouth – not the ones I'd meant to say about it at all.)

I didn't know whether she was going to laugh or yell at me. Her face looked as if it didn't know what to do with itself.

'In *prison*!! Oh, God, if only he were! If only I knew that's where ... But why on earth should you think ... '

I burst into tears. Seeing my genuine distress, I suppose, she came over and cuddled me while I stammered and sobbed out the story of the old lady.

Once I'd calmed down she said, 'OK. End of scene. Now, you've got to promise me, solemnly, that you won't truant again. I can't live with the constant terror of where you might be or what's happening to you, do you understand? And I don't care whether you like school or not, so don't try the "it's boring" thing on me. Be grateful for the decent education you're getting.'

She must have seen the hesitation in my eyes and, quite uncharacteristically, resorted to male authority of the 'just-you-wait-till-your-father-gets-home' kind.

'And if you don't promise, I'll write and tell Jack what you've been up to.'

Just the mention of his name was enough to lift my heart.

'You're talking as if he's my father.'

'I thought that's what you wanted. That's what this little drama's all about isn't it? And just in case you're in any doubt about the matter, there's as much chance of Jack becoming your stepfather as there is of the moon falling to Earth ... even if he were to divorce Myra for whatever unimaginable reason, even if she were to die, even if he were to ask me, even if ... '

'No. He's not really your type, is he?'

'What do you mean by that?'

'I don't *mean* anything. I'm just stating a fact. Agreeing with you. That's what mothers want, isn't it?'

'I have work to do before dinner. Go and do your homework. And don't forget to revise for that French test.'

I paused at my bedroom door. 'Mumsie ... you will write me a note, won't you? Otherwise I'll get into terrible trouble if they know I've ... '

'Maybe you should've thought of that before you ... '

Her voice trailed off and she looked as though she were ... somewhere else. She looked worried. Defeated. She looked very alone.

'Mumsie ... I promise I won't do it again. I'm sorry.'

She just nodded. When she thought I wasn't looking, she rubbed tears from her eyes with the heels of her hands.

'You OK?'

She nodded again. 'Just a bit tired.'

5

'METAMORPHOSIS'

❦ ELOISA ❦

Eloisa Hardiman 3A 1st Nov

Book review on reading homework

I chose question B: compare 2 animal stories
I read: "Animal Farm" by George Orwell
"The Old Man and the Sea" by Ernest Hemingway

In the Introduction it says "Animal Farm" is a political allegory. This means it's a story about politics where the animals stand for people (a bit like Aesop's fables). It is talking about what happened in Russia and it's very clever the way he makes the different animals stand for e.g. Napoleon (pig) for Stalin who was in charge of Russia and quite cruel. The sadest bit is when the horse is old and ill so he can't work anymore and is sold to be killed for glue. It was a clever book but not happy at all.

"The Old Man and the Sea" is just about an old man who goes out and catches a great big fish. The fish is really too big for him to manage and it is very hard for him to bring the fish back. It is also a sad book. I think it is supposed to have a meaning, like "Animal Farm" does, but I am not sure what it is.

I thought "Animal Farm" was better because it taught you about Russia and I like learning things about other countries and about history.

B+ Well done! I'm glad you chose stories from the more demanding part of the reading list. Don't worry if you don't understand 'The Old Man and the Sea'. I will explain it to you. Come and see me in Room 25 Tuesday lunch-time if you can. (For the next review, try to write more details about the characters. This is what we normally enjoy most about a story, isn't it?!)

❧ GEORGINA ❧

In her early teens, Eloisa suddenly begins to resemble her father in more than just her body and her facial expressions.

He lived life *con brio* – the result of being interested in *everything*, I guess. One day he'd be reading a thriller, analysing the tricks by which the author kept you reading; the next day it'd be a book on Egyptian hieroglyphics or Arabic architecture or the biography of a Russian composer. He loved discovering new words – in my language as well as his own (he was in ecstasies over 'flimflam', 'daddy-long-legs', 'flummox', 'doodle bug', 'yobbo'). As ardent out of bed as he was in it. And his restless energy and 'fizz' were catching. I thought I was living with greater zest and intensity than most people, but I met more than my match in him. With him, I simply lived *more*.

My step-family had always seemed half dead to me – or only half alive, whichever way you like to think of it. They never read anything except second-rate newspapers. Their politics consisted of a generalized moaning against whatever the *status quo* happened to be at the time. Their conversations were largely about food, illness, each other, or the misconduct of neighbours (whose lawns were never sufficiently tended). It was like living with a pillow over your face – though my more compassionate, older self hints that they were possibly just defeated by the effort of living and the lack of opportunities to become otherwise (none of them had had my grammar school advantages).

I knew I would never, ever introduce him to 'the family'. And it was a while before he introduced me to his, actually, and he seemed oddly nervous when we encountered *tante* Aline, by chance, in the Luxembourg Gardens that day. But I'd misread the signs, thought he was embarrassed about *me* when, in fact, he was anxious about how *I* would take to *them* (or so he

144

said). But once I *had* met them, I told him how lucky he was to come from a family who knew more about art than Van Gogh's 'Sunflowers' and had major wall-space given over to bookshelves. I told him about Miss Rose and Miss McHale and their little front room crammed with books and about their old grey Citroën in the school car park, packed for escape on the last day of term. But I'm not sure he really understood. He'd been able to take so much for granted.

And I so want Eloisa to be able to do the same – to have the advantage of growing up with books, art, ideas, music, *enthusiasm*. It's one of the reasons I gave in and accepted that modest legacy from Colette. A single mother in London in the inflationary 'seventies, how else could I do it? How else could we afford to live in a place with easy access to all that seems valuable to me?

Yes, it's a compromise. Our life is, possibly, compromised. I never really manage to forget that. Then, aren't we all 'compromised' in one way or another? But people don't refuse to visit the Pyramids because they were built using slave labour.

Is that an excuse or a reason? How can one be weighed against the other? I want to give our daughter what her father had. I guess that's why I get so rattled when she shows signs of rejecting her education and wanting nothing but a big house and lots of children.

But maybe I don't need to worry too much. She's beginning to change. She's his daughter, after all. And, ironically, the change was partly thanks to Alma's daughter, Apple, of all people – now metamorphosed into 'Angie'.

She's never got on well with Apple. Apart from being born in the same week in the same hospital, they have nothing in common whatsoever.

Sausages. (Raw ones.) That's what one thinks of, looking at 'Angie'. And she isn't too bright, either. Probably the most intelligent thing she's ever done was to insist that, when she went to secondary school, she would be known as 'Angie': a name like 'Apple' would've been a recipe for disaster.

Alma hates her daughter's new name and scarcely bothers to conceal her disappointment that she's turning out to be passive and conventional and not crisp and shining as she's always hoped. 'Angie' isn't exactly fat, but looks squashy just under her pink skin, and the poor girl's breasts are beginning to push out in a round, saucepan-liddish way. The skirts she wears are too short for straight, solid legs, and she never quite knows what to do with her hair.

I arrange for Eloisa to stay at Alma's for the weekend while I go to a 'popular fiction' writing convention in another part of the country (being desperate for a break from bubbling hormones and moods).

Although I find the convention really tedious, I have a better time than my daughter that weekend. (And I don't suppose it was that great for Angie, either.)

By the time I pick Eloisa up on Sunday evening, she's seething with resentment, and as soon as we're back home she removes the cork and lets it all gush out.

'Don't you ever, EVER, *EVER* … ' (both fists banging the table with each 'ever') 'make me stay with Alma again.'

'Whatever happened, my little Fury?'

'Nothing. Absolutely NOTHING. I've never been so bored in my entire life … except at school sometimes.'

'What did you do? You must've done something: Alma said you were holed up in Apple's room most of the time.'

'Exactly! I had to watch her "dance", and it was *so boring*. She played the same song over and over again. Then she wanted us to do each other's hair and I had to say I didn't know how because hers was greasy and I really didn't want to touch it. Then she kept on about "the wedding". You'd've thought she was one of Lady Di's bridesmaids or something, the way she went on. Then she said she had this big secret and I wasn't to tell and she locked the door so her mum wouldn't come in, and it was just a bottle of pink nail varnish she'd bought with her lunch money. And when I said why was it such a secret, she said her mum'ld kill her if she found out and I said I didn't think that was likely. Then she started asking me whether I minded not having a dad and living with just my mum and … '

'If it's any comfort,' I say, 'I had a pretty lousy weekend, too.'

'You didn't manage to pick up a new … "friend", then?'

(So *that's* what it's really about! The last time we were apart for more than a few hours – when she'd gone to Suffolk with Jack – I'd teamed up with Stephen.)

'Actually I *did* make a new friend.'

She gives me a withering look, but she's so het up over 'Angie' she doesn't even ask for details.

'I'll tell you something, Mumsie, I never in a million years want to be anything like Angie. She doesn't *know* anything. She doesn't *read* anything. She's not *interested* in anything.'

And that, I believe, is behind my daughter's conversion.

She starts to read obsessively – *because Angie doesn't*. She starts to open her eyes wider to everything in the world because Angie stays in her room with her eyes half closed, 'thinking about a boy at the bus stop who probably wasn't even looking at her anyway.'

Her father would be proud of such a *ravenous* daughter.

… Though sometimes, when she comes on a bit strong with it, it can be quite … *wearing*.

❦ ELOISA ❦

I didn't like my mother's new friend. Even before we met.

'Why are you trying to impress your new friend?' (My mother was on her hands and knees in the communal bathroom. I was leaning against the door-frame, a copy of *Pride and Prejudice* dangling from my right hand, my index finger marking my place.)

'I'm not trying to impress *anyone*. I'm cleaning the bathroom.'

'But you wouldn't be doing that if ... '

'Could you possibly lower yourself to go and fetch me the Ajax from the cupboard under the sink?'

'Sarcasm is the lowest form of wit: my English teacher says so. You should be pleased I'm reading.'

'I am. And I'd be even more pleased if you could just nip through and get the Ajax for me between paragraphs.'

Ajax. Funny word ... if you kept saying it. Age-axe ... Eh-jacks ... Ay-jacks ... Aige-acs ... The word slipping the loose knot holding it to an object in the world, drifting away from its moorings further and further with each time I said it. Two ugly sounds in a meaningless marriage. What had it got to do with a cardboard cylinder of cheap, smelly scouring powder. I handed it to my mother.

'A-jax ... It has no meaning. They should've called it "Devil's Talcum Powder" or something.'

'Ajax was a Greek hero who fought in the Trojan Wars.'

'That's silly.'

'No, it's not silly. It's metaphor ... as your English teacher would no doubt tell you. The powder's being likened to him for its strength and its ability to tackle a difficult job – like conquering the Trojans.'

She sprinkled the powder and scoured the basin, then turned

on the tap to rinse the stuff away. And I saw all the little Trojans struggling and throwing up their miniscule arms in the whirl-pool of water sucking them down the plughole. I really felt for them. But Ajax had done his job, prised them away from the side of the basin: you could hear them gurgling as they were pulled down and drowned ...

Never one to miss an educational opportunity, my mother enlightened me further as she breathed on the mirror above the basin and rubbed at the little white splats of toothpaste. 'Not much of a hero really, old Ajax. Brave but not bright. Killed himself in a fit of pique when they gave Achilles' armour to Odysseus instead of him. Jealousy is rightly called one of the Seven Deadly Sins.'

I saw a sword gouge the side of the none-too-bright cylinder (the Greeks used to fall on their swords, didn't they? ... or was that the Romans?), saw the horrid white powder come trick-ling out ... trickling and trickling ... until the half-empty tube toppled over, rolled a little from side to side, then lay still. 'The death of Ajax' ...

Someone else in the house had left a sliver of old soap – grime in the cracks of it, a suspiciously curly hair stuck to the top – beside the basin. She removed it with a sheet of loo-paper and replaced it with a new bar of Lux.

'Most brand names come from Greek or Latin.' She pointed to the soap. 'Like this.'

'Lux! That means light! It was in our Latin vocab list last week.'

'I told you Latin was useful.' She polished the taps.

We went back to our kitchen, working through some of the other words that inhabited the flat with us – Omo ... Ty-Phoo ... Persil ...

'And what about frurd?' I ask.

'What do you mean, "frurd"?'

'It's a word, on the spine of that big book on the shelf by the mirror.'

'Oh, "Froyd"! F–R–E–U–D. He's a man who had theories about everything to do with people. You'll learn about him one day. You're too young at the moment.'

'So it's about sex … '

There was a ring at the bell. The 'friend' had come early.

Amaranth Oort was enormous: large and sturdy as a Dutchman (her father), exotic as an Indonesian (her mother). Not fat, just very large all over. 'Amaranth' was the name she'd given herself in later life because no-one could pronounce her Indonesian one.

She told me how lucky I was to have such a lovely mum … to have any parents at all. Hers had died most horribly in a car crash when she was three: something involving a ravine. (A person who looked like *her* just wouldn't have been connected with run-of-the-mill deaths in bed.) The little orphan was taken in by friends of the incinerated parents, a sweet little English couple, the Selbys – childless missionaries – who later moved back to Surrey. I couldn't help thinking that if the Selbys really were a sweet *little* couple, as she said, they must've been terribly alarmed at what their adopted child became: huge and exotic. A bit like buying what you think is a wallflower plant and it turning out to be a sunflower with a face as big as a dinner-plate.

She was wearing tight black trousers, a loose velvet top in startling aquamarine, and entered bearing an enormous bunch of purple flowers we had to put in a bucket because we didn't have a vase even nearly big enough. Her earrings were long, intricate constructions hung with moons and stars, and the mass of her black, frizzyish hair was gathered into an overwhelming bush held in a silver clasp engraved with heraldic birds.

I knew they'd met at that 'Popular Fiction' convention, but I just couldn't imagine Amaranth hunched over a little type-writer – though I couldn't really imagine her working in an office or a shop either: she'd have been knocking things over all the time. And I began to wonder whether my mother had actually prepared enough food.

But at least it wasn't some man she'd picked up, so that was something.

Then Amaranth brought out a photo of the two of them together at the convention, saying, 'I finally finished the film, Georgie!' In the photo, her arm was around my mother in a way that made me feel ... uncomfortable. She looked 'protective', but also 'possessive': a 'she's mine' gesture, like you sometimes saw in pictures of men with women. Was it just because she was so much bigger? Perhaps she couldn't help looking possessive and in control. Or ...

A terrible truth stripped itself bare in front of me.

NO! *The last thing I wanted was* ANOTHER MOTHER! And especially not this giantess who'd stomped her way into our lives.

My response was to sit sullenly in the corner, playing the part of the silent intellectual while they babbled on about 'popular fiction', my eyes boring into my mother's old copy of *The Metaphysical Poets* (chosen because the 'metaphysical' bit sounded impressive, though I had no idea what it meant). I was half way through a poem called 'Go and catch a falling star' when the Oort turned to me with, 'So this is the important young lady you had to hurry away for at the end of the weekend' – which switched on another red light of suspicion with a very loud click: had this *woman* tried to delay my mother's departure at the end of the weekend? WHAT FOR??!!

My mother replied with unusual banality, 'Yes. The best girl in the world.'

'And a very studious one, too, by the look of it,' flattered the Oort.

I gave her the kind of smile I thought an 'intellectual' might bestow on a lesser being, then turned to my mother and pointed to the second line of the poem. 'What does this mean, "*Get with child a mandrake root"*?'

'I'll explain later, Tootsie.'

'Don't mind me,' said the Oort. 'If the child wants to know something … '

(*Child*?! Huh!)

'Later will do, won't it, Toots.' I heard my mother's not-to-be-argued-with tone beneath the smile.

Putting my eyes back on the poem ('Donny' – as I thought the poet was called – had obviously been having a bad day, too, when he wrote it), I tuned my ears for clues to the nature of their relationship.

'What's she reading?' asked the Oort, in a lowered voice.

My mother hesitated at the unlikelihood of her answer. 'Seventeenth-century poetry.'

I glanced up and caught the Oort staring at me. As our eyes met, she switched on a smile. 'Must be lovely having a daughter, Georgie.'

I was dying to say, 'You could. It's quite easy to make one, you know. But it does have to be one of each sex.' I didn't say it, of course. Just went back to the poem with its *'mermaids singing'* rhyming with *'envy's stinging'* … one ear still on *them*. But all they talked about was their writing so it was really boring, and the Oort had one of those sonorous voices that stopped you being able to concentrate on anything else. I went to my bedroom to read – but her voice came through the door. So in the end I took myself and 'Donny' off to the communal loo on the landing where I discovered his sonnet 'Death be not proud' and the satisfaction of substituting 'Oort' for 'Death' to come up with lines like, *'Oort be not proud though some have called thee mighty and dreadful'*, and a splendid ending: *'Oort, thou shalt DIE!'* …

'You all right in there, pansy?' (My mother on the other side of the locked door.)

'Yes. Why?'

'It's just that you've been some time … and Amaranth needs to have a wee.'

I flushed, for form's sake. Amaranth was already outside the door. She put her great hand on my head as she passed. I followed my mother through to the kitchen area and hovered at her elbow. It took a few seconds to find the courage to ask a more or less direct question.

'Are you and Amaranth … really close friends?'

She shrugged. 'Yes and no. There was lots of flirting going on at the conference. I wasn't interested, not with that seedy crew, and Amaranth didn't get a look in, being so big. We kind of stuck together. Not literally, of course … ' she added, with a wry smile. (Had she sussed the real tenor of my question?). 'She's lonely and unsure of herself. She writes very sweet romances – fantasies of what she wishes would happen to her, I guess. All she longs for is a home and family of her own.' Hearing Amaranth return from the loo, my mother lowered her voice. 'Let's be generous, Tootsie. We have each other.' She gave me a quick, reassuring hug. It changed my mood like the flick of a switch.

'Mumsie, why don't you go and talk to Amaranth and I'll finish doing the salad and getting stuff ready for lunch.' (She hesitated.) 'I'll wash the lettuce properly. Honest!'

I almost wished I hadn't closed the door in a fruitless attempt to muffle the Oort's voice because I could hear she was quizzing my mother about my father. My mother was keeping her voice low, so I only heard the questions, none of the answers. Some of them were quite long. Was she telling this new friend more about him than she'd ever told me? I thought about quietly opening the door, just a crack, but she'd have noticed and would probably have changed the subject. I put my ear to the closed door, but all our doors were the thick, solid, old-fashioned kind and not much came through them … apart from the voice of the Oort!

I wondered if my mother was telling her the truth or just making things up to satisfy her friend's curiosity – the way I sometimes did. I so wanted to hear what she was saying, but I couldn't, and it made me feel cross again. Cross with this 'woman'. Cross with my mother. Cross with myself ... because I never knew what questions I really wanted the answers to when it came to my father.

But I took my revenge. The lettuce received the most cursory contact with water. I did see the two greenfly ... and let them live a bit longer. After all, there probably wasn't much to choose between being washed down the drain and being washed down the throat of the great Oort by her no doubt copious digestive juices.

❧ GEORGINA ❧

Some memories seem to become more vivid with the passing of time – floodlit on a stage, a play performed over and over, to an audience of one. You can talk about your past in general terms to other people, but you can't easily take others into the actual performance. And no matter how hard you try to write down the script, there's always something missing: the physical 'actuality' of the actors. I can see him so clearly, hear his voice ... but stretch out a hand and the flesh melts. Nothing. Nothing. Nothing.

'Tu m'accroches comme un air de jazz ... ' he says. You cling to me like a jazz tune. (From him, that was a compliment.)

'You should write a song that begins like that.'

'Too late,' he says. 'Somebody made it already.'

'So I'm only worth second-hand compliments?'

'Ah, but when the first-hand is Boris Vian ... ' He puts on a record of Vian songs.

'So, how many girls have you used that line on?'

'Girls?! Never! Women ... not so many. Fewer than you are thinking, I expect.'

'I want to know.'

'What is it you want to know?'

'How many girl-friends – lovers – you had before me.'

'You do not want to know that.'

'Yes I do. It's better to know than imagine.'

'I don't remember.'

'Yes you do. Nobody forgets that kind of thing. Besides, you just said it was less than I'd think. And if you don't tell me I'll ... I'll make a hole in your head and search in your brain till I find them.'

'Au secours! Au secours! She's going to kill me!' He runs to the window, pretending to call for help.

'Women can be just as violent as men in matters of love,' I say, tears blurring my eyes, and feeling unaccustomed fury with him for trying to joke his way past my needs.

But he never does tell me, and the record plays on in my head. ' ... *Et la musique tourne, tourne, et les danseurs ...* '

'Music is a metaphor for the many things we do not have words for,' he says. 'That is why people who are not sharing a language can feel emotions from the same music. Music is a good manner to heal the world ... to make smaller the spaces between peoples and cultures.'

'But do different peoples hear each other's music in the same way?' I say. 'After all, there's "purr", "*ronronner*" and "*schnurren*" but it's all supposed to be the same onomatopoei-cally happy cat in England, France and Germany. And God only knows what it is in Japan or Vietnam.'

'Are there any cats remaining in Vietnam, *tu pense?*'

'Don't let's talk of Vietnam now.'

'*But it was you who ...* '

'Yes, I know it was me. But I can't get rid of those pictures from the television last night. How can people do such things to each other?'

'*Trop de grandes idées, absence d'imagination. Et ils manquent de la musique ...* '

Too many big ideas, too little imagination. Not enough music ...

> '*Put another nickel in*
> *the nickelodeon –*
> *All I want is loving you*
> *and music, music, music ...* '

My father always singing old songs to me, giving me my bath when my mother's 'poorly again'. All sorts of old songs. American, mainly. His childhood songs.

'Gimme crack corn and I don't care
Gimme crack corn and I don't care
Gimme crack corn and I don't care
My master's gone away ... '

'There's a hole in my bucket, dear Liza, dear Liza.
There's a hole in my bucket, dear Liza, a hole.

Then mend it dear Henry, dear Henry, dear Henry.
Then mend it ... '

I've tried. But it still leaks a bit.

Drip ...

Drip ...

C–O–L–L–A–B–O–R–A–T–E–U–R–S

... containing, for the French, CUL (as in *'mon cul'* – 'my arse': so 'arsehole'); RATS (which speaks for itself); OR ('gold': how much of it was done for greed?); BOL (as in *'bol alimentaire'* – a disgusting gobbet of chewed food, from the Greek 'Bolos', a clod or lump) ... leaving an A and an E (Adolph Eichmann in any language) and also another O ('Oh! ... Oh! ... '). And A's for the other Adolf, obviously, and also for Auschwitz and ash and *abbatoir*, for 'ARBEIT MACHT FREI', for absence, abyss and abomination, for *'adieu'* and anguish, for agony, anger, annihilate, appalling, for Azrael the Angel of Death. Then all the Es come tumbling ... evil, eugenics, enslave, experiment, emaciated, expendable, extermination ...

It drips and drips and drips.

C–O–L–L–A–B–O–R–A–T–E–U–R–S

❧ ELOISA ❧

In History we 'did' the Second World War.

Nazis. Fascism. Hitler. Anti-Semitism ... The words sent me back to that Suffolk beach again, where I first heard talk of such things. I was back with the heave of the slimy black sea and the rectangles of light from the houses where people were reading and yawning and discussing the papers and playing Scrabble and Monopoly, the dim gold windows too feeble against the blackness.

And I thought of Jack's voice calling us in, rescuing us from any more of that unspeakable telling.

Mrs Appleyard explained how the Second World War was partly the result of the First World War.

The ripples of war go on and on and on and on and on, she said.

❧ GEORGINA ❧

Jack comes back just after Christmas. His first wife's father has died and he's come over for the funeral. He rings me the morning before he's leaving to ask if he can call round and discuss a favour. (It turns out to be using us as an address for communications about an art school place for Dee, who wants to come back to England to continue her studies.)

So, returning to Miranda Road on the first day back after the Christmas holidays – cold and fed up because three of the teachers were off with flu and had left really boring work – Eloisa walks in to find Jack sitting there with me. She blushes deeply and is suddenly shy with him. She's grown a lot since he left, and is starting to 'develop' (as they call it). And he's changed, too: he seems sadder and older … which isn't surprising.

Before Eloisa arrives, Jack has begun to tell me his troubles (which is probably the real reason for him wanting to come around: the other thing could've been dealt with over the phone). Soon after their move to America, Myra was drawn into some right-wing religious group. He's been trying to stop her from influencing the younger ones – especially Natasha who, despite her sturdy looks, is emotionally quite vulnerable, he says. He thought living in another country would be a good experience for the whole family … instead of which it's sliding into disaster. I reassure him as best I can: I am sure Myra will 'see the light' before long, I say. 'That's the trouble,' says Jack. 'She thinks that's what she's done already.'

Here I must admit to a most uncharitable thought regarding Jack – a thought prompting laughter inside me … as well as panic. Is there a divorce on the horizon? Am I being lined up as a possible next 'Mrs Jack'? Is he really just a chap going through a hard time who needs a friendly but detached ear to tell his troubles to? Or is this another version of 'my wife doesn't understand me'? – that tedious old psychological foreplay technique.

The element of panic comes from my fear that I won't be able to withstand a concerted campaign from both Eloisa and himself. A panic that my life will be stolen from me for a second time. All those children!

I imagine that, when Eloisa goes into her room and closes the door to change out of her still loathed school uniform, she's grinning, dancing, thanking a god of personal destiny neither of us believes in, and saying a great big 'AT LAST!!!!' at the sight of Jack and myself so unexpectedly sitting there cosily together in the midst of a serious and possibly 'intimate' conversation.

He can't stay much longer, but we do all have a cup of tea together and he asks Eloisa how she's getting on at school *et cetera, et cetera*, and she asks after all the children and whether they're all happy in America. He winces slightly at this and says, 'It's … all right. But I think, all things considered, I'll be glad to come back to England' – which, of course, makes Eloisa very, very happy.

Perhaps that's why seeing Jack again seems to upset her less than I expected – though my hope is that she's growing out of her obsession with him … unless, growing up, she's just becoming more reticent about letting her feelings show. I hope she isn't becoming hard-hearted. I sometimes felt there was a fine, cold thread running through her father – a kind of 'absoluteness' and lack of empathy for and sensitivity to certain human emotions – and I hope she hasn't inherited that from him. But maybe it was just a 'male' thing …

This new spirit of detached 'inwardness' (that's not quite right, but I can't find the precise words to describe it) is much in evidence soon after Jack's visit when my stepbrother, Samuel, dies suddenly of a heart attack. I cry and cry.

Eloisa's eyes remain utterly dry and the only 'comfort' she offers me is an irritable sigh and, 'Oh, for goodness sake! He was *dreadful* and he ate too much. What is there to be so upset about? Think of all the starving children in Africa, dying every day. They don't even get a chance to live.' (But she's too young to know that reason and grief keep little company.)

It's a small, sad funeral. The fellow conducting the service hasn't bothered to find out much about 'the deceased'. He just goes on about 'our brother Samuel' being a reliable employee of the County Council and a 'very private person' (euphemism for 'had no friends'). No mention of the way he helped his brother recover after being hospitalized for acute depression, nor how very fond he was of his young niece – always talking about 'little Eloisa' to his colleagues (so it emerges during the post-burial sandwiches). Nor how tenderly, when we were young, he'd place the soft-feathered birds in the earth (always the one to bury their tangled remains left on our lawn by next door's violent cat) ... as well as the starving kitten I'd found under a hedge (it only lasted a day) ... and the goldfish won at the fair and which we over-fed and killed within a week ...

He'd been a big, shambly teenager with no sense whatever of how to be smart or sexy. Other children's parents were always nice to him because he was helpful and reliable and never took offence (or if he did, never showed it) when he was teased for being slow or flabby. He was never unpleasant to his stepfather (my father) and was probably kinder to me than a real brother would have been.

So, with these words, I try to save a little of his goodness from oblivion. And that's a good enough use for words.

I like to think, as Samuel lay on his back in the garden (that's where it happened), his eyes open to, but no longer seeing, the sky, that a bird – a song thrush, say, or a blackbird – hopped up onto the mountain of his stomach and sang for all it was worth.

❧ ELOISA ❧

I asked to go to the funeral (to get a day off school), but she said I was too young. Really I think she was afraid I wouldn't be upset enough. She was probably right. I couldn't get rid of the ridiculous image of enormous Uncle Samuel being rowed across the Styx, the Boatman panting as he pulled on the oars, the stern low in the water from Uncle Samuel's great weight, the slack hugeness of him watching for the shores of Ever-and-Ever-Land, his loose and plentiful buttocks spilling over the boat's little wooden seat ...

A few weeks later, Uncle Archie came to visit us – the first time I'd ever seen one of the uncles without the other – to deliver my 'inheritance'. He handed me a smallish cardboard box that shared the mould-and-mothballs smell of their clothes, the smell of them coming closer and closer for those obligatory kisses. With all the dignity of a magus presenting myrrh, he placed the box in my hands with, 'Your Uncle Samuel wanted you to have this. He often said so and, although he didn't leave a will, I know I am honouring his wishes by giving it to you.'

An inheritance! I was *so* excited. All those years, Uncle Samuel – funny old Uncle Samuel – had been putting a little aside for me out of his modest County Council salary, and it had built up to a considerable amount. An 'inheritance'. Maybe I could visit Jack in America. Or pay for my mother and myself to spend *the whole summer* in France ...

But it didn't feel like money. And if it was a cheque, it would surely have come in an envelope, not a box. Trying not to look disappointed, I said, 'What is it, Uncle Archie?'

'A babushka.' The word wobbled his jowls.

'What's that?'

'It's a Russian word for headscarf,' began my mother ... at which point Uncle Archie knocked over his cup of tea as he tried to lower his bulk into our modest-sized armchair and had to be mopped up and another cup had to be poured for him – after which it was all about the funeral and how 'bereft' he felt (I'd never heard the word before). 'Bereft … ' he kept saying, 'I just feel so *bereft*.' And he went over and over the scene of death – Samuel, only just recovering from a severe chest infection, insisting on doing 'the spring dig' in the garden. It was such a nice day – warm sun of early spring, birds singing, the bulbs showing already.

Uncle Archie had found him laid out next to the vegetable patch, like Gulliver, eyes to the sky, as if watching the high little white clouds drifting gently across the blue …

As I sat and listened, holding the unopened, smelly little box in my lap while Uncle Archie consumed cup after cup so my mother had to keep refilling the tea-pot (*surely* he'd need the toilet soon), the eccentric cinema of my mind banished boredom by turning the previously-imagined Stygian rowing-boat into a vast, squarish coffin floating on a river of sugared tea to a soundtrack of spring-time birds that gradually twittered into Wagner's *Siegfried Idyll* … It was one of Miss Enderby's favourites. (She often had us do 'creative writing' to music and, when we'd finished, she told us about the music.) I saw Miss Enderby gently conducting an invisible orchestra from a little cloud as Uncle Samuel's coffin floated downstream to the great ocean of eternity where it joined hundreds and hundreds … thousands and thousands … of other coffins bobbing gently with the slight movement of a calm sea, coffins all different sizes for the people in them – though Uncle Samuel's was the biggest …

Eventually there was Uncle Archie's dreaded goodbye kiss to endure. And as he wobbled off down the front path, alone, he seemed to trail the word 'bereft' behind him on a piece of string, like a child pulling a sad little toy dog on wheels.

While my mother cleared the tea things I took my 'inheritance' into my room, put the box in the middle of the floor and stared at it. Babushka. Headscarf. If it smelled anything like the rest of their clothes – mothballs and sweat – there was no way I was even going to touch it. What would I have wanted with a headscarf? I was thirteen, not fifty-three. AND WHAT' WAS UNCLE SAMUEL DOING WITH A HEADSCARF ANYWAY??!!

Maybe it'd been his mother's. Perhaps he used to dress up in it after she died. Kinky! Did he use to take it to bed with him? – like a security blanket? ... like I used to my mother's old vest? I was certainly not going to touch it if it'd been in bed with Uncle Samuel! And why pass it on to me? Some inheritance! Maybe there was a curse on it. Maybe it was meant as a punishment for me not being nice enough to him. *The Curse of the Babushka* ... Wear it and you'd begin to swell and smell and end up like Uncle Samuel ... I blew out my cheeks, distended my belly, waddled across the room intoning under my breath, '*The Curse of the Babushka* ... *The Curse of* ... '

But then the thought struck me that there might be a cheque in the box *as well as* the headscarf. I pulled off the lid. Polythene packing. For a scarf?

Which, of course, wasn't one. I lifted out a smooth, bright-painted object, its shape something between a very large egg and a pear. Wooden. I turned it ... to find I was looking into an impassive little face painted on it in black lines. The face was framed by a painted scarf with little flowers on it. Red, pink, yellow, green. It was one of those Russian dolls with smaller and smaller dolls inside. I twisted it so it came apart in the middle. (Perhaps there was a cheque curled up inside, wrapped around one of the smaller dolls.) Just red, pink, yellow, green and an inscrutable little face. I twisted the next one. It came apart revealing ... just another doll. And again ... Nothing. And again ... until I came to the solid little heart of them all.

I was sitting there among the mad scatter of top halves and bottom halves – hollow half-bodies with raw, unpainted insides – when my mother walked in.

'Huh! Some inheritance!' I flicked one of the bottom halves of the babushka so it tipped over and rolled across the floor, disappearing under my bed.

'Some people, Eloisa, don't have much to leave behind except their goodness. And sometimes those who dole out legacies and bequests have acquired their wealth at the expense of others – occasionally in a dreadful way.'

'You sound as though you know someone like that, the way you looked when you said it.'

She shrugged and turned away.

'We've got a legacy, haven't we? I remember you saying something about an old lady and I used to think it was "leg at sea". I used to imagine this leg sticking out of … '

'A very, very small legacy,' she said, sounding oddly defensive. 'Put the babushka back together and give it to me if you don't want it.'

'Why did you tell me "babushka" meant headscarf?' I asked her, my voice sullen with disappointment over my non-existent wealth.

'Because it does. Sort of. It comes from the Russian for granny or old woman. They'd always wear headscarves. When I was a child, we called this the "babushka" – though some people call these nests of dolls "matrioshki". It belonged to my stepmother – Archie and Samuel's mum – and that's what *she* called it. The fat old granny has all the following generations inside her, right down to the baby in the middle.'

'That's me … '

'You could say so. For the moment. Then if you have a baby, you'll be the next one up.'

'But there's only room for one baby each time and I want to have more than one. I want *lots* … and a big house to keep them all in and nice furniture and I'll have a lot of friends and they'll bring *their* children to play because we'll have a great big garden with swings and a slide and a Wendy-house and maybe even a tree-house and … '

My mother made a kind of grunting sound and walked out of the room, muttering something about mother ducks and father ducks and all the little baby ducks, and 'so much for Eloisa the rampant intellectual …' I found her so weird sometimes!

6

'A MOVEABLE FEAST'

❧ ELOISA ❧

Dear Jack,

I thought you would like to get a letter from France with a French stamp on it. My mother and I are staying in Paris. In a flat not a hotel. I like it better than last time because I have a friend here now and we go places together. There are lots of interesting things to do and see I know you would like it so you should come here for a holiday when you come back from America. When will that be do you think? It seems like you have been there a very long time allready.

How are 'the babes'? Does Josephine still play the violin? Does Natasha still miss Rags and has she got a new American dog?

I know you are very busy but if you have time please write a short letter to let me know you are allright.

With lots and lots and lots of love from,
                    Eloisa

PS My mum sends her love as well.

(One of the many letters I wrote to Jack but never sent.)

❧ GEORGINA ❧

Eloisa looks at me in disgust. 'You shouldn't use rude words like that – especially about a woman.'

I probably replied with something like, 'I don't count *her* as a woman. Our first female Prime Minister, and she acts worse than a man! Taking us into war … against Argentina, of all places!' – furious and bitter that a woman has let us down so badly. The flag-waving lunacy. The nauseous propaganda. The inhuman headlines yelling from the tabloids. The face of that woman. And her handbag. Like a defeat of all my generation had stood for.

It's Eloisa's first war. We still don't have a television, but one day, passing a shop where there are a number of them in the window tuned to the same news programme, she's riveted by a ship on fire in a dark and heaving sea. 'Our side' or 'their side', she asks me. Without the sound it's impossible to tell. 'Does it matter?' I say. 'There are sailors on that ship, burning maybe … or drowning.'

Then, on my birthday, they sink the *Belgrano*. A couple of days later I tell her I am going with Alma to attend a vigil for the three hundred and sixty-eight men who died in that dark and heaving sea. She asks if she can come too.

Alma brings Apple along – against her will, I imagine, from the way she behaves: she sits on the ground, head down, picking at her cuticles most of the time. Eloisa (possibly to prove how very different she is from 'Angie') is a model of maturity and consideration, taking her turn at holding one end of our banner and, when we're getting cold, going to fetch teas and coffees for us from the little stall nearby. I am so proud of her.

Of course, it's a useless kind of thing to do, really: what good can a 'vigil' do for those dead young men? But I need to be with people who feel the same as I do about the war. It's so depressing, the way it's brought out the worst in most people – the worst kind of patriotism and xenophobia.

In some ways it's like a faint after-echo of 'old times' – those demos against the Vietnam War, when we were young and had long hair and funny clothes and stuck flowers in gun-barrels, enraging our parents' generation. We couldn't understand them: we'd grown up in the shadow of 'their' war, heard their stories of it over and over, all the horrors and the sacrifices. Was it surprising we objected to Vietnam? Weren't they trying to turn us against war by giving us all the ghastly details of the air raids and the terror and uncertainty? And, anyway, weren't we carrying on *their* fight, as we understood it? Different uniforms and music, but it was a fight against the spirit of fascism, just the same. We wanted freedom, tolerance, the celebration of people's differences, an end to Man's inhumanity to Man (and Woman). The big stuff. We didn't want to be telling war stories to our children or live in fear of seeing them burn – as the children of Vietnam had burned, nightly, on our television screens. Napalm. Agent Orange.

I just have to get away for a while. France is calling more loudly than ever.

And, I must admit, I have personal reasons for wanting to go, too – sparked by Amaranth giving me her latest story to read. From the uncharacteristic, shifty look on her face when she gives me the envelope, I guess something's afoot.

The title is 'Choosing' – untypically spare and abstract for Amaranth, who is more the 'dawns' and 'bird-songs' and 'lavender sunsets' brigade.

This is how it begins.

'Joy allowed the neat tip of her right index finger to trace the path of an errant raindrop taking a drunken, unpredictable course down the windowpane of her second-floor bedroom

overlooking a lovely London square. September again already. Almost ten years since the accident, an accident caused by a sudden downpour on a long-dry and therefore oily road. Ten years since the brief, passionate affair with Joseph was brought to its tragic, irreversible end even before they could carry out their plan to marry.

She lived still with the ghost of him created out of their past. But with no new memories being created by a life lived together in the world, the old ones – and the ghosts made from them – were wearing thin … thin as a too-fine net curtain through which the outside world appeared with increasing clarity, colour, and vividness. In spring the weighty, sugar-pink blossoms of the big almond tree in the square waved for attention against a nursery-blue sky. In summer … '

But it soon becomes a bit more 'experimental' than Amaranth's usual stories, giving two parallel versions of the woman's future. In the first, she lives only with the ghost of her past great love, gradually turning into a ghost herself – the ghost *of* herself … no longer a proper mother to Saffron, the child of their brief union, eaten away by her own grief and sadness. In the other version she … BUYS A DOG. *BUYS A DOG*!!? (Oh, Amaranth, *please!*) … a dog she calls 'Grief' and which she begins to take for walks on a firm lead around the 'lovely London square'. Gradually she ventures further afield with the dog until, one day, she lets it off the lead on Hampstead Heath … and it runs away and a nice chap tries to help her find the dog. And the inevitable happens. (Amaranth's stories always end with a wedding. Or, at least, an imminent wedding.)

'So, what did you think?' (Amaranth on the phone the following week.)

'I think the dog should turn up again. Poor little Grief doesn't need to disappear or be killed, and I think it should live with them in that nice house in Hampstead. And the child needs to be less wishy-washy … maybe even a bit awkward. How does she react to the prospect of a new man in her mother's life after all that time? And the mother … couldn't she be a bit more resilient? – coping pretty well, all things considered, but maybe … missing sex? And wouldn't she see her dead lover's face or personality in the child sometimes?'

Silence. Then, 'It's a lousy story, isn't it, Georgie.'

'Well, maybe not up to your usual standard … in some ways. But I guess that's the trouble when something's written with an "agenda" – for a single, particular, and very obvious purpose.'

Silence again. Then, 'It's only because I love you, Georgie, and don't want you to end up lonely. You should really try to find someone before … Well, you're heading for forty.'

'I'm only thirty-seven.'

'That's nearly forty.'

'He might come back. He disappeared. I don't know for sure that he's dead.'

'Oh, come on, Georgie … '

'Besides, I've tried finding someone else to love.'

'Try harder, Georgie.'

'Why are you telling me this?'

'I just said: because I love you.'

I think I've laughed the story off, but its insidious little seed has taken root in some dark, fearful but fertile corner of my mind and is beginning to germinate. (I guess that's how stories do their work. Even lousy ones.)

Perhaps Englishmen just 'aren't my type'. Maybe another Frenchman …

❀ ELOISA ❀

Miranda Road, soon after five in the morning. I think it was the first time I'd seen it that early. It was light already, being July, but darker than it might've been because the sky was overcast. As we stood on the front step and did the last minute passports-money-tickets check, it began to rain gently. The air was so fresh and, as I breathed in the morning, my whole body felt alert for adventure.

We caught one of the first tubes of the day. The carriage was very silent. A few people read newspapers with shouting black headlines. Some dozed, heads jerking forward or back every now and then.

By the time we reached Dover, the morning had opened its eyes properly: the weather had cleared to a beautiful summer's day, the sea utterly calm, the sky utterly blue, the sea-gulls, the cliffs and the wake of the boat dazzling white in the sunshine. And beside me, leaning on the ferry's railings, smiling towards France, her hair pulled back by the breeze of the boat's movement, my mother looked beautiful. Grabbing the 'air camera', I lined up the shot and make a loud 'click' sound. She turned, saw what I'd done, and laughed. It was the first time I'd seen her laugh properly in ages.

We'd have a whole week in Paris, then a week at a little country house in Normandy owned by Maude and Maurice. Alphonse and Aline were in Italy, and the Bonnats were on a business trip to Canada, so their daughter, Monique, was staying with Maude and Maurice (her mother was Maurice's sister) in rue Claude Bernard. And so were we.

I hadn't been prepared, mentally, for Monique to be part of the holiday. My spirits withered, remembering that cool, well-groomed, aloof little girl who ignored me in the restaurant the first time we'd been to Paris. The happy energy I'd started out with that morning left me in the lurch and I felt suddenly defeated even before the holiday had started. But at least the *apartement* was spacious and cheerful, not nearly as polished as Pierre and Claudine's place. I liked it a lot better. There were lots of quite modern paintings in all the rooms. Light colours. Landscapes and objects, mainly: just a few of people. And loads and loads and loads of books.

My mother was given the guest room all to herself. I was to share with Monique. Two mattresses on the floor. White walls. One long window. Shelves and shelves of books and records and photo albums and expensive-looking equipment for listening to music. A cello in the corner. A jumper and a book on one mattress. Monique's. I tried to catch my mother's eye and show my desperation: maybe we could rearrange things so I could share *her* room. She was stumbling her way through a conversation in French with Maude, though, and seemed totally oblivious of my pleading looks.

But who was this bare-footed, jeans-wearing, crop-haired girl with a charming smile giving me the French double-kiss treatment? Monique! And speaking English (of a sort).

'I am 'appy to see you again, Eloise. You are very grown!'

My heart did a triple somersault, shocking a smile to my mouth. 'You too,' I said. 'And your hair! It's so different!'

She ran her hand over the not-much-more-than-stubble. 'Oh, *oui*. It is all right for you we share the same sleeping room?'

'Yes, that's fine. *C'est bon. Je suis très heureuse,*' I risked.

She smiled and looked at me as if she couldn't decide whether to say something or not. Then she did.

'You know, the first time I am meeting you I think you are going to be very "snob" because my parents, before we come to the restaurant, they say me many times I must behave good – very, very good – because I must give to the English family a positive impression. They make me put on a skirt and the new shoes that make bad on my toes and … '

I began to laugh. 'My mother made *me* wear a skirt!'

She shook her charming head. 'Why are they doing this to us, the parents? Sometimes they are very, very strange, the parents, no?'

Monique: sophisticated sister with her thighs astride a cello. She made such talented music and went to one of the best *lycées*. I fell in love with the movement of her neat hands, the turn of her cropped head, her smile, her green eyes. *Oh, brave new world that has such people in it ...* I wanted to *be* Monique.

An exquisite picture hanging in my memory – like a painting with sound.

Monique did cello practice every day: she had an exam coming up in the autumn. I watched her in her black jeans and tee-shirt, sitting on an old chair fetched from the kitchen, cello between spread knees, turned just sufficiently towards the flood of morning light from the long window to be able to read the music on the spindly silver stand without being dazzled. She was almost a silhouette against the brightness, her nice neck and her cropped, hazel-nut head moving with the music. The rise and dip of her elbow. The warm, glossy brown of the cello. Practising a piece by Tchaikovsky. His name and the title across the top of the music: *Valse Sentimentale*. Her shadow moving on the white wall. She had a recording of her teacher playing the piano part. If she made a mistake, she reached forward, pressed the button, rewound the tape, played the passage again. I watched her, then I watched her shadow. I was sitting on my mattress looking through some of the old family photograph albums, not really paying much attention to them because I was more interested in watching Monique but I didn't want her to realize it: it would have been embarrassing.

The only photo that caught my attention was the torn one. It was an old photo of a bride, but there was a jagged tear beside her left arm. You could see a bit of dark sleeve. I supposed it was the bridegroom's. Maybe somebody didn't like him. Or maybe they did. Maybe they liked him too much and took the picture of him for themselves … I began to spin stories around it. Secret loves. Illegitimate passions.

When Monique finished her practice I asked her about the photo. She gave me a strange look, as if she wasn't quite sure what to say. Then she told me it was Aline and Maude's older sister. She seemed to be expecting a reaction from me, so I asked, 'Does she live in Paris, too?' She looked puzzled, but told me the lady was dead.

As I went to replace the albums on the shelf, some loose, black-and-white photos fell out of the back of one of them. There were three photos all the same – photos of a baby, dark-faced and curly-haired. The kind of photos taken by a professional photographer. I was about to put them back when I saw a name and date on the back of one of them. I didn't note the date: I was too busy recognizing the name. It was my mother's friend Amadou as a baby! She was so cute!

I asked Monique if she thought *tante* Maude would let me have one of the photos – as there were three the same. Monique went to ask *tante* Maude. The answer was yes: I may have any photo I liked.

It would be a lovely surprise for my mother. She might not have ever seen this picture of her friend as a baby. Would she recognize her? I stowed it away carefully in my rucksack, inside a book. And promptly forgot about it.

Later, Monique and I went out together. We went to a record shop as Monique wanted to buy something for her father's birthday. He liked Bach. We went to the Classical department. They were playing a beautiful duet: two women singing. I imagined it to be Monique and me together in a lovely room … or maybe beside a lake … or in a garden … or on top of a hill … We were grown up and our voices were clear and beautiful and we were still friends.

'What lovely music!' I said.

'Yes. It is the 'Flower Duet' from the opera called *Lakmé*. You want to buy it?'

'No. It's all right. I haven't got any money.' (The old story.)

❧ GEORGINA ❧

Maude is in her element, having the two girls staying with her. It's such an unkind caprice of Fate that, loving children and even married to a children's medical specialist, she's been unable to have any of her own. She's the youngest of the three sisters, a little too young to be a mother-figure to me, a little too old to be one to Eloisa and Monique. But she calls us, collectively, *'les filles'* and shines her thwarted motherliness upon all three of us.

Eloisa is in seventh heaven: she clearly idolizes Monique. And when Maude discovers she loves *pains au chocolat* and provides an endless supply of them, life is perfect for her!

It's useful that Eloisa has really hit it off with Monique and that they are happy to spend most of the time together: it leaves me free to go out and about on my own. And, yes, I hang shamelessly around appropriate places, hoping for a miracle, hoping – ridiculously – that Fate will deliver love on a plate, 'love-to-go', someone to rescue me from the lonely future Amaranth has predicted will be mine if I don't take 'positive action'. Why not a suave Parisian? A new life in Paris?

I watch myself being slightly ridiculous, one half of my mind laughing at such a crazy and humiliating 'project', the other half deadly serious, applying itself with animal-like tenacity to the luring of a suitable mate – while a little gobbet of self-hatred sits in my stomach: it means I've given up hope, that I've become cynical (or just realistic) enough to face the truth that 'he' is never going to come back to me. He has chosen to disappear, to start a new life. I didn't matter enough to him in the end. If he has found it so easy to start a new life, why can't I? ... Answer: it can never be entirely new for me: he looks out at me every day from Eloisa's eyes. I will never be free of the past. I can only walk backwards into the future.

And how do I go about it, trying to trap my ideal Parisian man? Spending ludicrous amounts of money on coffee and wine, consumed at an extremely leisurely pace on the terraces of what I think are appropriate cafés. Table for two. Empty seat opposite me, in a good position. A reasonably stylish woman (*not yet forty*) in sunglasses, with whom one might strike up an interesting conversation ... if one were an interesting (and interested) man ... a man who speaks reasonable English, of course.

I try a couple of museums, too. And bookshops, of course. Browsing with intent ...

So, how does it go?

I've been in the Louvre for two hours before it dawns on me that not many sophisticated Frenchmen of the right age will be there, alone, on a weekday morning. They'll all be *at work*. It's mainly tourists. I'm so stupid! And, anyway, I all but forget the original purpose of my visit as the all-involving interest of art takes over from 'life'.

Good-looking chap in 'La Hune' – the philosophy section. But he turns out to be Canadian and, before we can both reach for the same book, his wife comes over with her 'great finds' from photography.

Gibert Jeune is too crowded – with memories as well as people: I was silly to try there. *He* was looking over my shoulder the whole time, pointing out the books I should have read.

And the cafés?

The first time, an overweight American asks if he can take the spare chair ... and doesn't replace it when his party leaves. (I can hardly go and retrieve it!) So that's a waste of money.

The second time I think I've struck lucky. The only free place is at my table. A French guy asks if I mind ... (tall, not bad looking; greying a little at the temples, stylish specs). He sits reading *Le Figaro* in total silence (can't he hear my heart thumping away in there?) for fifteen minutes while he sips a tiny cup of very black coffee … then leaves without so much as a nod in my direction. Not good for my ego … though he may be happily married, of course. Or gay.

The third time … Well, never mind: I don't need to humiliate myself any further.

Net result: I drink too much coffee and get through too much money. And but for the life-enhancing effect of Paris itself, I would no doubt end up utterly depressed as well.

But nobody can say I haven't tried. It's only for a week, anyway. Then we go off to Normandy. Unlikely hunting ground.

❧ ELOISA ❧

There wasn't enough room for us all in the car, plus the luggage and all the food *tante* Maude insisted on taking with us, so my mother went with Maude and Maurice, and Monique and I took the train. Monique was used to doing that kind of thing on her own.

Oncle Maurice drove us to the St Lazare station and put us on the right train. We were to 'descend' at Bayeux and he would meet us there, outside the cathedral, at six o'clock, after he'd delivered '*les dames*' and the luggage to the house. They gave us money for lunch, drinks, and the museum … plus a bit extra. I was *so* excited: it was like being grown-ups.

We had seats by the window, opposite each other. The train moved slowly through the jumbled outskirts of Paris, but soon the countryside was slipping swiftly and silently past. More than two hours for teenage confidences.

I told Monique I thought she was very lucky, having both her parents and being part of a large, nice family with nice homes. I told her about Jack.

'But you are in the family, too! It is making everyone very happy. And Maude is the most happy, I think, because she is always liking your mother very much and was so sad she did not stay in France. She speaks about it sometimes.'

I told her I was very happy, too, that my mother had decided to visit her old friends in France from when she was young.

'But you must not say "friends"!' She sounded a little exasperated. 'You must call us "the family"!'

I said it was very kind of them to make us feel part of their family. I said I was sorry if my mother made Maude sad.

'She was already very, very sad,' said Monique, 'because she loved very much your father and when he died she … '

182

I'm not sure what my face looked like at that moment, but if the explosion of 'realization' in my head was reflected in my expression, it wasn't surprising that Monique stopped mid-sentence and stared at me.

'Something is not good with you? ... I am sorry if I speak of your father and make you sad.'

'No ... it's all right ... It's just that ... well, my mother, she never tells me anything. I didn't know ... She always says he went away ... disappeared. I think she's always hoped he'd come back ... '

'I do not understand. How can she not know he died? In Senegal. And his mother she died just a few months after she has the news. They say she had something – I don't know how you call it English – something bad with blood in her head because she is so *bouleversée* by the death of her son.'

'But how did Maude know him?'

'He was the son of the most old sister of Maude and Aline. It is very strange your mother tells you nothing of these things!'

I began to cry a little, lowering my face so Monique couldn't see. But she did.

'Oh, Eloise ... I am sorry. I did not mean to say things for making you unhappy.'

I shook my head, meaning it was all right. Then, once I felt in control of my voice, I looked up. 'I honestly don't think my mother knows he's dead ... not *definitely* and for certain. You are sure, aren't you? It really is ... '

'*Mais, oui* ... It is written in the newspaper. I am sure Maude has the paper still. She is a person to keep such things.'

'How did he ... die?'

'I don't know this. I am not hearing the family talk of it. It is certain that Maude knows. She admired very much the courage of her sister to marry a man who was black when her parents were so opposing it. And Maude loved your father very,

183

very much, too. I think this is a reason she loves also you very much … But also for yourself, of course!'

I couldn't say anything for a long time. My mind was busy rearranging the furniture in the strange room that had been my life so far. I didn't even really know what I was feeling.

Finally, I managed to speak again. 'So, I really *am* part of your family … And I am half French!' I tried to smile. 'But I wish my mother had stayed in the family. I wish I'd grown up here so you and I could have … I would've been happier, I'm sure I would. I wonder why she left … '

'Perhaps it was for the *scandale* that is in the family at that time. Sometimes when they are talking about it in the family, they make joke and say the big troubles in France at that time were very small comparing with the big troubles in the family. Many arguments and bad feelings!'

'What were the big troubles in France?'

'*Les événements*,' she said. 'That is in 1968. I think Maude says your mother was living here in '67 and '68. Is that right?'

'I don't know,' I said, 'but I was born in 1969 … in February.'

Monique did some silent counting on her fingers, her lips moving slightly through words I couldn't hear. Then she laughed. 'That means they are making you in May of 1968. A good time to make a baby! In the middle of a revolution!'

The 'me' who got off the train at Bayeux was a different me from the one who'd boarded it in Paris. And I quite liked this new person living in my old skin. She seemed more confident for 'knowing who she was'. And even, strangely, more settled, now she was sure that an unknown father (I didn't even know what he looked like: did we really not have a single photo of him?) wasn't going to suddenly walk back out of the past and tip everything upside-down.

But what was I going to do with that knowledge? I was convinced my mother really didn't know he was dead – for sure.

She was too sensible to pretend about something like that. I'm ashamed to admit, even to myself, that it gave me a rather pleasant sense of power over her. I would probably tell her one day, of course ... but when it suited *me*. After all, she'd kept so much from me for so long ... And if she thought he might still come back, at least she wouldn't marry someone else. Though if Jack were to become 'available', of course I would say something.

I asked Monique not to mention anything about our conversation to anyone in the family: I told her I wanted to tell my mother at the appropriate moment, in my own time and in a way that wouldn't upset her too much. She said that was very, very '*sympathique*' of me – which made me feel dreadful: my motives were anything but altruistic.

We found a little restaurant in the centre of Bayeux and had a late and leisurely lunch, wallowing in our freedom and the new, conspiratorial closeness between us. It also gave me a chance to enjoy being my new self. For the first time I felt I could almost match Monique in confidence, intelligence ... even good looks!

My buoyancy lasted until we got to the cathedral and went to see the Bayeux Tapestry, leaving the sunny afternoon for the sombrely lit room displaying the famous embroidery. Another war. A battle, anyway. 1066 embroidered into a cartoon strip – a cartoon king, with enormous eyes, on a cartoon throne; little cartoon soldiers falling off their cartoon horses. The buildings too small for the people. Cartoon Harold with a cartoon arrow in his eye. Except none of it was very funny.

What would it be like, a cartoon tapestry of the war that had just stopped? The 'Falklands War'? ... People looking at the tapestry in hundreds of years' time and not realizing about the reality of the dark and heaving sea and how it would never, ever be over for the mothers. A too-small ship up-ended, half-disappearing into a regular pattern of little harmless-looking wavelets, the word BELGRANO embroidered a bit crookedly above it. Or if there wasn't room for the whole word, just some of the letters (like in the 1066 one): BELGR, maybe, expecting people would remember what it meant. The little sailors (but too big for the ship) with their arms flung up, their mouths open as if shouting whatever the cry for 'Help!' was in Argentina. Some of them right down under the waves already, one half-swallowed by a fish with a too-big eye ...

❧ GEORGINA ❧

On the third day Maurice proposes a trip to the *Plages de Débarquement*. His godmother had lived not far from Arromanche and her family had suffered particularly at the time of the Normandy landings.

So, having come to France to get away from images of the Falklands War, we are plunged into those of a worse one. Maurice means well, of course: he thinks it will be 'educational' for Eloisa and Monique. In the museum we have to sit through a film of terrible things happening in the water and on the vast, flat beaches. Even though, for me, it is familiar enough knowledge, it's newly upsetting to confront those stark images – uncompromising black and white – in the stuffy, crowded dark.

It makes me think of my father, of course. I've sometimes resented the way he made the war so horrendously real to me by naming the friends he'd lost. ('LOST': such a soft, innocuous little word, as if they are still wandering around somewhere other than in the memories of those who'd known them. Better in French: '*PERDU*' … the mind hooking it onto 'perdition' with its reverberations of suffering.) Charlie Brunswick … 'Buffer' Pearce … Don Schelling … Patrick Wiseman … 'Gizmo' Bersani … Irving Schumaker … And the one who lost his legs – Johnny Wimsatt – and with them his fiancée who couldn't face a life without them. 'And all the fine, courageous people that might've been their children,' he said. 'Have you ever thought of that, Georgie? – All the talented and brave people whose children we don't have in the world because of that goddam war.'

When he was talking like that, he seemed to forget he'd once told me that if it hadn't have been for the war he wouldn't have come to England and met my mother and I wouldn't have existed. It was as if he were saying I didn't count against all those might-have-been people. I was young and easily hurt.

I wonder about the life he's living now, my broken, abandoned father, with his sister in some remote town in the USA. I should have stayed in touch. None of it was his fault.

When the film is over and we walk outside into brilliant sunshine, blue sky, and a glimmering sea, the loveliness of it seems illusory, manufactured.

We take our picnic to one of the beaches. Eloisa in her new green bikini, Monique in a red one. After lunch they sun-bathe side by side – beautiful young bodies on blue-and-white striped towels. Then Monique blows up the beach-ball and the three of us play 'piggy in the middle'.

As we're throwing and catching and running along the sand after the ball, the soldiers from the film swarm darkly back into my head, then out of my head and onto the beach. Their ghosts – still in uniforms and hard helmets and weighed down with guns and heavy equipment – are running between us, ducking under the thrown ball, weaving past us ... crowds and crowds of soldiers, always running over the beach where they'd landed and where so many of them had died, still there after years and years, different times of history going on at the same time, the soldiers growing more and more real, more and more solid so that, instead of them seeming to dodge *us* as we play ball, I now feel *we* are dodging *them*. We are insubstantial: they are the real things, hard and heavy, sweating fear and pain and courage. The violence of their terrible deaths. We'll never free ourselves from them.

Then Monique's voice: 'Shall we go into the sea, Eloisa? Do you want to swim?'

My daughter go into that sea? – where those dreadful things happened? How could they even contemplate it? Surely the two of them haven't forgotten so quickly what had happened there …

Then I tell myself not to be silly. It isn't fair if the dreadful things of the past should steal from them this lovely summer afternoon. It's what those armies fought for, after all … freedom for people like my daughter – without blue eyes or blonde hair or the right tone of skin – to live without fear and do things like enjoy a beautiful afternoon on a clean, wide beach.

The last ghosts sink into the sand and it's just the two girls standing there together against the sun. They've grown very close during this holiday – which makes me glad.

'Race you!' I hear Eloisa say. Then they're both running towards the glittering sea, the sand flying up from their feet.

❧ ELOISA ❧

I wanted to have all my hair cut off so it was very, very short, like Monique's. But my mother said it wouldn't look like Monique's: we had different sorts of hair, different shaped heads and faces. She said it looked really nice the way it was and that if Monique had hair like mine, she'd probably let it grow long. I was moody for a while, then we reached a compromise: she cut off about three inches.

Just before I went back to school after the summer holidays, photos arrived from *tante* Maude – including a lovely one of Monique and myself holding up ice-creams from that day we'd gone to the beach in Normandy. It convinced me I looked fine the way I was. We bought a cheap frame and I kept the photo beside my bed.

The arrival of the photos jogged my memory about the one I'd asked *tante* Maude for as a surprise for my mother. Remembering the resulting drama still makes me feel uncomfortable: I prefer to remember it as a scene from a play ...

Scene: *A living-room in a flat. A Saturday morning in September. A shaft of sunlight coming from the window falls on the figure of the* MOTHER *sitting at her desk, typing. After a few minutes the door (Downstage Left) opens silently and the* DAUGHTER *enters, smiling and holding something behind her back. Her approach covered by the clatter of the typewriter, the* DAUGHTER *creeps up behind the* MOTHER *and, taking advantage of a momentary pause in the typing, thrusts a small photograph between the* MOTHER*'s face and the typewriter.*

MOTHER: *(Pulling back her head as if startled, baffled.)* What ... ?

DAUGHTER: *(Turning the photo over and pointing to the back.)* Look! It's the name of your friend. It's Amadou as a baby! *(The* DAUGHTER *smiles; the* MOTHER *doesn't.)*

MOTHER: *(Looking puzzled and sounding a bit cross.)* Where did you get this?

DAUGHTER: *Tante* Maude gave it to me when we were in Paris.

MOTHER: She *gave* it to you? *(then, sounding even more cross.)* She had no business doing that.

DAUGHTER: Well, not gave exactly. More … let me have it. It fell out of an old photo album and when I saw the name of your friend on the back I thought … I thought I'd make you happy. I know it's only a baby picture, but she looks so cute.

MOTHER: She? Oh … I see. *(Less furious but still clearly not happy.)* Maude didn't actually talk to you about the photo?

DAUGHTER: *(Tearfully.)* You're not pleased with it, are you. I thought you'd be pleased. *(She begins to cry.)* I thought you'd be *so* pleased …

MOTHER: *(Gets up from her desk and puts her arms around her* DAUGHTER.*)* Please don't cry, sweetheart, please don't cry. It was just such a surprise. A bit painful, if you must know.

DAUGHTER: *(Between sobs.)* How am I … supposed to … know … what's … painful for … you and … what's … not when … you don't tell … me any- … thing about … when you … were young … and … being in France and … what happened there.

MOTHER: *(Doesn't say anything but carries on hugging her* DAUGHTER, *rocking her as if stifling some kind of grief. She begins to cry silently.)*

DAUGHTER: *(Looks up at her* MOTHER'S *face.)* Why are you crying?

MOTHER: Because you are. *(She tries to smile.)* Like smelling other people's sick and your own stomach starts to heave.

DAUGHTER: I don't believe you. You're crying because of the picture.

MOTHER: *(She is silent, but her silence seems to indicate that her DAUGHTER is right.)*

DAUGHTER: This Amadou, did you fall out with her then?

MOTHER: *(She looks away from the DAUGHTER's face and towards the autumn sun streaming in through the window. She takes a deep breath before she speaks.)* Not her. Him.

There is a silence during which MOTHER and DAUGHTER look directly at each other. Eventually the DAUGHTER speaks.

DAUGHTER: Was he your boyfriend? Did you ... sleep with him?

MOTHER: *(Quietly.)* Yes.

There is a long silence during which the DAUGHTER moves over to the desk and picks up the photo. She looks at it for a while. Her back is to the audience so her expression cannot be seen. Then, turning so that she is facing the MOTHER, she holds the photo up beside her face. The MOTHER remains very still.

DAUGHTER: *(Her voice is strange, neither smiling nor sad.)* I do look a bit like him, don't I – only not so dark. Which country did he come from?

MOTHER: France, of course. *(She tugs a tissue from the box on her desk. She wipes her eyes and blows her nose.)* But his father was from Senegal: that's a country in Africa that used to be ruled by France.

DAUGHTER: *(Silent and thoughtful for a moment. Then she smiles a little.)* That's good. It means I'm a bit like Jack. He's Indian and English. Only I'm more mixed up – African and English and French and American and Polish.

MOTHER: And it's a known fact that mixed-raced children are among the most beautiful and intelligent in the world. Did you know that? It's good for species to mix the different genes and …

DAUGHTER: *(Interrupting.)* How did you meet?

MOTHER: Oh, you don't want to know all that old stuff. It's so boring when grown-ups go on about their past. I remember what it was like when my father …

DAUGHTER: *(Suddenly angry.)* No, it's *not* boring. I want to know about my father.

MOTHER: Not right now, sweetheart, please. Let's go out. I'll finish this later..

DAUGHTER: *(She moves to the door, stands in front of it, blocking the only way out of the room.)* I'm not letting you leave the house until you tell me how you met … Amadou … my father.

MOTHER: *(Turning away, hesitating, not sure what to say, then turning back to face the DAUGHTER. She looks her in the eye.)* In a shop.

DAUGHTER: He worked in a *shop*?

MOTHER: No. He trod on my make-up there.

❧ GEORGINA ❧

At the counter, about to pay for a magazine. Somehow, as I'm getting my purse out, my bag tips over and the contents fall out onto the floor. He … is walking towards the till but is so busy reading the newspaper he's about to pay for he doesn't notice what has happened and … He's very tall and has big feet and has crunched almost everything before I can pick it up. He gets pink lipstick and blue eye-shadow on the bottoms of his shoes and, before he realises it, has spread it all over the floor as he's trying to get out of my way so I can pick up the few things he hasn't destroyed. Then the manager comes and asks him to take his shoes off before he makes it any worse. So there he is, a great big chap in his socks, shoes in hand, apologizing to everyone. He walks out of the shop in his socks without paying for the newspaper and the manager comes after him and … I go to a café with him to help get the make-up off his shoes. He insists on replacing the make-up. And we happen to be going in the same direction …

❧ ELOISA ❧

Eloisa Hardiman   28th September, 1982
RE Project: (Mr Vernon)   **Who am I?**

Introduction

My name is Eloisa Gabrielle Hardiman. I am 13 years old and live with my mum in a flat (part of a house) in Miranda Road which is not far from Archway Station. Miranda is a character in 'The Tempest' who has to live on a small island ruled by her father, and there's a road near us called Prospero Road which is the name of Miranda's father in the play. I don't have any brothers or sisters.

My mother and her family

My mother's name is Georgina Alicia Hardiman. (She writes books but not using that name.) Her father was Conway Hardiman, an American soldier (airman) who came to England in World War Two. Her mother, Alicia Krajewska, was a librarian. Her parents were Polish. Conway would go to the library to read the newspapers and fell in love with her. Lots of young women had to work in factories in the war, or on farms, or they joined the army or navy or air force. But Alicia (my grandmother) was asthmatic and had a heart problem, too, so they let her work in the library still. She fell in love with the big American with the nice manners, even though he was older than her. Before he was sent off to the war in Europe, they started an affair. After he left, Alicia discovered she was pregnant. They had planned to get married after the war but Alicia's parents were so furious about the baby they threw her out. But a friend took her in and she lived there, even after the baby (my mother) was born, until Conway came back from the war and they married and lived in a little house in South London. But my mother's mother died when she (my mother) was very young and her father married again so she would have a mum to help bring her up. She also got two step-brothers older than her.

My father and his family
My father's name was Amadou Marc Camara. His mother was French (called Colette Gabrielle Ménard) and his father, Assane Camara, was from Senegal. (That's why I have darkish skin and curlyish hair.) My mother says my French grandmother, Colette, was very courageous to have a boyfriend from Senegal at that time. Her parents did not like him because he was from Africa which was really horrible of them. They made things hard for him and Colette, and then, when Hitler started his bad ideas in Europe, my grandfather could see it would soon be too difficult for him to live there. So he left my grandmother and her baby and went back to Senegal. My grandmother brought up my father on her own, like my mum and me. My mother met my father in Paris. He was very tall and played the saxophone and taught music in a college. He went to Senegal to find his family but never came back. My mother doesn't know why. Sometimes I am very sad I didn't know my father, especially as he was very nice (so my mum says).

Conclusion: About Me

I am a bit like my mother and a bit like my father. But my mum says we don't just take after our parents. Everyone is an individual otherwise we'd be like those Russian babushka dolls, just being the same as the people who came before. My mum says it also depends on the people we meet and what happens to us and the things we have the chance to do and what happens in history. I would probably be different if I knew my father and lived in Paris like I might have done if he hadn't gone away.

A— Well done, Eloisa. Careful and thoughtful work. Very interesting, and you come to a very mature conclusion.

7

'LES LIASONS DANGEREUSES'

❀ ELOISA ❀

Chère Monique,

   J'espère que tu vas bien. I hope you like this
Christmas card of London in the snow. It is the
famous Trafalgar Square and the big building at
the back is an art gallery. Are you going ski-ing
again this Christmas? It must be very nice to do
that. I expect we will just be at home as usual.
I have been reading some 'très bons livres'
recently. One of them I recommend to you. It's
called 'Metamorphosis' by Franz Kafka. It's 'très
bon' though I haven't finished it yet. Sorry I
cannot write much in French yet. Most of the stuff
we learn in French at school isn't very useful for
what I want to say to you.

   Give my love to tante Maude. I hope she
received my Christmas card. I will write you a
longer letter next time. 'Bon Noël'.

With love from

         Eloisa x x

❧ GEORGINA ❧

Nearly Christmas. Again. Another year gone.

'But what have I done with my life,' thought Mrs Ramsay, taking her place at the head of the table ... *Tick–tick–tick–tick–tick–tick–tick–tick ... That old skin-scratcher, Time. The Age of Wrinkles is coming ... is coming ... But Virginia Woolf made Mrs Ramsay fifty. I'm not yet forty. Quite. But hang on ... From Eloisa's birth to now ... same again and I will be fifty. FIFTY!*

But what have I done with my life? ... What have I done ...

I don't look nearly forty, do I? Maybe I do. Just because I still feel twenty-two inside ... some days. 'Big ideas' still bumping against the inside of my skull ... butterfly shut up in an old shed smelling of creosote, fluttering against the dust of a warm window.

Sometimes I think I'll go stark, raving mad if my life doesn't change soon.

Perhaps we should move ... though Eloisa went very sulky when I broached the subject the other day. But she goes out into the world every day while I'm stuck here over a type-writer, yanking stories out of my head like some mucky magician pulling strings of dirty handkerchiefs out of his sleeves.

I should get 'a proper job'. But what? I'm not 'trained' for anything, and jobs are scarcely two a penny these days. I can't even type properly. Quite fast considering I only use two fingers, but I still have to look at the keyboard. All right for what I do, but I wouldn't last five minutes in a 'business situation'. And, let's face it, I'd go even madder working in an office than I'm going here. And one sexist comment from some smart-arse and I'd be breaking jaws. I'm the proverbial fish out of the prover-bial water now. Thatcher's Britain. Or is this just a mid-life crisis on the horizon. A cloud of dust. Dust around the corner.

Fear in a handful of it ...

Please, not another wave of existential angst ... not just at the moment. It's bad enough with Christmas coming on.

'Nothing to be done.'

Yes there is. Put the decorations up before Eloisa gets home from school. Try to make her happy.

❦ ELOISA ❦

School had just finished for the Christmas holidays. I was in a suitably jolly mood as I turned into Miranda Road.

It was nearly dark already and I could see the outline of my mother looking down from the lighted front window, a human-sized moth on the other side of the glass. She was looking out for me.

The boy across the street was lurking by his front gate again, trying not to look as if he were watching me. I waved and called out, 'Happy Christmas!' and he scuttled away, like some miserable cockroach, into their overgrown front garden.

My mother had put the usual Christmas 'branch' in the window and had looped the usual silver pine-cones and little golden baubles onto its twigs. Some windows in our street had proper Christmas trees. With lights. Mostly little white ones. They looked so pretty in the dusk. I felt a sudden jab of jealousy. I so wished we could afford a proper, live Christmas tree with white starry lights.

I was scarcely through the door before I sensed my mother was specially happy about something, and there was a letter open on the table. My mind whizzed about like a bat in a barn. Had some distant, forgotten relative died and left us lots of money? Could we afford to go out and buy a proper Christmas tree … with lights? Would I get a lot of Christmas presents this year?

❧ GEORGINA ❧

I greet her with the usual hug.

'Phew! I smell school dinners. Worse than usual.'

'They had turkey. Disgusting. All I had was the potatoes and a mince pie – *without* custard.'

'Some really great news, Tootsie.'

'What??!!'

'Amaranth's getting married.'

'Oh. Is she?' (Said with the enthusiasm of a bonfire damped to ash.)

'I've had the loveliest letter from her. She's finally found someone big enough. We're invited to the wedding at the end of February. Coming?'

'But what do you think she'll wear?'

'What's that got to do with *anything*, Toots?! Amaranth's in love. She's happy. Her dream's come true. The last thing that matters is what she'll *wear* at the wedding!'

'It's just that it might be really embarrassing if she wears one of those Princess Diana things with the big skirts and puffy sleeves and loads of material everywhere. It was all right on *her*, but it wouldn't exactly make the Oort look like a fairy-tale princess, would it. And she might be too wide to get down the aisle, especially if her husband's big, too.'

The conjured image makes me laugh. 'I'll try and advise her to keep her sartorial ambitions quite modest. No princess gear. And talking of celebrations … we've had an invitation for Christmas Day.'

Something guarded in my voice raises her suspicions as she narrows her eyes and says, 'What kind of invitation?'

'To spend the day … ' (wincing before I say the next bit) ' … with Alma and … '

'NO! Absolutely and utterly NO. I'd rather spend Christmas

doing *algebra* on the *toilet* than under the same roof as "Angie". You didn't say we'd go, did you?'

'I … didn't make a *definite* commitment. But it's hard when you're face to face with someone who's trying to be kind. Perhaps one of us can go down with a bad cold: it'd only be a "social" lie. Better for everyone, really.'

'Especially Angie. I'd probably end up putting a pillow over her face … And sitting on it.'

'I see. "Joy to the world", eh? … Anyway, we've had a card from Jack.'

Knowing more about her father has, it seems to me, taken the edge off her Jack obsession. He's no longer the filler of that empty paternal space in her life in quite the same way as before. She now *has* a father – in her head. I sometimes wish I'd told her everything earlier: but then the questions it might have provoked would have led to the partly 'compromised' nature of our life – what I had to swallow to afford London and to live as a writer (of sorts!), trying to hold onto the vestige of dreams.

The Christmas card from Jack is an oval photo of the whole family – a very American affair, posed, smiling, framed in a holly-wreath and around it, in old-fashioned gold lettering, '*Family Greetings in this Joyous Season — Xmas 1982*'. It's a shock to see how much 'little' Josephine and Edward have grown: she's a leggy nine-year-old and he a confident-looking eleven. Tasha has slimmed down quite a bit: her hair is longer and her smile shows a mouthful of teeth-straightening metal. Myra appears rather haggard and strange with her long hair worn loose, and her eyes look … elsewhere. Jack … is Jack – though his eyes look sad even if his mouth is smiling beneath the moustache. Jamie and Dee haven't changed. The picture must've been taken back in September, before Dee came over to art school.

Eloisa looks at it for a while. Her expression gives no clue to her thoughts.

'Is there a letter or anything?'
There isn't.

We don't need to lie to Alma. By the next evening Eloisa is clearly sickening for something. A burst of manic energy and unpuberty-like helpfulness send her whirling around the house, tidying up, singing, asking me to put on *my* favourite records, then being *so* pro-active when we go shopping – holding doors open (and not just for the usual little old ladies), smiling, saying 'Happy Christmas' to the wan, lank girl sniffing her weary way through a shift at the check-out. Back home, she makes me sit down while she puts the kettle on and unpacks the shopping. She even puts my favourite Debussy on the record-player, turns on the table-lamps, turns off the harsh overhead one, and delivers a mug of tea (my favourite blue mug) that, for once, is exactly the right shade of brown. She sits on the floor at my feet, resting against the armchair, her left arm against my legs. The Debussy ripples around us like a bath of exactly the right temperature. We're quiet together for a few minutes. (We *do* have perfect moments together – though they're rare enough to seem a little weird when they happen.)

Then I say, 'You all right, Toots?'

'Fine. You?'

'Fine, sweetheart. Can I stroke your hair?' I love to do that. I used to do it so often when she was little that she once asked me if I was trying to smooth the curls out of it. When she turned twelve, she started objecting and I now have to ask permission to touch her head like that. I don't ask too often and have learnt to judge her mood.

Then the bloody phone rings and spoils it. (Archie. He needs someone to talk to. Still utterly 'bereft'. I even ask if he wants to come and spend Christmas with us, but fortunately he says no.)

By the time he's finished and I come back to Eloisa, her eyes are closed, her head resting on her arms on the seat of the chair.

'You sure you're all right, Toots?'

'I feel lousy all of a sudden … and my head hurts.'

I place my hand on her forehead. Burning.

'I thought so.' When she was small she was always full of manic energy just before she was ill. 'I think we'd better take your temperature.'

A hundred and two degrees.

'Bed. Cold flannels. Lots to drink. And don't cough in my direction if you can help it.'

'I'm being punished for our plan to lie to Alma.'

'That's rubbish, my rainbow, and you know it. The world doesn't work like that.'

Despite Eloisa starting the year with a bad dose of the flu, the first half of 1983 is one of our sweetest times together. Eloisa turns fourteen in the February and has all the beauty of a young sexual being without the sexual self-consciousness that all too soon hardens the look and confuses the emotions. In some unfathomable way, her being ill and the presents we give each other that Christmas melt the sometimes icy edges of two people living their different worlds beneath one not very large ceiling. She seems easy in her skin perhaps for the first time. Her smile comes readily and we both go out of our way to please one other. She even comes willingly to Amaranth's wedding at the end of February – a low-key affair at a registry office, Amaranth in a lilac trouser-suit (rather than the vast, Princess Di 'meringue' Eloisa had dreaded) and her husband is a very nice South American divorcee who takes a particular (fatherly) shine to Eloisa as she reminds him of his daughter back in Brazil.

But daffodils always start browning so quickly …

Is it my fault?

Probably.

The old lady who's been living downstairs is finally persuaded into a home and the flat is let to what seems at first to be a quiet couple – quiet but a little … common. The smell of cheap, sickly scent and a pair of greying Y-fronts in the bathroom, along with a dreadful black stocking – all catches and ladders – dropped on the landing and unclaimed for days. A scratched old record of tango music sometimes seeps up through the floor.

Our new neighbours have been there three weeks before we even catch a glimpse of one of them. 'Mister', we see, going out, closing the front door quietly, considerately. We are just a few yards from the front gate, but he manages to slip away in the other direction without even making eye-contact. A tall, pale chap. Thinnish. Round, flat sort of face. A moonface. Over-large, old-fashioned cream raincoat. Hard to tell how old he is, from a distance, but he looks pleasant enough. Can't see him being an enthusiast for the tango, though. We decide it must be 'her' who is into all that. She seems a bit of a floozie: the scent and that stocking say as much.

Eloisa is the first to see her. The back view. Slipping into the bathroom.

'Dreadful hair, Mumsie, and a *terrible* taste in dressing-gowns.'

If it hadn't been for the fire, maybe everything would've gone on as before and we might never have got to know our new neighbours.

We are out at the time, but come back to an alarmingly huge red engine in the narrow road and hefty, helmeted men hanging about in our front garden with an odd air of nonchalant mirth. First response: thank God it isn't our flat. One of the firemen tells us it's a chip-pan fire on the ground floor. Not a bad one: just a bit messy.

We step over hoses across the front path and, from the hallway, look in through their open door. We glimpse Floozie in an armchair: pink satin dressing-gown (at that time of day!?), head bowed, looking utterly tragic. Awful black hair. Acrid smell from the put-out fire. We stand in the doorway and I call out, 'Can we do anything to help? Are you all right?'

Floozie raises her head slowly. But it's Mister Moonface looking at us. Yes, it's definitely him, but ... lips bright red, cheeks powder pink, and just one eye smouldering beneath heavy, fake lashes. And it's obviously a wig.

I thrust our door-key at Eloisa with, 'Go up and put the kettle on, Toots.'

The three of us sit around our table, 'Mister' still in his floozie gear, except he's taken the wig off – but not the left eye-lashes.

'I was getting ready to go to a party.' He glances at Eloisa and adds, 'Fancy dress ... as you can see.' (His voice a bit ... Norfolk?) 'I put the oil on to do a few chips before going. There's never enough to eat at parties, is there? But I must've been longer doing my make-up than I realized. It's the eye-lashes that take the time, don't you find?'

I look down and stir my tea (pointlessly, since I don't take sugar). Eloisa tries to fill the awkward silence with, 'It was a good thing you already had the fancy-dress stuff ... like the stockings ... and that ruby ring. I remember you left it in the bathroom once.'

'Have another biscuit,' I say, before things can go any further.

'You're very kind. I will.' He stretches out a large hand to take one, the ruby ring odd against his hairiness – modest though it is. 'Then I really must be getting back. Quite a lot of clearing up to do, as you can imagine.'

'So you won't be going to the party, then?' says Eloisa.

'Party? ... Oh, that! No, I don't think I quite feel like it now.'

A last adam's-apple-bobbing gulp of tea, then, in a sweep of pink satin, he's gone.

Eloisa sits on at the table, staring at the biscuit crumbs. In the end, she comes right out and says, 'What do you call someone like him? Isn't there a special word for men who like dressing up as women?'

'Yes. It's "transvestite". But personally I'd rather say he was a refugee from the repressive country called "Conformity". It's no big deal, Eloisa. Everybody has a bit of the opposite sex inside themselves.'

'I don't,' she says, indignant, challenging – and looking just like her father.

❧ ELOISA ❧

My mother announced we were having a party. A party for three. She'd invited Joe Moonface to supper and asked him to bring his tango records. She'd always wanted to learn the tango, she said. (First I'd heard of it.)

Seven o'clock … five past … ten past. He obviously wasn't coming. Relief and disappointment battled it out somewhere in my skull.

Then a timid knock at the door. My mother, in her black, French polo-neck and black jeans, smiled as she went to open it. A very *un*-timid voice – thrillingly energetic, if rather stagy – erupted into the room.

'How kind of you to invite me! These are for you.' A glamorous woman was presenting my trousered mother with a bunch of long-stemmed, deep red roses. '*Lovely* jumper, darling. *Very* Existentialist.'

During supper I tried not to look at his face – though it was better than last time: as least he was wearing a matching set of false eye-lashes.

After a short while, he gradually dropped his exaggerated, female persona and sat there talking like a normal man – as if he'd completely forgotten he was dressed up as a woman. My mother had always been good at putting people at their ease. They talked a lot about themselves. Once or twice they tried to bring me into the conversation, but I successfully resisted their efforts. In the end they gave up.

When my mother blatantly told him she wrote 'willy books' – soft porn and slushy romances – he tipped back his moon-head on its long stalk of a neck and laughed. It was a joyous kind of laugh. He wasn't laughing 'at' her. He was just laughing. His laugh almost made me like him.

Joe worked with a small theatre company, doing all sorts of things except act and drive the van. He supplemented the meagre income from this by decorating people's houses. He came originally from a small town on the Norfolk Broads. A very watery place where, if you were a boy, you had to go fishing, he told us.

'The very first time I saw those little silver joys squirming out their lives, a hook through their palate and gasping to be returned to their natural element, just to give some snot-faced boy a moment of boasting, I knew whose side I was on. It was the fishing that made me vow to get away. The fishing finished what the hairdresser's started. Every week my mother went. It was like a social club for her and her friends. I was bored out of my mind when I had to go with her, hanging around her knees, nothing to do but watch a slow, sweet girl called Trixie sweeping up the hair and making cups of tea. Trixie used to smile at me and slip me sweets. We were sort of in league against all those unnaturally curly women who gossiped about their husbands as if they were cuts of meat. I like to think Trixie got away, too … but I don't suppose she did.'

'So you're an escapee, like me,' said my mother. 'Your Norfolk is my Kent.' And she told him about Paris and 1968 and falling in love.

'Don't tell me,' said Joe. 'You met on a demo. He rescued you from a *gendarme*'s truncheon. He carried you, bodily, away from the tear gas … '

'No. We met in a shop. My bag tipped over and everything fell on the floor and he trod on my make-up.'

'Darling, how *terrible* for you.'

They both laughed. I didn't. I got up from the table, went into my room and slammed the door … then called out 'Sorry', as if the slam had been an accident.

I heard Joe say, 'Ouch! I felt that.'

'So did I,' said my mother.

Good, I thought. You were meant to.

I heard them clearing the dishes away, then moving the furniture. They put on a tango record. My mother called out, 'Are you going to come and join us?'

'No. I've got a headache.' My voice was as graceless as I could make it.

I could hear them having a good time. There was a lot of laughing as Joe tried to teach my mother the tango.

I managed to stay in my room for half an hour. But I was bored. And I wanted to make sure they weren't kissing or anything. To come out of my room I used the excuse of needing a drink of water. My mother looked happy and relaxed. She was having fun. She looked younger.

'Come on. You be the judge.' Joe pointed at me. 'Give her marks out of ten.' He put the record on again.

Der – RRRRHHUMMMM – da – da – da (rrhum) – da – da – di – da – derr – RRRRHHUMMMM – da – da – da ... My mother with a red rose between her teeth.

Joe said, 'You realize, George, you're probably the first Existentialist to do the tango.'

My mother removed the rose from her mouth and tossed it to me. 'I doubt it. They were quite into enjoying themselves, you know. They needed as much fun as they could get, I should think, in Paris after the war ... ' She did a kind of backbend over Joe's arm.

'Just think,' said Joe, 'if the Nazis had learnt to tango ... instead of marching ... '

My mother performed a very nifty move and looked pleased with herself. Joe smiled over his shoulder at me and gave a huge wink – huge and slow – the kind of wink only false eyelashes can give, as if the weight of them slows the eye down.

Der – RRRRHHUMMMM – da – da – da (rrhum) – da – da – di – da – derr – RRRRHHUMMMM – da – da – da ...

All the things I'd heard about the Nazis came into my mind. They wouldn't have tolerated men like Joe. Men had to be thick-skulled and burly, capable of doing terrible things ... even to babies. Joe wouldn't have stood a chance among those high-kicking boot-boys. (And nor would my grandfather: they didn't like people with black skins.)

But maybe some of them *had* been like Joe and had liked dressing up and wearing make-up. Maybe some of them had secretly longed to tango in a scarlet dress and would've looked terrific in eyelashes but they'd had to pretend they didn't. I imagined it ... instead of shooting out their arms, like everyone else, as they high-kicked past old Beady-Eyes, heads turned towards him, one of them (it would only take one) pausing to deliver, with wonderful eyelashes, a huge, slow, wink. The whole show would've been ruined ... all bumping into each other, falling over, making the onlookers laugh. It might've made all the difference.

❧ GEORGINA ❧

Whether it's my relationship with Joe that's done it, or whether it would've happened anyway, I don't know. But that special period of sweetness between Eloisa and myself melts away, exposing the more normal rocky ground of life with an adolescent daughter.

It probably isn't wise to have a relationship with someone living in the same house, but I'm in desperate need of some adult company – and a bit of fun. Eloisa is all intensity and hormones most of the time, and though she isn't as appalling about Joe as she was about 'Stunt', she's making life ... less than easy. For all his 'idiosyncrasies', Joe is kind and intelligent and treats Eloisa nicely, so she can't take it out on *him*. Maybe the problem is she's reached the age for starting to fall in love herself ... and she hasn't yet done so.

She keeps the ultimate punishment for a Sunday afternoon in late November.

It's nearly midday when Joe comes up to plead for some coffee, still in his Wee-Willy-Winky nightshirt and puffy-eyed. I give him the jar.

'Make it strong,' Eloisa says. 'You look dreadful, Joe.'

'What are you girls doing today?'

'After lunch we're going for a walk on the Heath, if the weather holds. And you're coming with us. You could use some healthy fresh air, from the look of you.'

'A walk! Is there no end to your mother's sadistic energy?' He winks at Eloisa, and sleepily rubs the back of his scrabbled-looking head. 'I mean, it's *Sunday*. The day of rest.'

I see Eloisa's eyes go to the pale legs below his nightshirt: they're sprouting stubble. 'So maybe you should stay in a shave your legs,' she says.

He looks down. 'I guess you're right,' he says, good-humouredly. 'A girl's gotta do what a girl's gotta do ... So I won't be able to join you on that *invigorating* walk. I'll bake a cake and you can come to my place for tea when you get back – as long as you promise not to smell too much of the fresh air when you come in: we're a little delicate today, my body and I.'

'You're coming with us, Joe,' I insist. 'You don't get enough proper exercise. It's not healthy.'

He sighs, shrugs, addresses Eloisa. 'Your mother is ... *irresistible*. OK. What time does the torture begin?'

'One-thirty ... so we're back before the light starts going.'

The last time we walked on the Heath it was still flamboyant autumn. Now it has all dimmed to muted, Constable colours – walnut, mouse, caramel, sepia ... and the few greens left are washed-out sage, dull olive, a darkish kind of reseda. But, above, the sky is an unsuitable forget-me-not blue, as if the earth and sky didn't belong to each other and are darkly stitched together: on the hill-top, skeletons of trees reaching up into the blue and down into the heavy, rain-soaked earth, holding them together with dark embroidery. The smell of decaying leaves coats the nostrils and hangs in the mouth and reaches down into the lungs, generations of past leaves making a dark squelch that oozes up through the new fall where the ground dips and the water collects. The old mulch is trodden into the leathery, caramel oak-leaves, turning them black before their time.

❧ ELOISA ❧

When we set out on the walk I had no intention of telling her.

They had this way of talking about adult things as if I weren't there. And I don't think it was just them wanting me to believe they were treating me as a grown-up.

Joe was asking my mother about her past relationships and whether she'd ever considered getting married. She told him she'd never considered it because she'd always held onto the hope that Amadou might come back.

Joe stopped dead. 'After fifteen years?! You have to be joking, George.'

My mother looked embarrassed. We were at the top of the hill, looking out over London. She made the excuse of taking in the view not to reply.

And that's when I said it.

'He's dead.'

My mother took a deep breath. 'We don't know that for certain, Tootsie.'

'Yes we do. Monique told me. There's a newspaper clipping where it says so. *Tante* Maude's got it.'

My mother's face turned redder than I'd ever seen it. She stared at me. Then she had me by the shoulders and tried to shake it all out of me ... until Joe gently took hold of her and the shaking stopped.

We sat on a seat. Joe held both her hands, as if he was afraid she might hit me or something. She wanted to know the exact circumstances (the train journey to Normandy, I told her, beginning to cry) and the exact words Monique had used. And why hadn't I told her before?

'I ... I didn't want to upset you,' I stammered.

'So what's changed your mind about that?'

'I ... I ... I don't know, Mumsie. It ... just came out ... ' – which was probably as near the truth as I could manage, because one of my reasons for not telling her before was so she wouldn't marry – or link up 'properly' – with someone else. And there she was getting rather involved with Joe and you'd think I had every reason to still keep it from her. Or maybe I wanted to hurt her because of that. Or maybe the pressure of the knowledge was finally too much to bear ... I really don't know. (Even now.)

When we got home, she demanded Monique's telephone number (she knew I had it on the smart, headed paper Monique used when she wrote to me) and rang the Bonnats. She spoke briefly to Thérèse, but her English wasn't very good so she passed her over to Monique.

I was in my room, but the door was open and I was listening and wondering if everything would be different now. Now that she knew. For certain.

Part of the way through the conversation, she began to cry – really sobbing. I was about to go through and ask if she wanted me to take the phone and speak to Monique, but she mumbled, '*Merci* ... *au revoir* ...' through her tears, and put down the phone. I didn't know what to do – whether I should go and put my arm around her or ... But in the end I thought I'd better just leave her.

❧ GEORGINA ❧

It comes down to my inadequate grasp of French. I'd misunderstood a word in Maude's telegram – the one that told me Amadou's family in Senegal had contacted them and confirmed his '*disparition*' . I thought it meant 'disappearance' – which it does. But it also means death. It's as simple as that.

Maybe if he hadn't insisted on speaking English to me most of the time – showing off ... but also impatient of my stumbling through his language. If he'd only been more patient. If only ... If ... If ... If ... Here we go again ... That old mongrel and its fleas.

Apparently the family took my lack of response to the telegram as a sign of how very deeply I'd reacted to the '*scandale*' of that time. Colette's legacy was all the more remarkable bearing in mind that I hadn't even written to her at the time. Confirming a 'disappearance' ... What was there to say? But confirming the death of her only beloved son, the father of her grandchild ... whom she never saw ... Of course I would have written if I'd realized ... If ...

Once the initial shock of Eloisa's revelation is over, we have a long talk. She asks me if it was because of the 'big problems' and the arguments or whatever it was going on in the family at the time that had made me leave France, as Monique said might be the case.

I say, 'Partly, perhaps ...'

'But the arguments are over now, aren't they?' she says. 'They all get on well together. You could have gone back to France once the arguments were over.'

'The arguments are over because the people who caused them are dead – the parents of Colette, Maude and Aline.'

'What were the arguments about?' she persists.

'You really want to know?'

'Yes. I told *you* something important, so now you ...'

'OK. The parents of Colette, Maude and Aline were very rich and the father was quite an influential person, but ... not particularly nice. Very right-wing – and, in 1968, when there was a kind of left-wing revolution in France, someone discovered information about what the parents had done during the war and made that information public. During the Nazi Occupation they had been ... collaborators. That means they'd helped the Nazis. Many people did it – some because they were afraid, I guess, but some because, well, they agreed with what the Nazis were doing. Of course, there were also many, many brave people who fought against them – and lost their lives doing it.'

'Was that the "Resistance"? I think we saw a film about it in History.'

'Not just those who were full Resistance members, blowing up enemy trains and things like that. There were lots and lots of ordinary people doing brave things day in, day out – hiding Jewish people ... particularly the children. Things that put their own lives in danger. So you can imagine how terrible it was, if you were decent people, to discover that your own parents had collaborated with the Nazis, and possibly benefitted financially from doing so. It was a huge scandal in the family: the atmosphere was dreadful. Your ... father couldn't cope with it and used it as a reason to finally go and seek out his own father's family in Senegal. He promised he'd be back within three months, to start the autumn term in the college where he taught. But ...'

'Did he die in an accident, then?'

'Something like that, Toots. Can we leave it there for now?'

❧ GEORGINA ❧

No word. Nothing.

I'm not a French citizen. I'm not married to one. There's no justification for me staying on.

Maude says they will support me. I can live with her and Maurice. Colette wants to contribute to my support. They can all afford it. Easily.

But *why* can they afford it? Some of their wealth has come from their parents.

C–O–L–L–A–B–O–R–A–T–E–U–R–S

Where will that leave me? – morally. Living on money that …

But how am I supposed to support myself? And the baby?

To begin with I stay on my moral high horse. I manage to get work in a big London bookshop until the January, a few weeks before Eloisa's birth.

It's December when Colette has a massive stroke and dies. I'm informed of the legacy by her *notaire*. It's small enough to tempt me to accept it – not *all* Colette's money was from her parents, was it? – and large enough to solve the immediate problem of supporting us.

Compromise.

Or 'compromised'?

I come to rely on it. It means I can just about afford to stay in London rather than move out to some cultural wasteland. It means I can try to pick up my writing ambitions again, rather than training as a teacher or something. It means I can stay at home and bring up our daughter myself rather than risking her day-to-day development to child-minders.

Justification.

But always a fidgety little voice at the back of my head muttering accusations. A voice that wears a yellow star.

❦ ELOISA ❦

It didn't make so very much difference, as far as I could see, knowing for certain that he was dead, rather than just suspecting that he might be. Of course she cried a lot for a few days and muttered 'I'm so stupid!' a lot under her breath. And I suppose it was ironic that, for someone whose life was so taken up with words, she should have been so misled by one. But, as she said, she never had been very good at languages.

For reasons I couldn't understand, the whole thing seemed to bring her and Joe closer together and I began to worry that she'd marry him and I'd be stuck with him as my stepfather. Imagine him at parents' evening! True he was always very nice to me, but he lacked … *gravitas*. And that, I decided (having just learnt the word) is what I required of a father. I would try to make sure things didn't work out between them. And anyway, it should have been *me* having a boyfriend, not my mother! I was nearly fifteen. I needed the chance to grow up. I needed to know what it was all about. I needed to fall in love.

8

'SENTIMENTAL EDUCATION'

❧ GEORGINA ❧

Is 'lust in action' the 'expense of spirit in a waste of shame' ... or simply a bit of fun? – giving the body what it asks for and not taking any of it too seriously? Fun. Functional. Sex for grown-ups. A bit heartless? Maybe, even though Joe was kind and considerate, as well as humorous. I really liked him, but ... But like plus sex doesn't really equal love.

I'd never properly fallen in love when I was young – *really* young. I went straight from a chaste, school-girl crush on Veronica (two years older than me, beautiful, confident and clever: everyone adored her) to seedy sex with that lecturer who thought we were all fair game. It was one of the perks, he told me (during that terrible scene when I confronted him after finding out he'd been doing the same to at least three other girls in the seminar group), getting awe-struck students into bed. I'd been all at sea, at first, at university (I nearly gave up after the first term) and Mr Carpe Diem had dressed himself up as a rock. Though he turned out to be one of the polystyrene kind: theatrical. It was all an act, his 'concern'.

So with Amadou it'd been complicated: the sweetness of a first tender love but with the experienced bodies we both had for each other. His more experienced than mine. He was a very good lover.

It would be silly to expect too much from Joe. And I don't. It's nice not to be lonely, though. And he likes to dance.

When Fate places the hand of a first love in my daughter's hand, the person attached to it turns out to be as different from Joe as watercress from cornflakes.

❦ ELOISA ❦

I developed an obsession with bookshops. I wanted to own lots of books, like Monique. When we'd gone out together in Paris, she'd thought nothing of buying four or five at the same time.

'Buy them second-hand,' said my mother, when I started bemoaning our poverty. 'They sometimes smell a bit, but you get more for your money. The words inside are the same, and that's what counts.'

I started haunting a second-hand bookshop I used to pass on my way home from school. Many of the books had tear-jerker inscriptions: I lingered over them, mawkish. All the love on birthdays and Christmases and anniversaries … all that love between parents and children and aunts and uncles and teachers and pupils and friends and lovers and husbands and wives, not to mention the School Prizes so dearly earned – none of it had lasted. It had all been scraped off the plate of 'Life' into the bin of a musty old shop run by a sallow-faced man with no sense of humour: Mr Jolly (that really was his name). He tolerated my regular presence in his shop no doubt because it looked better having *someone* in there rather than no-one.

Then came the day of 'the other customer'. And he was perusing the very volume I'd had to put back the day before from want of a few pence which I now had and was all set to use for the purchase of Flaubert's *Sentimental Education* (I'd seen Monique reading it). It had once been owned by a Margaret Jane: a birthday present from her aunt (called Julia) in 1949. I remembered the inscription clearly from the previous day, having thought how enviable it was to have an Aunt Julia to give you Flaubert for your birthday.

I wanted Margaret Jane's book. And it was in *his* hands. Thwarted!

I pretended to be looking at the Gs while giving him a surreptitious 'once over'.

He was a bit older than me – a year or two, maybe. Slightly stooped with a long, pale face and steel-rimmed glasses. Baggy brown jumper and over-large trousers. And his shoe-laces didn't match.

He glanced at me. I turned my head away then, suddenly having an idea, I walked to the till where Mr Jolly was leafing through some papers and muttering to himself. 'Excuse me,' I said, as loudly as I dared (drowning the boom-boom-boom of my heart), 'do you happen to know if Flaubert's *Sentimental Education* has been sold since yesterday? I didn't have quite enough money on me, but now I have. It's just that I can't see it on the shelf anymore and I wondered if you'd sold it or maybe someone's put it back in the wrong place.'

'Don't remember selling it.'

'Well, if you come across it, could you possibly put it aside for me. The name's Hardiman. Eloisa Hardiman. I come in here quite often.'

'I know.' Mr Jolly gave me a fed-up kind of look.

I took myself and my thumping heart out onto the pavement and stood there for a moment. WOULD IT WORK? Would the Other Customer put it back? Or say something to Mr Jolly?

A few days later – a Saturday – I found the book on the doormat, in a rumpled brown-paper bag. 'For ELOISA HARDIMANN' (double N) it said, in letters made shaky by the creases of the bag. Inside was half a sheet of file paper, raggedly torn. Peculiar writing.

Dear E.H.

Hope you enjoy it as much as I did. Sorry to beat you to it.

Best wishes, T.G.

HE MUST'VE FOLLOWED ME HOME!!!!!

Realising I'd been followed, I felt hot and fluttery. I went back upstairs and hid the book in my room. Was it something I needed to tell my mother? I couldn't imagine that a skinny, book-loving boy with odd shoe-laces was much of a threat, but he might be even stranger than he looked …

I decided to give it a day or two … keep my eyes open … make sure he wasn't hanging obsessively around Miranda Road or outside the bookshop, waiting for me. If I thought he was watching or following me, I'd tell my mother; if not, I wouldn't.

But as the days passed and I tried to concentrate on *Sentimental Education*, a tincey-wincey bit of me grew increasingly disappointed: there was no need to tell. No sign of T.G. (Thomas Green? Terence Goring? Timothy Gardner?). The 'adventure' was over before it had even begun. And it took me twice as long as T.G. to finish the book. And still no sign of him.

Eventually I plucked up courage and went back to the shop. I was looking to see if Marcel Proust had written anything a bit shorter than the volumes on *tante* Maude's shelf. The Ps were at the very bottom and I was squatting, trying to read the battered spines, when there was suddenly a voice beside me.

'Did you enjoy it?'

I should've stood up. I must've appeared extremely silly, squatting with my head tipped back to look up into the face looking down at me.

I said, 'Do you want it back, or shall I pay you for it?' – which sounded so *inadequate* I just wanted the floor to open up and swallow me whole.

'Keep it,' he said. Then, putting on a shaky, old-lady voice, he added, 'It's a birthday present for you, Margaret Jane, from your old Aunt Julia.'

I decrouched with as much dignity as I could muster while putting on a lispy, little-girl voice and saying, 'Thank you, Aunt Julia.'

I noted his odd, horse-shoe-shaped smile and the sloping-in shoulders of an asthmatic.

In his normal voice, he said, 'Seems a shame Margaret Jane … '

' … should get rid of the book from her aunt?' I finished his sentence for him.

'Yes.'

'Perhaps Margaret Jane died. Perhaps whoever sorted out her stuff didn't realize. It'd be just an old book to them.'

'Sad, though,' he said, though he was still smiling.

'Yes.'

Conversational fizzle-out.

Frantic for something to say into the silence, I asked, 'Are you looking for anything special today?'

'Something on Arnold Schoenberg, if I can find it. I like his music. Don't suppose you do by any chance?'

'I might if I knew it, but I don't … even though my father was a musician.'

His eyes lit up at this piece of information. He plunged his hand into the deep pocket of those same baggy trousers he was wearing the first time I saw him, and pulled out a handful of coins. 'I can just do two coffees. Schoenberg can wait.'

The conversation in the café went something like this.

'You have an unfair advantage, knowing my name – which, by the way, has only one N. What's T.G.? T has to be Thomas or Timothy or Terence or … '

' … or Theo. Theodor, actually, but everyone calls me Theo.'

'Then I'd better call you Dor so as not to wear out the first part of your name.'

It made him give his horse-shoe smile again. Such a long, thin face. Long teeth, too. Grey eyes.

'Second name?'

'Goldmann – two Ns.'

'Theodor Goldmann … '

231

'Theodor Otto Goldmann, actually – the Otto is after my grandfather.'

' A palindrome!'

'What?'

'Otto. It's a palindrome – you know, spelt the same backwards as forwards.'

'That's jolly clever of you. Are you always like that with words?'

'My mum's a writer. Of sorts. I can't get away from them.'

'Wow! I suppose you're called after some literary heroine, are you?'

'I have no idea. I've never thought about it.'

'What do you want me to call you? "Eloisa" seems a bit of a mouthful.'

'Take your choice: you could call me "Hell", from Helloisa … from a certain incident in my childhood that I won't go into now. Or Lou … or Louisa … of just "Ouisa" … '

'That's what *I* should be called, "Wheezer" – me and my asthma.'

(So I was right. Those shoulders. Dead give-away.)

'Well?'

'Hell.'

So I become his 'Hell' and he becomes my 'Door'.

He wasn't exactly my idea of a proper boyfriend, but he was easy to talk to and had a lovely smile and wasn't like most boys of his age (sixteen going on seventeen) and I began to like him very much.

I didn't tell my mother about Theo at first. But the third time we met he brought me a little bunch of roses (the kind that come from a garden, not a shop) and, as we passed 'our' bookshop, he took my hand and I thought I would melt or fly away over the rooftops. So, in order to explain the roses, I had to tell her when I got home.

My mother was busy on a book she jokingly referred to as *The Way of All Flashers* (it was really called *Journey into Love*). When I appeared beside her with my little bunch of roses, she stopped typing.

'Oh, thank you, Toots!' she exclaimed, thinking they were for her.

'Actually ... they're for me ... from this boy I've met ... '

There was a moment's silence. I didn't know what was going through her head and couldn't predict what she was going to say.

'That's ... nice, Toots.' She turned so that she was properly facing me. 'At least, I hope he's nice.'

'Oh, you'd like him. He's not at all sexy.'

She laughed. 'What's that supposed to mean?!'

'Mother's always worry about ... that stuff, don't they? He's only sixteen.'

'And you're only fifteen, sweetheart.'

'I know: I'm not "legal" yet. But you really don't have to worry.'

'I'm your mother: I'm allowed to be worried. It's my privilege and my duty.'

'When you meet him you'll see what I mean. He's more into Schoenberg than sex.'

'*Schoenberg*! At sixteen?! That probably makes him about as safe as any male on the planet. I can't wait to meet this extraordinary young man, who goes by the name of ... ?'

'Theo. Theodor Goldmann. Two ns.'

'Probably Jewish, then.'

'No idea. We've only met three times. We haven't got onto religion yet.'

'Well, if you want to invite him round, just say the word. I'll be on my best behaviour.' She turned back to Qwerty.

I looked over her shoulder and read what she'd just typed: ' *... and kneading her willing little breasts in his practised hands, he ...* ' But she covered the page with her hands.

'I'll ... er ... leave you to it, Mumsie.'

Later, I asked my mother if she knew anything about Schoenberg: I wanted to impress Theo – intellectually. She told me he'd been a very avant-garde Jewish composer and that he'd escaped the Nazis by going to America. The only titles she could remember were *Transfigured Night* and *Pierrot Lunaire*, and she thought he'd also written the opera *Moses and Aron* in which Moses doesn't sing and Aron does, though she didn't know why.

'Ask your Theo,' she said. 'He'll probably know.' ('My' Theo! It sounded wonderful!) 'I think there's even a record of *Pierrot Lunaire* in my pile somewhere, if you want to dig it out. There's a picture of Cleo Laine on the front. I remember getting it from a jumble sale. But it's heavy stuff … '

Next time I met Theo I asked him why Schoenberg made Aron sing but not Moses.

'Well, it's sort of to do with the purity of an abstract concept in contrast to its embodiment in … Sorry, I'm not being very clear, am I … '

'*Perfectly* clear. Carry on … '

'I say, you have an awful lot of hair.'

(*What*??!!) 'Is that a compliment or just a *non sequitur*?'

The Door laughed and I was thinking, 'This isn't the way people in books talk when they're falling in love. I'm sure it's not how Mumsie's people talk. It's all too jolly.'

INTENSITY – that's what it lacked. We were just really good friends who held hands when all the time what I wanted was Luv, Lerv, *L'amour*, blind Cupid … arrows and all. I wanted him to *KISS* me. But it looked as though I'd have to engineer that first kiss myself.

I imagined the scene – had it all worked out.

The evenings were drawing in so it would happen by starlight … And it would go something like this:

ME: *(After being mysteriously silent for a while, I'd tip back my head and gaze at the star-spangled night sky. I'd sigh …)* Oh, Door … (No, that sounded silly: it'd have to be 'Theo' for this.) ... Oh, Theo. What do you think it all means? Billions of stars ... billions of light years ...

HIM: I've often wondered the same thing myself, Eloisa. But when I'm beside you, it doesn't seem to matter any more. The only thing that would matter would be if ...

ME: If what, Theo?

HIM: If I couldn't see you ... if you didn't ... love me.

ME: But I'll always love you, Theo ... *(At which his face would draw close to mine, pausing for a moment as if for permission to go on ... then our lips would meet and ...)*

And so to the event itself. It was dark by six o'clock so he insisted on walking me home. We turned the corner into Miranda Road. It was now or never.

ME: *(Tipping back my head to gaze, very pointedly, at the night sky ... What! No stars?! ... Damn. OK. Adapt the script.)* No stars tonight.

HIM: Never see many in the city anyway. It's the light ... and the pollution. Cloudy tonight, too.

ME: *(Here goes ...)* Probably just as well. All those billions of stars ... billions of light years ... It always starts me off wondering about the meaning of life.

HIM: I don't think there *is* any meaning ... apart from what we make for ourselves.

ME: *(Help!)* But ... But there's ... music and art and flowers and ... love ...

HIM: Not to mention raindrops on roses. Just a wonderfully embroidered tablecloth over a table that isn't there. Forget the table, enjoy the cloth: that's what *I* say.

Then ...

At first it was only words in my head. 'I am being kissed. I am being *kissed* ... ' Then I began to really 'enjoy the cloth'. And even the words 'I am being kissed' seemed part of the pleasure.

Well, we'd arrived where I'd hoped we would, even if by a different bus (so to speak).

Then comedy struck. My hair. His glasses. He had to let go of me to catch them, still tangled in a bit of hair I couldn't see. Him, half-blind, trying to extricate them ... just as my dear mother arrived on the scene with a bag of shopping and removed, without a word, the glasses from my hair, placed them back on the Door's face and said in her most charming manner, 'I'm assuming you're Theo. Hello, Theo. Very pleased to meet you. Do feel free to come round any time.' And she walked on into the dark.

After supper (my body wanting love, not food) it was my turn to wash up. My mother was popping out to the post box. Once she'd gone out I put Schoenberg's *Pierrot Lunaire* on the record player. Loud. I cleared the table and shook the table-cloth into the sink (table-cloths coupled with kissing from now on), laughing inside. 'I've been kissed! I've been *kissed*!' I put too much washing-up liquid in the bowl. There were bubbles and bubbles and bubbles ... I blew a handful and they landed on the parsley pot ... I scooped another handful and held them up to the light ... They made a big, round fairy moon ... *lune* ... I began to sway, my body wanting to move in time ... to move ... to move ... *lune* ... *Lunaire* ... finding myself doing a weird kind of dance to *Pierrot Lunaire*. It was eerie, spiky music – heavy and light at the same time. No proper rhythm ... Impossible to dance to ... But I'm dancing anyway ... dancing to Schoenberg ... Theo's music ... Wanting Theo ... wanting to like Schoenberg ... Wanting to dance ... Dancing ... dancing ... even though it was Schoenberg and so hard to dance to ...

I didn't hear my mother come back. I just saw her, as I turned, standing in the doorway, smiling. I stopped dancing, a pile of washing-up bubbles wobbling and wilting in my cupped hands.

I said, 'Sorry. I haven't quite … started the washing-up yet. I was just sort of … dancing … to Schoenberg.'

She closed the door, her smile turning ironic. 'Welcome to the club, Toots.'

❧ GEORGINA ❧

What a relief when I meet him! Seeing someone groping blindly for a pair of spectacles caught up in your daughter's hair somehow takes away the sense of imminent doom that attends the idea of one's offspring venturing, for the first time, into the realms of love.

It can't be many mothers who undergo the sweet trauma of witnessing a daughter's first kiss. Not that I know it is at the time – though she clearly hasn't had a lot of practice. And I don't think he has, either. Which is reassuring. How would I have reacted if it'd been some skanky, stubble-faced old *gigolo* I'd caught her with? ('Blood on Miranda Road' …)

I like Theo because he's light-hearted and serious at the same time. Rather old-fashioned. And, imagine! Into Schoenberg! I almost envy my daughter. What did I have? Joe. Yes, he's amusing. And the sex is … OK. But there's something 'insubstantial' about him, even though he is decent and good company.

Eloisa tolerates Joe more readily now that she has Theo. She needs someone to love. But when I catch her gazing at engagement rings in a jeweller's window, my radical heart sheds a tear – though I resist pointing out to her how rare it is for one's first teenage romance to last … which would have been a little cruel of me.

❦ ELOISA ❦

He came to our house. I went to his – which was long, narrow, and rather dark, apart from the kitchen which was a modern extension with blue gingham curtains and a big pine dresser of blue and white china. When it didn't smell of food, it smelled of floral disinfectant. The rest of the house smelled of polish. There were many dark, shiny surfaces.

His parents were quite old. There were three children before him. He was 'a late mistake', he said (though his parents preferred to call him 'an unexpected blessing', a gift from God – which was what his name meant). I told him I was an early mistake.

Theo wanted to be a lawyer. If he'd had more talent, he'd have liked a career in music. But he recognised his limitations – though I thought he played the piano really well. 'Will you teach me?' I asked, imagining intimate hours, hip-bone to hip-bone on the piano stool. 'I've always wanted to play an instrument,' I lied, 'but my mother wouldn't have been able to afford the lessons. I told you my father had been a musician, didn't I? And even if we could've afforded it, I doubt she would've let me: I don't think she'd like the idea of me being too like my father.'

'Oh, I shouldn't think that would be the case. Your mum's too nice to think like that – much too nice.'

Yes. They were quite a little mutual admiration society, Theo and my mother. Sometimes I resented the fact that she liked him so much. Was her encouragement of our relationship a ploy to keep me from more 'dangerous' males? But then I got on really well with his parents. True, his father was rarely at home when I visited. And even when he was, he was usually in his study. (He was a History lecturer.) But his mother, Miriam, was nearly always there, usually in the kitchen making wonderful food. Theo was like his father – long and stringy: his mother was more ... substantial. Her bosom and stomach blended into one (too much 'tasting' in the kitchen?), but she carried them before her with a dignified and unapologetic cheerfulness. Her hair was short, grey, very well cut, and her nails – toes as well as fingers – were carefully manicured and always brightly painted to match her lipstick: camellia, magenta, and even geranium which was especially stunning with her grey hair and lightly olive skin. She looked much richer than they were.

Miriam worried that, being vegetarian, I didn't eat properly. 'Fish!' she said. 'You must at least eat fish! It's the brain food.'

Quite a lot older than my mother, feminism seemed not to have touched her. Although the Goldmanns weren't practicing Jews, Miriam was, to all intents and purposes, a traditional Jewish mother. And I liked the smell of her kitchen and the taste of the food she cooked – though I never did eat anything with meat in it (but gave in, occasionally, when it came to fish).

I tried not to talk about Miriam too much to my mother: I was sure they wouldn't get on and dreaded the idea of them meeting ... even at the wedding. (I had firm fantasies about the future – couldn't imagine Theo and myself ever arguing or falling out, so it could only end at the altar, surely. Well, the registry office ...)

I was happy – because of Theo – very happy, even though the heat was on at school with 'mocks' coming up.

But my mother clearly *wasn't* happy. She tried to hide it, but I could tell. Maybe she didn't like me spending so much time at Theo's house. Maybe she was jealous. Or was she ill??!! Had she found a lump in her breast or something? ... like the mother of a girl in my class?

The problem turned out to be Joe. Things weren't going well between them any more. In fact, Joe had definitively 'changed sides', as she delicately put it: he was going out with an oboist from an opera orchestra. Trevor.

She told me she and Joe still liked each other 'as people', but they'd decided just to be friends.

'You mean you won't be having sex any more,' I said, with unnecessary cruelty of which I was duly ashamed the next moment.

'Yes,' she said, with a twist to her smile, 'I guess that's exactly what I mean.'

Was Joe moving out? No.

Was 'Trevor' moving in? No.

'Well, that's something,' I said.

'Is it?' she said. 'I suppose so.'

But she was sad. I tried not to be too happy in front of her. I tried to be helpful. Once, while she was at the launderette, I even cooked some of the special coconut cakes Theo's mum had shown me how to make. But all she said was, 'You shouldn't be wasting your time cooking, Eloisa. You've got revision to do.'

Next time I passed Joe on the stairs, I ignored him. (*TREVOR*! Huh!)

❧ GEORGINA ❧

Eloisa suggests, rather ruefully, that Theo is a little in love with me. I try reassuring her that, if so, it's just a residual bit of the process by which boys often transfer love of their own mother to a substitute before finally maturing into the full, physical love of a female from their peer group. (She grunts.) But then Eloisa is a little in love with Theo's mum, isn't she? – which isn't quite the same thing, of course, but quite … understandable. Beside Miriam, I suppose I must seem insubstantial, almost spectral, sitting here at Qwerty, conjuring unreal people with unreal lives – lives and values so different from our own that even *I* sometimes wonder if those things I write (justifying them as 'little holidays from life' for the people who buy them) are as much for myself as for 'my readers'. Maybe I'm writing those stories to keep others at bay.

My daughter has lived her life to the arrhythmical tap-dance of an old grey typewriter. It's just part of the background sound-track of our life, along with the ticking of clocks, the growl and whine of traffic and planes. But with hormones now at a 'rolling boil' (Eloisa explained Miriam's jam-making recipe to me in great detail one Friday evening that I would rather forget), the clatter of Qwerty has, she hints, become the maddening rattle of a machine gun in her ears. She finds the sounds of Miriam's kitchen more gentle, less insistent. I guess one never has to be quiet if Miriam is rolling pastry or chopping vegetables for soup. She can do it and offer motherly advice at the same time. So Eloisa goes there more and more often. On one level I understand – though it would be dishonest to say I'm not hurt.

But it's once again coming up to that problematical time of year for the lonely, poor, and unattached. 'The big C.'

Everywhere they're playing the Band Aid song, 'Do they know it's Christmas'. Eloisa's Biology teacher (charming Mr Singh) has persuaded his pupils not to buy presents for each other but to give the money to the Bhopal Disaster Fund instead – a blessed relief for those who, like my daughter, lack both friends and money or are plagued with parents who reject conspicuous consumption in all its forms, especially at Christmas. I'm proud to say the latter point does not bother Eloisa unduly. Alma is less fortunate: I have reason to believe Apple gives her a hard time.

We have a card and letter from Jack. He and Myra are no longer living together. She's now been totally drawn in to the 'cult' and has taken Natasha and joined some kind of religious commune. Jack has managed to retain custody of Edward and Josephine, but because he isn't Tasha's natural father, his jurisdiction over her is limited, even though he adopted her. He's frantically worried about her and is still trying to persuade Myra to let her come home. He wants to move back to England.

Eloisa leaps on this piece of information. 'Does that mean they're getting divorced?!'

'No, Machiavelli, it doesn't. And if you so much as start thinking along the lines I think you're thinking along … '

'I can't imagine *what* you mean, Mumsie.'

So, goodbye 1984. Hello 1985. A momentous year – the year I'll be facing the big four ow; the year my daughter will become sexually 'legal' (further raising my anxiety levels); the year Jack might come back from America: and the year of Eloisa's exams and going into the sixth form. But it's a year that has something else up its sleeve, too. Not an easy year, but an interesting one.

9

'THE SUN ALSO RISES'

❀ ELOISA ❀

Paris (rue Claude Bernard)
31st July, 1985

Dearest Theo,

So, here we are in Paris and I'm missing you already. I just can't wait till you get here. I want to show you everything. We'll do all the romantic Paris-type things and you must promise to kiss me on the Pont Neuf which is supposed to be the most romantic bridge in Paris. (By the way, the 'Neuf' bit doesn't mean 'nine': my mum says it means 'new' because when it was first built it was 'the new bridge' and the name stuck.) Don't forget to bring your camera.

See you on the 7th, Gare du Nord at 12.40, if everything's on time. But don't worry if the boat or the train are late. We won't mind waiting.

As the French say, 'je t'embrasse bien fort'.

With many kisses,

Eloisa XXXXXXXXXX

☙ GEORGINA ❧

Once, my father was flying over a vast forest sparsely criss-crossed by roads when he looked down from the plane and saw two cars – the only vehicles as far as the eye could see – speeding towards the same intersection. The nearer they got, the more obvious it became that they'd reach the cross-roads at the same time. He said he felt like a kind of helpless god, looking down, witnessing what were probably the last seconds of at least two persons' lives while they themselves were completely oblivious that they were about to die. He saw the moment of impact. Couldn't hear it, of course, from way up there and sealed in a plane. Just saw the explosion.

The unbearable truth: if one of the two vehicles had been delayed by a couple of seconds, or had been travelling at a very slightly different speed, they wouldn't have collided.

And that, I suppose, is the essence of life's inescapable and terrifying contingency.

After Eloisa's exams we spend a whole month in Paris, living in Maude and Maurice's *apartement*. Maurice is speaking at medical conferences in America and Australia and they're building in some holiday time for themselves. It's dear Maude's idea to invite us to use their place while they're away. And it's my idea to invite Theo to join us for a few days. That makes Eloisa very happy. Sixteen going on seventeen, in romantic Paris with her boyfriend ... What could be better? – though with mother as (probably unnecessary) chaperone.

I really like Theo and it makes me happy to see the two of them together, even if it also makes me even more conscious of the empty space at my own side. You could say I am getting used to it.

Then, a few days before Theo arrives, we go to the *Musée* Picasso. A man steps backwards without checking to see whether anyone is standing behind him. We are looking at the same painting. I guess he's trying to get a little more distance on it. He steps on my foot. I am wearing open-toed sandals. He is wearing very smart leather shoes with a hard heel. It really hurts (and I'm not one to make a fuss easily). Eloisa helps me to a bench, him following, beside himself with apologies as he sees I am really in pain.

'Do you think it is broken? We should take you to the hospital for an X-ray, to be sure.'

He speaks perfect English – with a deep French accent, of course, but he doesn't get the grammar wrong or make odd mistakes in vocabulary. He's only a little taller than me and is the browner kind of Frenchman. Receding but very wavy (almost frizzy) hair. Features roundish. Not thin, not fat.

'I insist on taking you to the hospital. If your toe is broken, it must not be neglected.'

I relent. He and Eloisa help me to his car (smallish, blue, with a dent in the front passenger door: is he as careless with his driving as with his feet?) and he takes us to the hospital where my toe receives meticulous French medical attention. He waits with us for the X-ray results (not broken, just badly bruised: it'll be painful for a while), by which time we're getting on pretty well. So lunch in a café (paid for by him) is inevitable.

I'm laughing and crying inside, both at the same time, with the utter ridiculousness of it all, thinking of Amadou's big feet and going to the café after he'd crushed my make-up. I imagine the significance Alma might draw from it: my life being 'trampled' twice beneath the feet of men. I prefer to think of it as them maybe putting a foot on me to stop me blowing away into some loveless gutter.

But Paul (pronounced 'Pol', of course) Dupin is nothing like Amadou. He trained as a lawyer but now works for a big legal publishers. His mind is logical rather than creative, he admits, though he very much enjoys films, art, and some kinds of music.

That morning he was scheduled to attend a meeting not far from the *Musée* Picasso but arrived to find it had been cancelled at the last moment. He says he'd always promised himself he'd go there but never got around to it, so he seized the opportunity that day ... and is very glad he did. Not glad for the toe, of course.

I often wonder what the reason was for that cancellation: one of those 'contingent' events that shape the lives of people who have absolutely no connection with the event itself. Probably someone just had a cold or a stomach upset: just some little bug and then that almost thoughtless decision: 'I just don't feel up to that meeting: cancel it, will you, Jeanne ... '

Early on he makes it clear he's unattached. He's been married, but not any more. His ex-wife has re-married, moved south. He misses his daughter, Nathalie. Out comes the photo. She's about ten. She has his mouth, his smile. He seems rather lonely. He obviously isn't a stunningly wonderful man who would sweep you off your feet, that you'd fall head-over-heels in love with on a first meeting. But he's decent, straightforward, intelligent, had been a *soixante-huitard* (though you'd never guess it, looking at him). And he's broad-minded – which is useful when we get on to 'occupations'.

'I write books. Just short ones, about love. Romantic ones, but also, well ... sexy ones.'

He doesn't bat an eyelid. 'Are they popular in England too, then, erotic stories? French people sometimes think the English are sexually repressed. In former times, our "free thinkers" were always escaping to Britain to avoid persecution, and your "free lovers" would escape to France, I think. Two-way traffic. Perhaps they waved to each other as their boats passed in the English Channel!'

I wonder why his wife left him. How does his daughter feel about it? But it isn't the kind of thing I can ask. Yet.

At the weekend he drives us to Giverny. 'Yes, it is possible to go by train, but much easier in the car. You cannot walk properly with your bad toe, and you must give it the opportunity to get better. No, I insist that I drive you in my car.'

A real Frenchman: very attached to his wheels.

Eloisa is nervous. Me, too: I'm the one in the 'dent' seat! The French seem to have a particular way of driving. And we aren't used to cars, anyway.

❦ ELOISA ❦

The drive to Giverny was a bit hair-raising, but worth it once we were there. I liked Monet's house more than his paintings, actually. It made me feel very *domestic* and that I wanted nothing more fervently than a house of my own that I could paint beautiful colours and choose curtains for and arrange artistically. I wanted to put flowers in little vases and have a nice kitchen where I prepared delicious meals for my family and friends, and served sugared strawberries in pretty blue and white bowls to nice people sitting in wicker chairs around a white-linen-draped table in a shady corner of the garden ... And children ... yes, children having a happy childhood, playing in a beautiful, *beautiful* garden, my little girl running up to me with a bunch of daisies and a kiss. So much better than all the pressure of exams and the stress of waiting for the results (my stomach turned slightly when I remembered that envelope containing my results which would be waiting for us when we got back). Life would be so much easier if I could just trail around a garden in a long dress and a big hat, picking roses. And Monet's yellow dining-room took my breath away. I'd have one just like it! Essence of sunshine. My heart was a singing bird. Come, O love, O Theo, O future ...

... which I nearly didn't have. A lucky escape on the way back to Paris. It wasn't strictly Paul's fault, but I wished he'd drive more slowly.

A couple of days later we prepared supper for him at the *apartement*. Newly inspired to domesticity by the Giverny experience, I plumped cushions, smoothed throws, searched Maude's linen cupboard for the right kind of table-cloth, then set the table very correctly, very beautifully ... though it lacked flowers.

'Steady on, sweetheart,' said my mother. 'It's basically only mushroom omelette and salad. Let's keep it simple or he'll think I'm trying to seduce him.'

'Aren't you?' I said.

'No.' The telephone rang. 'Not yet,' she added, over her shoulder, as she went to answer it.

It was Paul. He wanted to speak to *me*. She shrugged, made a face, handed me the receiver.

'Eloisa, I need your advice. I want to bring some flowers for your muzzer' (the English 'th' sound was the one thing he sometimes found difficult) 'but I don't know her taste in such things. If I say a list of flowers, will you please say "yes" to any you know she especially likes?'

Being totally oblivious to my mother's taste in flowers, I decided that pink roses would best enhance my table arrangement and indicated to 'Pol' accordingly. Then he wanted to speak to my 'muzzer'. I could hear what he was saying: he was asking her what kind of chocolate I preferred. She said 'yes' to dark. Then, 'See you at seven thirty.'

I left her to answer the doorbell – or rather to call through the securiphone.

'OK, Paul. It's open. Come on up. Second floor.'

We heard the grinding of the lift, the clatter of the folding metal grill opening then closing. We opened the front door, and there he was, holding out his flowers with a smile.

'Oh, Paul. How lovely!' exclaimed my mother, with genuine delight. 'Yellow roses are my favourite!'

Paul Dupin: well-meaning, intelligent, educated, affectionate, though a little … 'all over the place'. Thoughtful enough to ring up and ask about my mother's favourite flowers … then forgetting what I'd said. And I was given a box of mixed chocolates because he'd also forgotten which she said I preferred. But it turned out that my mother really *did* like yellow roses best.

And Theo preferred milk chocolate to dark so we were able to share what was left of them when he arrived a couple of days later.

We soon realised this was typical of 'Pol' – meaning to do the right thing, getting it all wrong, but it usually turning out fine in the end anyway. Maybe that was what his wife had had trouble with – never being quite sure. Maybe it had caused her to feel insecure all the time, whereas my mother … well, she claimed she was used to living with 'uncertainty'. And Paul definitely improved with keeping, as they say. He got along fine with Theo: they had Law in common. Twice that week the four of us went for a long, after-dinner stroll by the river, where it was cooler.

It was a peculiar situation, really: my mother with her boyfriend, me with mine. More as if we were sisters than mother and daughter. As we strolled, two by two, that first evening we were all together, I deliberately slowed down so that 'they' would be in front, partly because it was embarrassing to feel them watch us hold hands, but mainly because I hoped Theo might pick up a few tips from a charming Frenchman who seemed to know exactly how to treat a woman. Theo was still quite happy to do nothing more than hold hands and talk about human rights and music – which was fine, up to a point. I enjoyed the intellectual side of our relationship, but … BUT couldn't he at least put his arm affectionately around me as we walked and talked – around my waist, my shoulders, my *neck* … anything! Some proper physical contact, for goodness' sake!!

Observing a particularly tender moment between Paul and my mother (his arm around her shoulders, he gave her an affectionate squeeze and they leaned their heads together, just for a moment), I interrupted Theo's monologue with, 'Look! Aren't they sweet together?! It's so nice, seeing two people falling in love, the way they … '

'Sorry. What were you saying?'

'Oh, nothing. It doesn't matter.'

But it did matter. For the first time a little niggling doubt raised its seedling head in my fertile heart, a doubt as to whether Theo really *was* the 'till-death-do-us-part' man of my dreams. And my pleasure in seeing my mother so obviously happy was, if I'm absolutely honest, tainted with a tiny drip of jealousy. Not that I felt anything in the least erotic towards Paul, but I longed to have a 'real man' treat me as the 'real woman' I already felt myself to be. Then I stamped down on the doubt sufficiently to go on holding Theo's hand, reminding myself that boys mature, emotionally, later than girls and that maybe he'd grow into Paul's charming manliness ... eventually.

The evening before Theo left, the four of us had dinner in a little restaurant off the *rue* Mouffetard (Pauls' idea – and he paid). The conversation turned to more deep and personal matters to do with my father's family and the reactions of both him and my mother to the matter of his grandparents' supposed 'collaboration'.

'So how is that connected with his decision to go to Senegal?' Paul asked.

'It was only with the revelations about the grandparents that he began to realise how very difficult they must have made his father's marriage to Colette. Once the cork was out of the bottle, so to speak, lots of things began to come out. You see, when he was young, Amadou had never forgiven his father for abandoning his mother, not really understanding the tremendous difficulties caused by the parents, or how serious it would have been if he'd still been in Paris at the time of the Occupation. He'd never tried to contact his father. When we were ... together, he admitted he'd now grown up enough to understand – especially having experienced the poisonous atmosphere in the family when the collaboration scandal came out. He just wanted to escape. I don't blame him, really. He just wanted to find his father, tell him he understood. He really did mean to come back, I'm sure of it. But ...'

My mother's eyes suddenly filled with tears, so I decided to finish the explanation for her. 'He was involved in an accident. We don't really know the details, do we, Mumsie?'

My mother just hung her head so we couldn't see her face. I thought Paul would have been sensitive enough to stop the questions there, but as soon as she'd wiped her eyes and looked up again, he persisted.

'And you? Why did you not stay in France, with the family? You too loved France very much, you told me. Life would have been easier for you and Eloisa, would it not?'

My mother sighed as if she didn't really want to be walking over this old ground again. 'I would have had to rely so much on his family for support, and I guess I felt uncomfortable that the family's wealth might in some way be connected to the deportation of Jews ... There was no way I wanted ... '

(My cheeks burned. Had she forgotten that Theo was *Jewish*? How could she talk about all that in front of him? I hardly dared meet his eye. But, glancing from under my hair as I manoeuvred salad into a mouth that didn't want it, I saw that he simply looked ... interested.)

'The whole thing made me more – how shall I put it? – "equivocal" towards France for a while. I'd been totally seduced and, well, though you *know* about collaboration *intellectually*, you think of it as being done by people who were obviously "evil" – not the kind you'd actually find yourself *related* to ... more or less. And, yes, I know that sounds naïve. But that's how it was for me at the time. And don't forget the war and everything was nearer then.'

'But you cannot always be taking history forward with you into the future.'

'Do we have a choice? It seems to follow us, even as we try

kicking it away. It goes on snapping at our heels, not allowing us to ignore it ... or it's like a heavy suitcase we're forced to carry with us to every new place, our shoulders always a bit skewed with the weight of it.'

'But if you reject all countries that have done some bad things in the past, then you reject all countries. Including your own. Would you not agree that it is not whole countries that do bad things: it is individual people.'

Theo chipped in. 'The plaques. Surely they remind you of the "other" France. I know I've only been here a few days but I've seen them everywhere, those plaques marking the places where brave French people were shot while trying to resist the Nazis – shot on the very streets they used to play on as kids, I expect.' (He'd never mentioned these thoughts to me! It made me feel a bit cross and uncomfortable. What else went on in his head that I didn't know about?) 'Shot for defending *real* French values. *Human* values. Yes, there were collaborators, but far more people who *didn't* collaborate, surely.'

My mother looked thoughtful, then stretched out her hand and placed it on Theo's. I felt an even stronger than usual pang of jealousy at that moment of indefinable tenderness between them. But I also realised it was at this moment that the last of her 'complicated' feelings about returning to France – feelings all tied up with losing my father – began to fall away, and she felt free to fall in love with France (and with a Frenchman!) again. In the candle-light, she looked calm and happy and beautiful. I could quite see why my father would have fallen in love with her.

Paul was more upset than we were, I think, when it came to saying goodbye. I could see he'd fallen absolutely and utterly head-over-heels in love with my mother. You don't think of 'love at first sight' when it's older people, but I guess it happens. And she'd grown fond enough of 'Pol' to invite him to come and visit us in London, soon.

When we finally got back to Miranda Road, there was a little brown envelope waiting for me. Exam results. I'd done well. There was a note of 'congratulations' from the Headmistress saying they hoped I'd be returning for the Sixth Form in September and could I confirm this as soon as possible, please.

I phoned Theo to tell him my results. Then I wrote to Jack: he'd asked my mother to let him know how I'd got on. But he didn't receive the letter. While we'd been in France, he'd moved back to England with Edward and Josephine, but without Tasha. A few formalities and the divorce would be complete. He was back in their old house and phoned one Saturday morning towards the end of September to invite us round to lunch the following Sunday. But that was the weekend Paul was coming to stay for the first time. My mother explained. He understood. But he didn't invite us again.

❧ GEORGINA ❧

' *"But what have I done with my life?" thought Mrs Ramsay … '*
And what am I going to do with the rest of mine?

Nothing like a brush with mortality to make you think.

Shortly after we return from our summer in Paris, I experience, on two or three occasions, signals that all is not completely well with my body. I try to convince myself, the first time, that the pains are muscular or something to do with the start of the menopause, maybe. Once it even gets so scary I go down to Joe and sit with him till I begin to feel better. He threatens to call the doctor, or even an ambulance, unless I promise to go for a proper check-up. Mindful of my mother's early death and recalling that little bottle of heart pills my father came to rely on in middle age, I decide to take Joe's advice.

A very careful doctor, unwilling to make a snap diagnosis. He wants me to have some tests in hospital as soon as possible. It might mean staying in overnight, so my plan not to tell Eloisa about the problem goes awry (though I play it down as best I can, of course).

Such a long day, that day at the hospital.

Good health – a bright sweet left in a dark pocket. Or like the moon. 'I want! I want!'

Doctors and nurses all very matter-of-fact. Suppose they have to be. Have to hang a curtain between themselves and your full, living reality. (Like people who eat meat?)

Explaining what they're doing and why. Do I have any questions?

Not that I can think of. Only the one that everyone wants to ask but usually doesn't. 'How long am I going to live?'

And there is the time before the diagnosis and the time after. The time after the moment that can change everything. And so much time spent waiting. Simply waiting. Perhaps it's deliberate. To give the mind time to adjust to what might turn out to be a new reality. A new time-scale by which to live. Possibly.

All around one sees the usually hidden functions of the body pulled into visibility. Tubes. Pulsings. Fluids. 'This is what you are'. Personhood shrinking away from the surface of the skin. A dry tuber in winter earth.

Suddenly insignificant, the usual filigree of questions. What would've happened if … ? Would he have … ? Did he just want a new life? Or did he love me and only me? Would we have been happy? Would it have lasted?

All that 'then' stuff.

But with my own mortality tugging at my skirt for attention, it all seems … rather irrelevant, really.

There's one known truth about it all, though: when Eloisa was conceived, we loved each other deeply. She is the child of a particular moment of deep joy, regardless of what happened afterwards. Or might have happened.

Heading for that crossroads where we'll collide with our death. Maybe nearer than I thought.

The patients have their disguises of individuality peeled away revealing the fear common to all – even those not seriously ill. Because you never know. And there are plenty of stories to feed the fear: going into hospital with a minor condition … mistakes being made … or an infection picked up … or discovering it isn't what they thought: not minor at all. The end. *FIN* (white letters on a black screen, or black letters on a white screen). Fear of dying before even having the chance to live the wanted life. And between the gaze of the doctors and the gaze of the patients the hologram of a grinning skeleton doing its usual old dance. (*Carpe diem.*)

❀ ELOISA ❀

It was when my mother developed a heart problem that everything changed. You could say she'd always had a 'heart' problem, but this time it was of the gory, blood and muscle kind that needed hospital tests. She might have to stay overnight.

I made her phone Paul … who was still in a state of high anxiety from having seen the Brixton riots on the news in France. (He wanted us to 'escape' to Paris and refused to believe we could live in London and not have seen any of it.) When he heard about the tests he panicked, and insisted on coming over. Which hospital? He'd find the nearest hotel. Wouldn't it be better to get checked by a good doctor in Paris? He'd find out the best cardiologist and pay whatever was necessary. Would even take out a loan, if necessary, he said.

I phoned Jack.

'If there's anything whatever I can do, Eloisa, you only have to say the word.'

On the spur of the moment, I said, 'Can I come and sleep at your place if she has to stay in? I … I don't want to be here on my own … without her.' (My voice went husky.)

'Of course you can, my dear, as long as it's all right with your mum. Josephine'll be thrilled to see you again. Try not to worry. I'm sure it won't be anything too drastic. It's probably just the doctor not wanting to take chances.'

It was only after I put the phone down I realised the obvious thing to have done would have been to ask if I could stay at Theo's place. But maybe there was something deep down in me that wanted the particular assurance I'd always felt with Jack.

She waved me off to school – a golden day in October – smiling down from the window, deliberately cheerful. Paul had arrived in London late the previous night and was coming for her by

261

taxi at ten o'clock. I could go and visit at five – if she was kept in.

I stayed in school for the morning. But I couldn't concentrate and when I went out at lunch-time, I took my bags with me and didn't go back (bunking double French).

I phoned home a couple of times, just in case she was back. No answer. I wandered aimlessly about, my ever-ready imagination coming up with different versions of what had been happening and what would happen later.

VERSION ONE

Chief Consultant: Terrible to see this sort of thing in a woman so young. Can't be more than forty. The condition's inherited, of course.

Second Consultant: So what's the outlook for her?

Chief Consultant: Not good. Hard to be precise, but …

VERSION TWO

Nurse: Now don't you worry Miss Hardiman. You're in good hands.

Consultant: You were wise to go to the doctor when you did, Miss Hardiman. You're a sensible woman so I'll come straight to the point: your only hope is a transplant …

VERSION THREE

Paul: Tell me the truth, doctor.

Consultant: Are you her next of kin?

Paul: I will be soon. We're to be married. There is a daughter, but she's not yet seventeen. If the outlook is not good, then …

Consultant: The outlook is not at all good, I'm afraid.

Paul breaks down in tears. A 'look' between the nurse and the consultant. A clock is heard striking five. The daughter arrives at the hospital to find the curtains drawn round her bed. The sound of crying …

Nurse: (Stopping the daughter as she goes towards the curtains.)

I'm sorry, my dear. I'm afraid you're just too late. She was worse than we thought. The stress of the tests … it was too much for her poor heart …

The daughter pushes melodramatically past the nurse, rips back the flowered curtain and sees her mother, death-pale, and Paul clutching her stilled hand, his lips pressed to it, sobbing …

Et cetera.

Tears lurking behind my eyes from the dramas playing themselves out in my head, I blinked into a bookshop window, trying to compose myself. It was Booker Prize time again and the six short-listed books were featured. A display-board covered in regularly-spaced holes had six metal book-supports hooked into it. The book with a bright orange cover was the first to catch my eye … then one with a blue cover showing a bi-plane and attracting attention by its peculiar title: *Illywhacker*. There was only one by a name I recognised. Doris Lessing. My mother had a book by her.

My mother. How she'd have loved to be up there in that display. How she'd have loved to have written a book that might even be considered for it. And now it was probably too late. Instead of prize-winning novels all she had to show for her life was a heap of soft porn and daft romances. And me. (The life of a woman.)

I invented a book she might have written – a bitter-sweet story of a mother and daughter … a lost love haunting their lives, trapping them on a small island … though I had no idea how it might end. I imagined smuggling it into the display. The seventh Booker … (Muffled gasps of indignation from the other six.) I invented a cover, my two-dimensional younger face (all hair and eyes) staring out at me through the bookshop window – a black-and-white photo. Above my child-face the title throbbed bright pink – though I didn't actually know what

263

the title was – while beneath my face was my mother's name. (I tried to banish the thought of it as carved in stone.)

A woman pushing a buggy full of sleeping child paused at the window. She had a small, intelligent face and a lot of auburn hair. She looked healthy and happy, her children's growing up – and most of her own life – still in front of her. She looked so nice. I wished I could talk to her ... tell her my troubles ... But she glanced at her watch and was off.

After a last look in the window (my mother's book had gone and I couldn't conjure it back), I tried to follow the woman's rust-coloured anorak, but she was going at quite a pace – hair bouncing to the rhythm of her buggy-pushing strides – and I was slowed down by the weight of my school stuff and over-night bag for staying at Jack's.

I lost her in the street that was suddenly weaving with women (and one or two men) pushing buggies, leading toddlers by the hand, or carrying a tired one. Some walked with others, some on their own, all heading in one direction. It was nearly three o'clock already: school finished soon. So many mothers and fathers and none of them mine. (Violins of self-pity in a rising *glissando*.)

And my imagination had me riding on the back of a pigeon, up, up, to the ridge of a high roof from where I looked down at the many-coloured iron filings being drawn to the school gate. Soon there'd be a swarming of smaller filings from the other side of the gate. They'd meet, mix, disperse ... until tomorrow when it'd happen all over again. And then they came, the first ones ... running towards their mothers ... Just like I used to.

Oh, please don't die, Mumsie, please don't die.

She'd seemed to like being a mother. And even though things had sometimes been difficult, we'd also had a lot of fun. But if she'd had a choice, if she could have a second chance at life and could choose between being a 'proper' writer, ending up with those Booker people, or being my mother ...

Suddenly I felt very cross with her. I didn't want to have to feel sorry that she never wrote 'proper' novels. I didn't want to feel *responsible*. It had been her choice: she didn't *have* to have me? And she could've written other things if she'd really wanted to, if she'd really been *able* to. I started to imagine her death-bed speech, full of regrets ...

I found myself in a slightly run-down little square with a play area for children and a couple of wooden benches. I sat down. There was a woman on the next bench reading a thin, rubbishy-looking paperback while her children played on the climbing frame. I wished she'd talk to me, but she was absorbed in her book. It was called *Never Too Late*. She was lumpy and pale, wearing white sandals despite the cold.

The plane trees around the square were losing their leaves and the low sun glimmered through them like a gentle, sporadic strobe playing over me as I sat, trying to be rational but feeling as miserable as a zoo-penguin staring into a dried-up pool.

After a while, I looked up and stared into the shifting dazzle of golden light. And out of the light my imagination conjured a face – a face made up to the hilt, a plastered crochet of wrinkles with false eye-lashes twice the size of Joe's and a hand holding up a wand or a glowing kind of pen. She was all in pink. Then her voice. 'Coo-ee. Can you hear me? You don't want to worry. Doesn't do a girl good. Your mother's quite happy really. As she once told you, she knows her stories have been a great deal more enjoyed than a lot of that Booker stuff. People get so terribly *critical* when they think they're discussing "Literature", my dear. But the kind of people who read your mother's books – and mine – simply *enjoy* them. Takes them out of themselves for a bit.' She became pinker by the moment. (It was Barbara Cartland ...) 'You really should cheer up a bit, sweetie. Face as long as a conger eel. Like one of those femi-what's-its with no sense of *pink*. We all need a little pink in our lives, a little hope, a little love ...' She waved a circle with the wand-pen, scattering a gentle shower of diamantés to catch the sunlight. ' ... especially women like the one on that bench. Our books give them ... a little holiday from *Life*.' Smiling, she tossed a few more diamantés from her wand-pen – then she faded, like the Cheshire cat. And when I finally looked down, I saw just a little crushed glass at my feet.

A sudden wail from the climbing frame. One of the children had fallen. *Never Too Late* was abandoned, face down, on the bench. Cuddling, investigation of the (very minor) wound. Kissing it better. Time to go home. But the older child didn't want to go. *He* wasn't hurt. 'Not fair!' Promise of sweets from the ice-cream shop 'if Mummy has enough pennies'.

The woman started to leave the square, carrying the still sobbing child as well as her shopping and the lunch-boxes and school bags, the uninjured child having refused to carry his own. I shivered, looked at my watch. I could start making my way slowly to the hospital. As I passed the bench I saw that the woman's book had been left behind: it had slipped through a gap in the bench and was lying on the ground beneath. I picked it up (*Never Too Late* was by Susanna Bell – not one of my mother's pseudonyms, as far as I remembered) and hurried after the woman. She was just turning out of the square as I caught up with her.

'Excuse me, I think you forgot this.'

The woman blinked at me, looked at the book as if it were something from another planet, then, with a distracted kind of recognition, said, 'Oh ... Thanks, love. You couldn't just ... shove it in the top of that blue bag, could you. My hands are a bit full.'

'Can I take something for you? Carry something home for you? I've got time if you don't live too far away.'

'No, 'sall right.' Her face closed, looked suddenly suspicious. 'I'll manage, but if you could just stick the book in the bag.'

I did. She smiled a guarded 'thank you' and walked on, the injured child watching me over her mother's shoulder, cheek against her mother's neck. I could imagine its warmth ... and I panicked afresh about a possible not-too-distant future when I'd never again be able to lay my cheek, like that, against my own mother's neck.

Still no answer when I phoned home so I went to the hospital.

I found the right ward but, looking down its length, I couldn't see my mother, or Paul. There was one bed with the curtains drawn around it ...

'Can I help you? You look a bit lost.' (Little Irish nurse.)

'My mother's meant to be here. Where is she?'

'What's her name?'

'Georgina Hardiman.'

'It rings a bell. Just a minute.' She looked at a list on the desk while my heart chunkered in my head and my eyes were pulled to the curtained bed of my nightmare. 'Oh, yes. We had to move her to one of the little side wards. Follow me.'

'Why? Why did you have to move her?' (Rising panic.)

'We had an emergency admission, and the woman needs to be in the open ward where we can keep an eye on her more easily.'

'Is she all right?'

'The woman?'

'No. My mother.'

'Here we are. Your father's with her.'

'My *father*?!' But the nurse had already hurried off.

She was sitting up in the high bed, beaming. Paul was in the low hospital armchair next to her, holding her hand. A huge bouquet of yellow roses sang out his love from the grey formica cabinet beside the bed.

'Are you all right?'

'I'm fine, Toots.' Her cheek was warm when I kissed it.

'What did they say? Have you had all the tests?'

'Yes, and it's nothing much to worry about.' (I saw Paul give her hand a surreptitious squeeze.) 'It's a minor condition. Loads of people have it. I probably inherited it from one or both of my parents, they say. There are some wonderful little tablets they can give me to help it. A bit more exercise, a bit less sitting at my desk and I could well make ninety. There's really no need to look so desperate.'

'But why are you still here if it's all right?'

'They were very late starting the tests, for some reason, so now I have to wait until the doctors come round in the morning and sort out my medication. They want me to start it straight away. And I'm only in bed because I'm tired, and they said my blood pressure was up a bit.'

'Are you sure that … '

Paul nodded reassuringly. 'It really is all right, Eloisa. I have spoken to the nurse who is in charge here. There is a problem, but it is quite a small one. And I am going to take very good care of your mother.'

The way he said it, and seeing them look so like a 'happy couple', I almost expected them to announce their engagement. My eyes even flicked to my mother's left hand. No. No ring. Yet. Anyway, they were a bit old to bother with that …

She asked me about my day. I lied. I asked her about hers and she told me what good treatment she'd had and how lovely the nurses were. It was just the food that was awful!

'So,' said Paul, 'I am taking her to a good restaurant for lunch tomorrow when we leave the hospital.'

'That's really nice,' I said, but suddenly felt absurdly tearful and excluded. A romantic lunch for two. Them. Not me. They were a 'couple'. The tender, sensuous way he held her hand in both of his. His … *attentiveness*. Suddenly I felt utterly fed up with the chaste little relationship I had with Theo.

❧ GEORGINA ☙

The longest day followed by the longest night.

How can anyone ever recover in hospital? The noise, all night. Bad enough in this little side room: on the main ward it must be impossible to sleep. Unless they knock everyone out with pills.

Hungry! So-called 'supper' too early. Wish Paul had brought chocolates instead of flowers ... or as well as.

Paul. What do I do?

Can I once and for all carve the past into a child and carry it on my hip, so to speak? – get on with the housework, as it were, one-handed? Or must I keep the past like a stone in my pocket, forever putting in my hand, surreptitiously, to check it's still there, closing my hand around it?

But this ... 'thing' with Paul has taken me by surprise. After years of looking over my shoulder at what *was*, even while wanting to fall in love again and have a 'life', it's so weird to have someone fall in love with me so utterly. Nothing like I expected, nothing at all ... now it's happened. Just feels very ... comfortable. God! How middle-aged!

It'd mean me going to live in Paris, eventually. His job. His daughter. And ... I think I'd like that. I always feel more alive there, anyway. But I can't possibly think of going until Eloisa's through school and away at university. It could be a relief to her, once she's off living her own life, not having to feel guilty about me being on my own, lonely, at Miranda Road. She gets on all right with Paul ... apart from his driving. He has a nice enough apartment with a little room I can have as a study, he says, if I want to go on writing. Not luxury, but he earns a decent amount to keep two ... plus a few modest investments.

Physical affection rather than wild passion. Fine by me. Especially now ... with this.

And anyway, I don't want to become just a lamenting old mouth spitting out the ashes of 'once upon a time'.

I do like him tremendously. I think we *appreciate* each other. I think, with him, life could be very … enjoyable. And that's not to be underestimated.

Will Maude be glad or sad? I like to think she'd be glad. I'll be living not far from her, in another couple of years. It'll go quickly, with visits back and forth. Life will be INTERESTING again … though it'll be hard to leave Miranda Road. Hope Eloisa won't mind: she's never known anywhere else … though she'd have preferred to live in Jack's house!

It's no good: I'll have to go out to the loo.

The night sister at her desk. A reading lamp whitens her face to a thoughtful moon watching over the sea of the main ward as it sighs and snores and jabbers through the almost dark. A beached whale moans from the third bed on the right – a vast woman I remember noticing when I first came in. Somebody's shouting obscenities in their sleep (presumably). Pebbles rasp in the chest of yesterday's emergency who was put in the bed I was down for. Mary Nash. They rubbed out my name and wrote up hers while I was gathering my things. They might've sent me home if it hadn't been for that blip in my blood pressure – and a bed in a side-ward unexpectedly free.

As I pass, Mary Nash coughs … groans … shouts. The night-sister stands up, walks to her on soft, heel-less shoes. I carry on towards the loo.

When I come back, I realize something is wrong. The curtains have been drawn around the bed. Urgent voices. Hurrying. Two white coats fly past me in the half dark. Someone's moving a heavy brown cylinder of oxygen. Voices urgently calming. Instructions. Strange sounds from Mary Nash. Light glows through the curtains, like a magical box in a film when some scary transformation is taking place inside.

I get back into bed and grope for my watch.

3 a.m.

Even less possible to sleep now. I can hear that something very bad is happening in the bed that was nearly mine.

5 a.m. ... and I've hardly slept. Sounds as if the hospital is beginning its day already. Desperate for a cup of tea. Wonder if they'd let me make one in the nurses' kitchen. No harm asking ...

The curtains are pulled back. The sheets have been stripped. 'Mary Nash' has been rubbed from the little white board above the bed. I don't want to know if this is because she's to be carved in stone.

No, not allowed to make tea. There'll be some coming soon, I'm told. I go back to bed to wait.

A locket hangs in my head like a small gold watch: open it and a tiny skull says 'tick-tock: tick-tock'.

One life.

That was then. This is now. I still have a future to fill. Some, anyway.

Like a full moon, I know the past will always come round again – again – again ... though growing paler each time, lately ... turning into a monument.

An in-creeping tide is finally filling the impress of feet that have, anyway, been walking away over the dunes for years now. Above are small, high clouds like white handkerchiefs of goodbye.

Dresdens of the heart.

❦ ELOISA ❦

The studio. I'd never been up there before. It was on the floor above where the 'proper' house stopped – looking out over the garden and the tall backs of the houses beyond. It used to be the room where Myra kept all her old art junk, and though she'd liked to call it 'the studio', I don't think a lot of art had actually gone on here. It sounded good, I suppose: 'I'm just popping up to the studio … ' She'd had to clear it out when they let the house, of course. And now it had been transformed.

The walls had been given a fresh coat of white paint and Jack had bought a comfortable bed for the room (in case Dee or Jamie wanted to invite friends to stay) as well as proper curtains – dark blue, right to the floor – and a big bright rug to soften the bare boards. There was no wardrobe, yet, just an old wooden chest of drawers painted yellow. A beer-mug of flowers had been put on the top. From Josephine. Did I like them? Her anxious face wanting reassurance.

Bits and pieces from the autumn garden – flowers from the straggle end of the year – gathered, just for me, by 'little' Josephine, now long, eleven, motherless, spiked with talent and needing so much to be loved. I gave her a big hug and told her the flowers were lovely. She gave me a clinging hug back, and for the first time I experienced a slight inkling of what it might feel like to be a mother, the way her arms tightened around my body in pleading and dependence and love.

'I wish you were my sister,' she said. 'I always wished you were my sister even when I was little and you used to take me to the beach early in the morning to practise my violin. You were the only one who understood.'

I hadn't *really* understood her obsession with the violin, an obsession which now takes her, every Saturday, to the Guildhall School of Music. I used to take her onto the beach to impress her father with how helpful and *nice* I could be. Hard to imagine that I was about the same age then as Josephine is now.

She was allowed to stay up half an hour later than usual in honour of my presence. Once she'd had her bath she was allowed to play me *one* piece on the violin. 'A short section from a longer work by Wolfgang Amadeus Mozart,' she announced seriously, standing there in pale blue pyjamas, an old pair of Edward's, clown-baggy on her slim body. Playing from memory, she created a stream of musical sunshine that made me think of the yellow room at Giverny. When she'd finished and we'd clapped, I said, 'I've got a sort of cousin in France who plays the cello really well, but you play the violin even better.'

Her smile was luminous. She went to bed happy.

I hardly slept, even though I was exhausted from the trampolining of my emotions throughout the day and well into the evening.

I stayed up talking to Jack. We talked about my mother. About Paul. About Myra. We talked about me and what I hoped to do in the future. He was so easy to talk with. At one point I even revealed my childhood machinations regarding him and my mother. In his amused expression I saw a spark of the old Jack, not the one turned sad and drawn-looking by all the problems he'd been dealing with since the 'American catastrophe', as he called it.

'Well,' he smiled, 'I always was a great admirer of your mother, and who knows, if things had been different ... But she seems to have found someone to be happy with. And that's great.' At which he got up from the armchair, collected the coffee-cups, and asked me what time I liked to get up in the morning: he'd give me a call.

I stared into the dark, the day churning its pictures in front of my eyes – a day that had started with my mother waving me off to school, smiling down calmly from the window like a figure from a cathedral niche, and ended with that momentary, uncomfortable encounter between Paul and Jack when Paul, at the end of visiting time, delivered me to Jack's house by taxi – eyeing each other, two middle-aged male rivals? ... probably thinking 'He's going bald' ... 'He's going grey' ... Quite funny, really!

And now I'm kept awake by the complicated emotions of being back in this house I'd fallen in love with when I was even younger than Josephine. Edward is now the awkward, almost surly but sensitive thirteen-year-old Jamie had been when I first knew him. And it was lovely to be with Jack again, being able to talk to him almost like an adult. But then he always did talk to me sensibly. Nothing has really changed since that first time I met him. What was it he said to me? ... What were his first words? ... Something like, 'Don't let this noisy lot scare you; they're really quite harmless.' Wanting to give me confidence right from the start, telling me not to be scared. And with him I never was. Am. I know, I just know that if anything terrible does happen to my mother, he'll make sure I'm well taken care of. Maybe that's how my mother feels with Paul. Maybe she just wants to be taken care of, for once ... wants to be loved and appreciated by someone she can rely on ... though I, personally, wouldn't find the kind of reliability I want with Paul – him and his big feet and dodgy driving and getting things 'wrong'. Though he has kindness and charm, I have to admit that. Probably all right in ... the bedroom. Not that they've had the chance for a lot of that, yet. Maybe it doesn't count quite so much once you're middle-aged. Maybe it doesn't count as much, anyway, as people pretend, if everything else works well between you. What's the point of brilliant sex if you loathe each

*other the rest of the time? Mind you, it's all very theoretical for
me, so far, with Theo still more interested in Schoenberg than ...
anything else. On the other hand, I don't like the 'musical beds'
way of going on, like it was in the sixties. Apparently. Before
AIDS. Were they really great, the sixties? What was Jack like
then? Did he have long hair? Would've been in his twenties,
wouldn't he? Teaching already. Were teachers allowed long
hair? Never seen any pictures of him when he was really young.
The most recent was the wedding picture with Myra. Silly cow.*

Won't this night ever end? Wonder what the time is?

Half past five. So I must have drifted off once or twice.

I got out of bed and tip-toed to the window, trying to avoid the
squeaky board I'd noticed the night before: Jack's room was
right beneath mine and I didn't want to disturb him.

*Jack sleeping on his own down there in the big double bed.
Does he dream of Myra? ... Of his first wife, even? ... Of sex?*

I pulled back the long blue curtain and looked out.

*Black bulk of bushes and trees, and beyond them the solid,
flat silhouettes of roofs and chimneys. A few lights on: some
people up and about already. I can see a woman in a kitchen ...
second floor: a house divided into flats. She's too far away for
me to see exactly what she's doing as she moves from one side
of the window to the other, back and forth. Probably laying the
breakfast table. Now there's a man with her. I see him come up
behind her and put his arms around her. I try to imagine their
life ...*

*Sometimes I long so much to leave school, to be a 'grown-
up', have a home and family of my own ... All the things I'm
not supposed to want instead of a career. Or as well as. Why
not? Is it 'hormones'? The nesting instinct now my body is old*

enough to reproduce. But knowing it's that doesn't make it less strong. Another year and a half at school. Then university ... four years if I do Modern Languages. You have to do a year abroad. A whole year in France might be nice ... as long as it's Paris. Don't want to be stuck in the middle of nowhere. Then what? Teach? Translate? Or work for a big company and earn lots of money? That's what everyone says you should do. Silly if you don't. It's there for the taking. Everyone out for themselves. But my mother hates all that. Mrs Thatcher and the fat City cats. Smug men in suits, bloated from too much food and drink, while in Ethiopia ... Those terrible pictures in the programme Mr Vernon made us watch in Current Affairs. Anita Clarkson calls him 'Lefty' Vernon just because he tries to give us a view of the whole world, not just our selfish little corner of it ... though he didn't know much about Senegal when I asked him.

Maybe I can go and teach in Senegal ...

I like being able to speak other languages. Especially French. Italian's lovely, too. Very musical. Miss Bassani says I should be fine for Italian 'A' level: I'm doing really well with it so far.

But supposing I was to fall in love. I probably wouldn't want to go off to Senegal then ... Though he did. And look at the problems that caused ... for my mother. And me.

Is it worse not to have a mother than not to have a father? How could Myra put some stupid so-called 'religion' before Jack and her children? Though she still has Tasha. Poor Tasha. Jack worries about her. But he has so much to do, looking after the other two. Money is clearly a bit tighter than it used to be – Josephine in her brother's old pyjamas. And their food's a bit basic if last night's supper is anything to go by. The washing up! We didn't do it because we were talking and it got late and ... maybe I can do it before going to school, to help him a bit. Merde! I forgot to finish that French translation, too.

That must be Jack's alarm clock ...

It bipped for ages before he turned it off. I heard him clear his throat. It made him sound ... *vulnerable*. I felt a flood of tenderness for him as I imagined his waking.

Doors were opening and closing, water running. Now that it was time to get up I felt perversely sleepy. There was a tiny bathroom next to the studio. A quick, cool shower to wake myself up ...

When I came back into my room, there was a hideously milky mug of tea on the yellow chest of drawers. The note beside it said, 'Love from Josephine xx'

Jack wouldn't let me wash up, but I cleared the breakfast things and did Josephine's plait for her, and just before eight o'clock we all piled into the car with our bags. Josephine had her big recorder and swimming things as well as her usual school-bag and lunch-box. Edward had contrived to leave his football gear behind (he hates 'Games'), but at the last minute Jack noticed it behind the kitchen door. There was a moment of tension between them.

We dropped the children off – first, uncommunicative Edward, then Josephine, who made me promise to visit again soon. Then, even though I could have easily made my way to school from there, Jack insisted on driving me right to the gates. He wasn't giving his first seminar until ten. We didn't say much, but I was sorry when the drive was over.

'Keep in touch,' he said. 'Let me know how things go ... with your mum.'

'Thanks for letting me stay the night,' I said. And it seemed the most natural thing in the world to lean over and give him a quick peck on the cheek before I got out of the car.

'Who was that I saw you kissing in the grey car this morning?' (Anita said this in the middle of the Sixth-Form Common Room, in front of six other smirking girls.) 'The old bloke with the moustache ... '

'Karl Marx,' I said, and pushed past her so she spilled coffee down her skirt.

My lack of sleep caught up with me in German and I nodded off during a television programme about Goethe. But the blinds were down so I don't suppose anyone noticed.

10

'ENORMOUS CHANGES AT THE LAST MOMENT'

❦ ELOISA ❦

Dear Theo,

Hope things are still going well for you at uni. Sounds like you have quite a hectic social life already! (Lucky you.)

My mum's had her heart tests now and they say it's not too bad but she has to take medication. Seems like she's definitely hooking up with Paul and will probably go off and live with him in Paris once I'm at uni. It feels a bit weird, knowing things will change so much, like leaving Miranda Road. I've never lived anywhere else. Part of me can't wait to get away and start 'my' life (like you have), and part of me feels scared at the thought of it. At least I won't have to worry about my mum being on her own, even if he isn't exactly my ideal stepfather. But he's all right.

Have you found anyone else who's into Schoenberg yet? Some clever, luscious blonde who can't resist you? (Only joking.) I'm getting used to you not being around. It was really hard at first.

I went to see your mum the other day. She invited me to stay when my mum goes off to Paris for a few days in November, but I'd already arranged to go to Jack's. It was very nice of her, though, and I hope she wasn't offended. I like your mum very much. Maybe you could ring her a bit more often. She's really missing you, you know. Your dad has offered to help me with my German. I might take him up on it. (Our teacher's not very good.)

Must go. Have French essay to finish and Italian vocab to learn.

Much love,

'Hell' x x

Theo and I began to drift apart – which was inevitable once he went away. He was so taken up with his new friends, his new life. Our letters and phone-calls became less frequent, less 'intimate'. There was no melodramatic point of 'rupture'. We just became more like affectionate cousins – not that our relationship had ever been much more than that anyway. It seemed to upset our mothers more than it upset us! – especially his mother. But I made sure I visited her from time to time. And his dad did end up giving me some German tuition: I needed an 'A' grade if I was going to take my French teacher's advice and try for Cambridge.

Putting down my mother's occupation as 'novelist' on the application form had probably helped. And when the first interviewer took the matter up, I passed it off as if it were quite normal to do things like that, in the family I came from, even mentioning that my French father had been a composer as well as a musician. When he said he hadn't actually heard of a novelist called Georgina Hardiman, I said my mother wrote under a pseudonym (almost true: she'd written under several). 'She doesn't like me to make too much of it – her writing. She's quite modest … quite a private person.'

What did I think of her books? Presumably I'd read them … (Moment of utter panic: I couldn't possibly have talked about *Pleasure Island*, *Babylon Baby*, *The Cage Game*, *China Virgin*, *Vengeful Loving* … not there, in that room, among all those weighty primary texts of the French Enlightenment! They might have started falling off the shelves in horror or something …)

'Actually, I … prefer her poetry … though she doesn't publish that much any more.' And we were soon well away on the communicative value of metaphor.

Just into October was nest-quitting day. I stood there between the two suitcases, looking my goodbyes to my room, tears in my eyes, heart in my mouth, brain telling me I knew nothing and would be sent home after one week. It was all a mistake. It had been meant for someone else, that letter. 'An administrative error,' they'd explain, when I arrived.

'What on *earth* have you got in this case?' She tried to lift it.

'Stop! You're not to take that one. It's too heavy for you ... Your heart. Promise me you won't lift heavy things while ... '

'But what's in it?'

'All my books ... and a few of yours. You don't mind, do you? Mainly Kafka and Flaubert ... and a few others. So people can see that even if I haven't got much money, I have ... '

She insisted on helping with the lighter case. Joe saw us struggling through the front door with the luggage and yelled out of the window, 'Put that case down, Georgina Hardiman!' (He was still in his night-shirt.) 'Give me one minute ... ' After which he emerged, more or less dressed, though uncombed, unshaved, and unwashed, but good-hearted enough to come on the tube with us to King's Cross, carrying the heavier case all the way.

I expected there to be lots of us on the train – lots of students all going up with their luggage. But there weren't. I even checked the date on the paper I'd been sent. But maybe they'd gone earlier, the others.

Joe bought us a large takeaway coffee to share on the train and waved us off, making funny faces from the platform as the train pulled out. The coffee was so hot that Hertfordshire was already running greenly and goldenly past the window before we could start drinking it. Then, as I was passing it back to my mother, the train lurched and brown liquid went all over my clean trousers ... which triggered excessive distress in me and 'a good talking to' from my mother about 'keeping a sense of proportion' because I was going to need it. If I got *that* worked up over a small coffee stain, she said, how on earth was I going to cope with ...

But I continued to rub obsessively at the stain with a tissue. (Displacement activity?)

She treated us to a taxi from Cambridge station.

Cars. They'd all come by car, of course, the 'others'. That's why there'd been none on the train. Boots up, doors open. Boxes, bags, cases, stereos, musical instruments, and all the mummies and daddies rather smart and terribly anxious. My mother winked at me.

'*Hic sunt leones*,' she whispered. Here be lions. (An old joke between us.) '*Mais prends courage, ma gazelle*. You're as good as any of them.'

We walked down the middle of the wide drive, between cars parked at odd angles, weaving past the unpackers and their heaps of stuff. Questions and instructions, reassurances that the squash racket had been found and that the dropped stereo-speaker didn't look damaged ... words from lives so different from mine flying through the air like ... But there was no time to think of a simile ... nor for translating the Latin above the entrance to the building at the top of the wide steps.

My mother waited outside the Porters' Lodge while I checked in. By the time I came out, she was chatting to someone's dad.

The rooms – built in the 1920s in memory of the young men from the college who'd died in the First World War – were arranged around grassed and gardened courts. At the entrance to each set of rooms, each staircase, the names of the students were hand-painted in white on a dark plaque. There I was: E.G. Hardiman. It wasn't a mistake: they really were expecting M E.

Footsteps were coming down the stairs. A tall young man with a mane of sandy hair and a wide, strong-toothed smile. 'Hi!' (American twang.) 'Hi!' (From me.) Wan smile from my mother: I think she imagined him sizing me up for 'prey'.

Next thing, the chap she was chatting to outside the Porters' Lodge was beside us with his son. (Subdued, dark-haired, nice eyes.)

'Are you on the ground floor, too?'

'No. One up.'

'Oh, of course. They probably don't put girls at ground level.'

In my mother's eyes I saw reflected those night-time lions squeezing in through raised sash windows … front half already in … hind-quarters slipping over the window-sill … matted end of a sandy tail disappearing … the silenced scream …

We picked up the cases.

'They look heavy. Seb, take those cases up for the young lady.'

'Seb' obliged. He deposited them at the top of the stairs, passed me on the way down with a head-lowered, shy muttering of, 'Probably see you later.'

Heart drumming against my temples, I fiddled the key into the lock and opened the door to my new life.

I'd never had so much space to myself. Two whole rooms! A wood-panelled sitting-room with all the cupboards and shelves and chairs I could possibly want. A large desk and a reading lamp. Gas fire. Sofa! I opened the door to the bedroom. Big wardrobe. My own wash-basin. My few belongings would surely look lost in all this.

I went to the window (to one of my *three* windows) looking out onto the central court. It was so beautiful. There was a magnificent tree and a full view of the 'Fallen Warrior' sculpture by Henry Moore I'd read about in the college prospectus.

My mother came and stood beside me, put an arm around my shoulders. We stood like that for a minute or two, looking. Then there was a distant flushing sound.

'Just like home,' I said. 'Having to share a loo.'

We laughed together, postponing tears.

We walked into town to stock up on a few things (easier than bringing them with us on the train). You had to cross a busy road, but a few yards to the left of the college entrance were traffic lights of the press-button kind for pedestrians.

My mother said, 'Promise me you'll always use the traffic lights for crossing this road.' (Cars roared past, a motorcycle snarled close to the kerb.)

'No, Mumsie. I'm going to leap out right in front of the cars every single time I cross,' I teased her. But she was not amused.

'*Promise* me!' Her suddenly mask-like face and brimming eyes told me her terror was real, biological, visceral: mother for her cub; bird for her fledgling on the edge of the nest.

I promised.

On the way back, she bought me some sunflowers from the market. Then we remembered I didn't have a vase so we had to find a cheap one. And she was determined to buy me my first Cambridge book, so we did a detour via Heffer's for a little paperback of *Jacob's Room*. It had been her favourite book when she was my age, she said. She hoped I'd like it. I started reading it while we were waiting to pay.

'So of course,' wrote Betty Flanders, pressing her heels rather deeper in the sand, 'there was nothing for it but to leave.'

Slowly welling from the point of her gold nib, pale blue ink dissolved the full stop; for there her pen stuck; her eyes fixed, and tears slowly filled them. The entire bay quivered; the lighthouse wobbled; and she had the illusion that the mast of Mr Connor's little yacht was bending like a wax candle in the sun. She winked quickly. Accidents were awful things. She winked again. The mast was straight; the waves were regular; the lighthouse was upright; but the blot had spread.

' ... nothing for it but to leave,' she read.

(A tear-jerker. Just what I needed. Thanks a bunch, Mumsie.)

We had to hurry back. At five there was some kind of get-together (and I needed to change my coffee-stained trousers). It was probably to make sure the 'mummies and daddies' had a deadline for getting out of the place. You could just imagine the lingering and fussing otherwise, and us just dying to get on with our new lives.

When we got back from town, 'Seb' had his door open as we passed. In his room there was stuff everywhere and he was playing jazz on his stereo. My room looked dead and empty, but once we'd put the sunflowers in water and *Jacob's Room* and a few of 'our' books on one of the shelves, I could already begin to imagine living here for the next year.

Then it was the big goodbye.

'I'll walk to the gates with you, Mumsie: I've got time, really I have.'

Most of the car parents had gone, or were just going. At the gates, a last hug.

'Take care, Tootsie, my sweetheart.'

'*You* take care, Mumsie.' Two big, brave smiles out-cheer-fulling each other.

She turned away and walked along to the traffic lights. It was only then that my eyes filled with tears. The entire scene quivered; the traffic lights wobbled, and I had the impression that the lamp-post nearby was bending like a wax candle in the sun. I blinked quickly. Partings were awful things. I blinked again. The lamp-post was straight; the traffic lights were upright … And she'd gone.

I walked back up the drive, up the steps, under the Latin inscription, past the Porters' Lodge, and followed someone to where the 'welcome' event was being held.

There weren't many of the girls there yet: it was mainly young men, a few chatting, but mostly standing about awkwardly, weighing each other up, every new arrival inspected (what was the competition like?). I hesitated at the door, scanning faces, looking for Seb … someone definite to make for. But he wasn't there yet.

I heard my mother whisper, in my head, one last, 'Take care, my antelope, take care … ' Should I turn and run? …

Too late. I'd been spotted. Some began whisking their tails. Their yellow eyes were on me.

❧ GEORGINA ❧

17th October, 1987

Dear Amaranth,

It was lovely to have all your news — and the photos. Pablo's family look so friendly and full of life. No wonder you say you could live in Chile permanently if Pablo really wanted to go back.

This year everyone seems to be up and away. My friend Alma's in Sydney for six months (hoping it will 'do something' for her daughter, I think!); Joe's just left for Italy (though only for a short time); Eloisa's gone off to Cambridge, of course, and I've started packing up ready for the move to Paris before Christmas. (I hope I'm doing the right thing!) You two must come and visit once I'm settled in.

I wonder what you'll make of Paul. He's kind and loving — though I don't recommend his driving! He's not a remarkable man, but he is a good one. In fact, better than he realizes and I've grown to love him a lot. And in bed he's ... very 'attentive'.

I miss Eloisa horribly and I worry about her all the time, wondering if the academic pressure will be too much for her, wondering if she's going to be too easily seduced to go to bed with some fellow just using her to get sexual experience. (I can't imagine many girls these days get through uni with their virginity intact — not that that in itself matters, but I don't want her 'exploited'.) I'm so afraid of her being hurt, emotionally and physically. But what can one do once they're technically adults? And they always think they know best!

Are you doing any writing while you're out there? Or getting any ideas or material for when you come back? I always wanted to travel when I was young. You're lucky to get the chance — though Paul has promised to take me to Greece in the spring, and he has friends with a house near Lake Como which we might be able to use. Not very exotic compared with your travels, but it'll be nice.

I'm not writing any more 'willy books', I've decided. I don't need the money now and Paul says he'd like me to be able to write what I actually want to (though he has no objection to the 'other stuff': the French are very liberal-minded about such things). There's a tiny spare room in his apartment (it's full of junk at the moment) which he's going to clear out and turn into a little study for me. Isn't that nice?! He really is a sweetie. What more could a girl want? The only thing that's worrying me is his daughter. I haven't met her yet but she's just hitting those difficult pubescent years and I can imagine she might not take too kindly to her father's 'girlfriend'. Anyway, we shall see ...

I think you said you were getting back mid November, so there'll be time for us to get together, maybe, before I leave. I'll give you my Paris address then.

Enjoy the rest of your trip. Say 'Hi' to Pablo for me. And I look forward to hearing all about your travels when I see you.

Much love,
Georgie

7th January, 1988

Dear Amaranth,

Happy New Year! Hope Christmas was OK and that you managed to get out of that party you mentioned (sounded dreadful!).

I've just finished reading your 'Gekö' story. I think it's really wonderful and was the best Christmas present you could have given me. It's quite unlike anything you've written before and, to be honest, a lot better. Your travels have certainly fed your creativity! So, congratulations. There's only one word I would change: instead of describing the woman's dress as 'yellow', use a more precise colour: 'saffron' or 'mustard' or 'lemon' or however you see it. But that's such a small point, it's hardly worth mentioning.

I've now got my own little writing room but haven't started writing properly in it yet. I guess undergoing such a radical life-change is bound to be distracting for a while. Paul has met 'the family' now (i.e. Amadou's family). Maude, inevitably, was a little dubious at first, but now she's met him a few times she's fine. With Maurice he got on splendidly right from the start. And Eloisa tells me Monique (her sort of cousin — I'm not sure what the precise term for the relationship is: something so many times removed, I suppose. But Eloisa's close to her, anyway) thinks Paul is 'mignon'.

I've met Paul's ex-wife now and we got on reasonably well, actually. She trusted me enough to allow their daughter, Nathalie, to come and stay over Christmas, for

291

which Paul was deeply glad. Things were a bit tense, especially at the start, and she's not at all like Eloisa was at the 'awkward age'. Less door-slamming, but less laughter. She's quite inward, maybe from witnessing the progressive disintegration of her parents' marriage. At least Eloisa didn't have that!

Anyway, as soon as I get down to writing something again, I'll send it to you.

Hope you're both well. Everyone in Paris seems to have a cold at the moment (I'm just starting one ...).

Much love,

Georgie x x

P.S. Enclose photo of Paul and me so you can see what he looks like, and that I'm happy!

Dear Amaranth and Pablo,

Having wonderful time in here in Crete. They say Spring is the best time here and that isn't hard to believe. To think what I've been missing all these years! It's so beautiful, and interesting and the air's so fresh (unlike Paris!).

Love from us both,

Georgie and Paul

3rd September, 1988

Dear Amaranth,

Found this under the bed after you left. Started flicking through it and am going to get myself a copy. I like the way she writes though the cover doesn't do it justice and would probably put me off picking it up, by chance, in a bookshop.

We so enjoyed your visit, especially that picnic in the Bois. Pablo is great fun and was a real hit with Nathalie. She's been a lot better with me since Eloïsa's visit. She's started calling her 'my big sister' and asked me if her father and I are going to get married!

Don't nag me about writing. Yes, I know there's no excuse now. But what have I got to write about? I never did make it to Katmandu.

Well, take care. Love to Pablo.

Much love,

Georgie x x

❀ ELOISA ❀

My time at Cambridge turned out to be rather ... mixed. Sometimes I was happy. Sometimes I was angry. Often it was about never having *quite* enough money when some of my friends had whatever they needed. I became properly aware of social inequalities and the insidious class system for the first time. I did very well in some of my exams; not so well in others. I made some good friends – and a few lousy ones.

I lost my virginity to a big chap called Anthony. The experience was a blend of the two kinds of books my mother wrote: he wined and dined me romantically (he could afford to: champagne, red roses ... which I had to put in the cheap vase bought for the sunflowers on that first day). Then there was the rest. I didn't particularly enjoy it and the relationship (if you could call it that) didn't last long. Anthony was only interested in his own pleasure, not mine. His charm and civilization were scarcely skin deep.

Then I got to know Titus. He was gay but 'not in a relationship' at the time. We became the best of friends. (It reminded me of my mother and Joe – but without going through the sexual stage first.) With Alisa and Mark we made up a foursome to go travelling through Europe at the end of the first year. We called in on Paris where my mother and Paul put on a very nice dinner for us. The other three really liked my mother. It made me feel good. Paul's daughter, Nathalie, was staying with them at the time. There seemed to be a bit of difficulty between her and my mother, so I paid a lot of attention to her. I promised to send her postcards from every place we visited. I told her I'd always wanted a little sister: could I please 'adopt' her as one? She said she'd always wanted an older sister, so ... problem solved, we decided. She was sad when we left. I made her promise to write to me at Cambridge so I wouldn't be so lonely ...

For my compulsory year abroad, I was sent as an *assistante* to a school in Tours (not Paris, as I'd hoped: but it was close enough for weekend visits).

My 'Finals' year started badly: a brutally terminated relationship with a young French science teacher from the school where I'd worked sent me rebounding into the arms of a PhD student (someone dreadfully double-barrelled) ... whom I caught fondling another girl the day after we'd made love for the first time.

By Christmas, the pressure of work was becoming intolerable. That, on top of everything else, led to me literally running away. I turned up on Jack's doorstep late one night. Fortunately he was in.

EPILOGUE

'IN SEARCH OF
LOST TIME'

MY NAME IS GINA-JO

I AM 5

MY EYES ARE BROWN

AND MY HAIR

I GO TO SCHOOL

IT IS NICE

I PLAY WITH LUCY AND ALI AND BEN

❧ GEORGINA ❧

Maurice's seventieth birthday coincides with the thirtieth anniversary of '68. Various events around Paris that year coax us old *soixante-huitards* out of the closet. Eloisa and family come over for Maurice's party (thank God for Eurostar!) – which is how we end up all going to the Magnum photography exhibition together.

'1968'. Easy to forget just how many things the world crammed into that one hectic year, resurrected here in the gloom and musty stones of the Sorbonne. Huge blow-ups of black-and-white photos, bringing it all dazzlingly back, each one a flash-bulb going off in the memory.

The terrible face of the Vietnamese boy weeping for his dead sister – and the anti-war protests everywhere: London, Paris, Tokyo, Washington … (the woman with a flower, approaching a row of guns and helmets).

Martin Luther King preaching his Civil Rights dream into a dozen microphones …

Then his wife dignified beside his assassinated body.

The living skeletons of Biafra …

And the reflection of Andy Warhol in a tin of Campbell's soup.

Bobby Kennedy, Democratic candidate for the US Presidency …

And his funeral.

Bob Dylan … Joan Baez … Jimi Hendrix … Janis Joplin … and the Beatles going off to India.

Russian tanks in Prague …

And the funeral of Jan Palach who set fire to himself in protest.

But most of all Paris, in May: *les événements* …

Eloisa is utterly absorbed by this 'bed' on which she'd been conceived ... so to speak. I'm holding little Gina-Jo's hand. Eloisa has Sam on her back in some marvellous carrier-thing. Gina is bored, tugging and swinging on my arm, or hopping experimentally with her body in peculiar positions.

'When are we going to play in the park like you said, Granny?'

'Soon, sweetheart, soon.'

... then his face is suddenly looking out at me from the photograph's black-and-white crowd. At least, I think it's him. And even after so long a time and ten years of happiness with Paul, that face (which, slightly blurred, is only *possibly* his, anyway) makes my heart throb against my eyes and blood rush to my face.

Gina-Jo saying, 'What's wrong, Granny?'

'Nothing, sweetheart. I think Granny's got a bit of a cold coming on: she needs to blow her nose. Go and hold Daddy's hand for a minute.'

'You all right, Mumsie?'

'Yes ... yes ... I'm fine, Toots.'

'Are you sure? ... Jack – can you hold on to Gina for a minute ... '

'Come here, poppet. Hold Daddy's hand.'

I love it when Eloisa comes over. Seeing her so happy, I really have got over the bombshell she dropped at the end of her graduation dinner (paid for by Paul – who couldn't get over the weird and archaic ceremony at the Senate House earlier in the day) regarding her wedding plans. We were worried, to say the least. After all, he's old enough to be her father. But it was Eloisa who'd proposed to *him*. (Was it a leap year?) He turned her down at first, doubting her motives – and her sanity. But she didn't give up. And, of course, he really did love her to bits, anyway. Always had.

Because of Jack's age, Eloisa was anxious to start a family of her own as soon as possible and – like mother, like daughter? – had no trouble conceiving. Gina-Jo was due on 7th July, but hung on until Bastille Day (getting on the good side of her granny right from the start!). A straightforward birth. Eloisa turned out to be a happy, competent mother and, I'm pleased to say, kept her hand in by doing a little translation work at home. Gina-Jo is not growing up to the tap-dance of an old grey typewriter, of course, but to the light little rattles and bips of a computer. (Even *I* have one now.) Gina-Jo was about three-and-a-half when Sam (Samuel Amadou) was born.

I love it when Eloisa phones for a chat, or I get an email with news of her large family. She has stepchildren older than herself, of course. Tricky at times? All I can say is, thank God Jamie's happily married …

And then there's the answer-phone. Nothing lovelier than when Paul and I come home after a film or an evening of jazz and hear that voice which, even now, catches my throat … always so full of plans for when we go over there or they come over here … that lovely moment after the long 'beep' when her words begin and …

❦ ELOISA ❦

Santiago, Chile
16/2/04

My dear Eloisa,

Thank you for your letter, though needless to say I was terribly, *terribly* upset by the news it brought. Fate can be so unkind. What words of comfort can I offer? None, I'm afraid. Everything seems inadequate and I can only say that I am so very, very sorry and send you all my love. Do try to be strong and brave, my love, for the sake of your children.

And now I'm going to make a suggestion. You have every right to groan and say, 'Oh, no! What's that mad woman, Amaranth, got into her head *now*?!' Well, if you do, you do. At least I'm too far away to hear you.

I don't know whether your mother ever mentioned it, but we were in the habit of sending each other things we'd written (the way writers sometimes do: it's not that unusual). Now, although your mother had a lot of books published (or should that be 'books', in inverted commas?!), we both know (at least, I think you probably know) that what she really wanted was to write a 'proper' novel. And of course, once she moved to Paris with Paul and didn't have to write for money any more (there's definitely something to be said for being a 'kept woman', Eloisa, as I've discovered ...), the conditions were perfect, weren't they? But 'nothing would come', as she put it. 'What do you mean, "Nothing will come"?' I said to her. 'There you are, living in one of the most beautiful and intellectually exciting cities in the world, a place you've always loved, and with a man who's utterly besotted with you, and Eloisa all happy and settled so you don't even have to worry about *her* any more.' 'But what have I got to write about? I never did make it to Katmandu. All I've done is bring up a child in a small flat and sit at a typewriter, churning out "willy books".' 'Well, write about that, then. It'd be a start.' 'Don't nag me, Amaranth,' she'd say. 'Don't nag me.'

Well, anyway, it was Paul who finally got her started, persuading her to write some things about her own life for *him*, so he could get to know her more deeply. From time to time she sent me some of the fragments she'd written. Some were better than others, I thought. Some were wry and amusing, some were quite intense and almost poetic. I'm sure Paul has copies, or they'll be on her computer. And now, this is my idea. I was thinking that maybe, as a way of coping with your loss, or simply as a tribute or 'memorial' to your mother, you might try putting those fragments together and making them into a little book – a book that tells her story, which is also the story of the time she lived through, of course. None of us is free of 'history'. It would be a lovely thing to give her grandchildren, when they're older, and also for Paul – and yourself, of course.

Now I know you have a writer's instinct, Eloísa: your mother often said so. I'm not flattering you: it's the truth. She was always showing me poems and things you'd written, so I know you could do it, if you have the time and inclination. You might even be able to fill in some of the gaps. You know how much your dear mother meant to me, so you won't be surprised to know that I've kept all the letters she wrote me since Pablo and I moved to Chile and am happy to send you copies if you think they'll be any help. (But only copies: the originals are just too, too precious.)

So, end of Amaranth's mad (?) idea. I won't be in the least offended if you just have a laugh at my expense and throw the whole idea in the dustbin, as it were. But I just couldn't stop myself making the suggestion. When I talked to Pablo about it, he actually said why don't I do it if you won't. But I really do think you're better placed. Anyway ...

Please give my best wishes to Jack. I found him a really charming man when we met him at your wedding. I hope the children are well and not taking the loss of their grandmother too badly. It must be so difficult to know how to comfort them.

With all my love and sympathy,

Amaranth

P.S. My email address here is amaranthoort-mendoza@hotmail. com. I can scan in the letters and email them to you. Do keep in touch.

Paul had no idea why she'd gone out. She was still recovering from a bad bout of flu and bronchitis. The weather was particularly horrible that day, so cold that the rain had some flakes of snow mixed with it – 'Though it never snows properly in Paris any more,' said Paul. 'That was something your mother remarked on when we were watching the weather forecast the previous evening and they said we might perhaps see a little snow settling the next day.'

He was devastated – utterly, utterly devastated.

'There was no *need* for her to go out, absolutely no need,' he kept saying, as if he thought I would blame him. 'I had done all the shopping. We had plenty of everything. She was finally beginning to feel better, she said. She was even up before I left for work and waved down at me from the window as she'd always liked to do when I went off in the mornings. She'd said she might try to do some writing.'

She was in the Tuileries when she collapsed. By the time Paul had been located and he'd reached the hospital, she'd had a second heart attack. She'd died in the ambulance.

It was quite a while before I could bring myself to ask Paul if I could see what she'd been writing about her life. I told him about Amaranth's suggestion. I wasn't sure I wanted to do it (too painful, too time-consuming), nor that I *could*. In the end it was curiosity: I wanted to see what she'd said about *me*! I took Gina-Jo with me to Paris for a couple of days and left Sam with Jack.

Paul let me go into her little writing room: he hadn't moved or touched anything since she died. He was quite a sentimental old thing. (Gina-Jo doted on him and insisted on calling him '*grand-père*', which pleased him enormously.)

On the shelf above her desk was an old blue box I remembered from Miranda Road, when I was a child. Expecting it to be full of old letters and bills, I didn't bother opening it at first. I turned on her computer and easily located the relevant files: there wasn't much else on there. While they were printing I took down the blue box, wondering if there might be any useful correspondence in it for if I *should*, eventually, decide to put the book together.

It was crammed with things *I*'d written – poems, stories, pieces of school work from way, way back. She'd kept them all. And for the first time for ages, I laughed. It was that poem about poor old Wriggles, my short-lived goldfish (and only pet ever) that did it.

At the very bottom of the box was an old brown envelope. I nearly didn't bother opening it (the printer had stopped: everything was done). But my mother had taught me to be infinitely curious.

There was a French stamp on the envelope, and my mother's name and the Miranda Road address, written in a hand I recognized but could not at first place. As soon as I looked inside and saw the note, though, I knew it was from Maude. Folded into the note was a yellowing, fragile newspaper cutting.

From the date-stamp on the letter I worked out that it had

been sent not long after that day on Hampstead Heath when I finally told my mother about the conversation I'd had with Monique, confirming that my father was dead. There had been some intense phone-calls between my mother and Maude immediately afterwards, resulting, I suppose, in my mother finally being sent the scrap of newspaper (which Maude had probably found it hard to part with). It was a very brief report, but confirmed that my father had died trying to save a child – though not from drowning, as my mother had finally told me.

He was, as they say, simply at the wrong place at the wrong time. Pure contingency, as always.

There was a lot of unrest in Senegal that year (as my subsequent research informed me). Political power had become increasingly concentrated in the hands of one man and there was only one political party. With long-term drought in the north, a declining economic situation and reduced aid from France, along with the general mood of the world that year, I suppose, there were continual student protests, union strikes and the attempt of 'illegal' opposition groups to challenge the status quo. 'A recognizable post-colonial situation,' as one article put it. Any anti-governmental unrest or violence was routinely crushed by the army.

Some armed group – possibly political, or maybe just criminal – had been cornered by the army in the centre of a town. In the shooting that followed, a child had been caught in the cross-fire. My father had, apparently, run out from his place of shelter, picked up the child and had almost reached safety when he was hit.

There weren't many details. It was left to my imagination – fed by constant exposure to TV news – to provide them. The film ran through my head again and again. A child lying in a dusty road, the growing pool of blood, the mercy dash of a tall stranger, trying to keep low to avoid the bullets … scooping up the child, its head hanging back over the strong arm of the rescuer, the run for cover ... then the violent jerk and the sudden bloom of red on the back of the white shirt ...

Had the child lived?

Strange to think of a man or woman, a few years older than me, walking about in Senegal, totally unaware that in England lived a person whose life had been largely shaped by the absence of that stranger who'd saved them.

What would I say to them if ever we ... ?

When someone dies, it's their voice you miss most.

Even now, several years on, I sometimes talk to her in my head. Sometimes I even argue with her. It's taken me a long time to put together her story – 'our' story. I've had to fit it in at odd moments between my translation work and looking after the kids (two more since Gina-Jo and Sam!) – and Jack, of course, who's not quite as robust as he used to be.

I think my mother would've liked me to have had a big career – a more demanding one, anyway (as if motherhood isn't!). Have I disappointed her feminist hopes? I don't know. I wish I'd got around to telling her the important thing to me is that I've had a choice. She gave me that. Choosing is freedom, no matter what it is you choose. I wish I could thank her, tell her not to worry, tell her I'm happy. Maybe later, once all the children have left home, I'll have more of a career. There's time. The doctor assures me I have inherited my father's strong heart.

The summer after she died we went to WOMAD, the wonderful festival of music and dance from all over the world. Josephine's Italian boyfriend was manager of one of the groups appearing and she very much wanted us to be there. She was sure we'd enjoy the global atmosphere of the festival. And we did. I loved the flags most of all: they were amazing – dozens of them, made of the lightest imaginable silk, running and rippling to an undetectable breeze above us. Not the flags of nations: no coarse reds and blues bounded by harsh, straight lines, but luscious ice-cream colours with soft, amorphous shapes on them that seemed to represent beautiful ideas and possibilities blending into one another ... though you couldn't quite put your finger on what they were. My mother would have loved it. Very sixties – in the nicest possible sense.

That year the fashion for fairy wings had really taken hold. You could buy them from a stall at the festival. Lots of little girls had them. We laughed when we saw them coming away from the children's workshops at the end of the day, all wings and wellies and needing the loo. But later they were transformed from damp and grubby children to become ... something else entirely.

We're all under the night sky: there's a stage lit bright as sunshine. There's not enough room to dance properly to the music, but people are moving up and down in time to it. Above the sea of bobbing heads between us and the stage sit silhouettes of the fairy children with their wings and wild-spun hair – little girls high on their fathers' shoulders, dancing their thin arms and pin fingers against the light. Their narrow wrists are dazzled almost away by the flood of stage light that turns them into fantastical little shadow-puppets doing a spiky dance. Children of the festival, up there in their own special realm, they look as if they're trying to break free, to rise up with the music, to escape ... only their legs (held by strong hands) are anchoring them, like roots, into the merged darkness of the grown-ups with all their musty histories.

Perfect gems of city writing
Edited by Heather Reyes

city-pick

Discover some of the best writing on our
favourite world cities with the **city-pick** series.

Berlin
Paris
New York
Istanbul
Venice

St Petersburg
Amsterdam
London
Dublin

'Brilliant ... the best way to get under the skin of a city.
The perfect read for travellers and book lovers of all ages.'
Kate Mosse

'Superb ... it's like having your own iPad loaded with
different tomes, except only the best passages.'
The Times

'A different point of view. Tired of the usual guides?
Can't be bothered with apps? Meet the alternative.'
Wanderlust

'What a great idea! A sublime introduction.'
The Sydney Morning Herald

'The beauty of this clever series is the breadth and reach
of its contributors.'   *Real Travel Magazine*

'We love the *city-pick* books. They're right up our street!'
Lonely Planet Traveller

Available from all good bookshops

www.oxygenbooks.co.uk

Heather Reyes

AN EVERYWHERE

a little book about reading

During several months of treatment for a serious illness, the writer decides to turn a necessary evil into an opportunity: the luxury of reading whatever takes her fancy.

An Everywhere: a little book about reading is a quietly passionate and witty defence of the joys and consolations of reading in both the difficult and day-to-day aspects of our lives.

'A brilliant travel guide to the city of book: the city we hold within us, and the one we share with all its other citizens. I love ... the blend of erudition and intimacy she brings to the discussion of what reading is and what books can do within a life. It is such a truthful book, honest about panic and anguish, and fascinating about what happens when the panic ebbs and the reader continues.'

Helen Dunmore

'A gem of a book ... Reyes writes with the imagination and skill of the writer, the heart of a reader, the forbearance and wisdom of the patient and the expertise of the well-travelled.'

Cheryl Moskowitz

£8.99   978 099263640 1

Available from all good bookshops

Oxygen Books

www.oxygenbooks.co.uk